P9-CEC-869

OLD FATHER OF WATERS

Center Point
Large Print

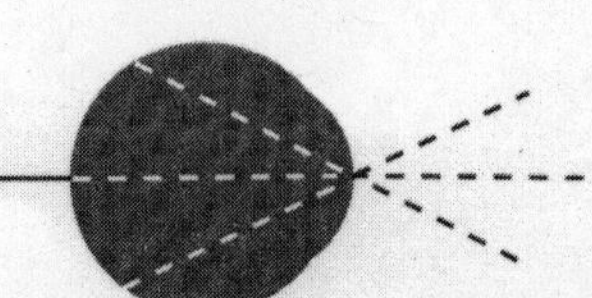

ALAN LeMAY

OLD FATHER OF WATERS

CENTER POINT PUBLISHING
THORNDIKE, MAINE • USA

BOLINDA PUBLISHING
MELBOURNE • AUSTRALIA

This Center Point Large Print edition
is published in the year 2003 by arrangement with
Golden West Literary Agency.

This Bolinda Large Print edition is published in the year
2003 by arrangement with Center Point Publishing.

The text of this Large Print edition is unabridged. In other aspects, this book may vary from the original edition. Printed in Thailand. Set in 16-point Times New Roman type by Bill Coskrey and Gary Socquet.

US ISBN 1-58547-304-9
BC ISBN 1-74030-944-8

U.S. Library of Congress Cataloging-in-Publication Data.

Le May, Alan, 1899-1964.
Old father of waters / Alan LeMay.--Center Point large print ed.
p. cm.
ISBN 1-58547-304-9 (lib. bdg. : alk. paper)
1. Large type books. I. Title.

PS3523.E513 O4 2003
813'.52--dc21

2002041277

Australian Cataloguing-in-Publication.

Le May, Alan, 1899-1964.
Old father of waters / Alan LeMay.
ISBN 1740309448
1. Large print books.
2. Western stories.
I. Title.
813.6

British Cataloguing-in-Publication is available from the British Library.

CHAPTER I

IN a night that seemed utterly without light the deep, ghostly blanket of the fog held a faint pearly color of its own, as soft as gray chiffon; beautiful in its dim mystery, but deathly treacherous, its limitless depths masking the unknown. Its cold wraith fingers wet the faces of the rivermen and held close to the water the faint smell of clay awash, and wet leaves. Under it the ancient river slid silently, smooth as black glass, its four-mile current majestic, perpetual, unhurried.

The watchman at Fairchild's landing heard the invisible steamboat *Peter Swain* go past, down river bound. Through the fog, with incongruous clarity, there drifted to him the steady churr of her paddle wheel and the soft panting of her steam. The chanting cries of her leadsmen, feeling her way, came unimpeded across the hidden water: "Ma-ark three. . . . Quarter less three. . . . Ma-ark three. . . ."

On the *Peter Swain* every gleam of light had been smothered. Even the red breath of the fire doors was masked by canvas screens, to give the eyes of the fog-blinded pilot every chance. Peering through the grayness the watchman thought he could glimpse for a moment the red and green pin points of her running lights, high on her towering smoke stacks; but that was all.

The watchman leaned back among his cratings, his eyes still turned sightlessly downstream after the receding boat. It was beyond midnight: he dozed; the long minutes passed. . . .

Far down the river there appeared a faint glow in the fog, tiny at first like a lantern smudged by the mist; then growing a little, as if a plucked-out bit of fog-cotton had turned to golden light. Over the water came a small murmur of raised voices, a stamping of feet; then the hoarse, deep voice of the boat whistling a long, two shorts, and a long, the signal for a landing where no landing was.

"Gaw'!" The old man ran stumbling up the path. His shouts rose shrilly, frightening the birds of the night. "Hank! Eben! Fire on the river! Steamboat burnin'! Hank—git up—Eben, run—run to the town!" Panting, almost hysterical with excitement, the watchman ran on to spread an alarm that was half an appeal for swift aid, half a summons to a great tragic show.

In his bunk on the *Peter Swain* Captain Arnold Huston sat up suddenly from a light and restless sleep, and stared into the dark. From the main deck, close down by the water, came a confused babble of exclamations, followed by loud voices, excited cries, the scuffling of feet.

Through the dark he could see only the gray square of his window, a dim page of nothingness, framed in utter black. He rolled to his feet, and his hands gripped the clammy sill as he tried to discover some sign on the fog-hidden water below. To his nostrils came the drenched river odor and the smell of water-touched paint; but for all his eyes could make out there might have existed nothing in the world but the swathing gray vapor, the frame of his window, and the rising, clamoring voices below.

A thin little whistle blew suddenly at his elbow. It was the speaking tube from the pilot house. "Yeah?"

"Fire in the deck room," said the small voice of the tube. "I just got it from below." The voice stopped, then Huston heard it again, faint this time, as the pilot spoke through another tube to the engineer. "Stand by, Dick—I can't step down on her fer a second. Git ready to tear the heart out of her, Dick—" Then a small mutter of something from the engine room, coming to Captain Huston by way of the pilot house through the tubes. It was odd how, in this moment of clamor and disaster, those whispers could run over the boat, slipping alike through noise and bulkheads and decks.

A chill like a settling ice block in Huston's stomach made him rigid. The boat beneath his feet represented everything he owned. More: it supplied almost the whole meaning of his life. It was the old story of river fire, old as the first boat, yet as perpetually new as death, the wastage of a floating village, the destruction of man-built hopes. A belated load of cotton in the open deck room below, tinder dust of cargo-ground wood, perhaps a spark from a pine-knot brazier at the last landing, careless niggers—these things had turned the trick again.

Another steamboat, Arnold Huston's this time, was hesitating on the brink of a destruction incongruously swift and certain. No stove-laid fire of dry pine was better adapted to go up in a great rush of flame than the flimsy superstructures of those white river-plying boats. Steamboats that caught fire were lost, in those days before the war of the states.

Bells jangled in the engine room, signalling full speed ahead. Huston felt the answering tremble of the whole boat to the surging thrust of the steam. Her engines heaved mightily with great slow sighs like overburdened giants laboring to gain way, fighting to get her nose against the unseen shore before she gave herself utterly to the flames and smoke.

The ice in Huston's body left him quivering with helpless wrath. He had been sleeping naked under his sheet, an old habit of his; now he jerked on his trousers, and kicked his feet into his shoes. The engine-room bells jabbered again, hysterically, to the yank of the pilot's cord: "Give 'er hell! Give 'er hell!" The dry reek of fire subtly penetrated the smell of the mist. Huston burst out of his stateroom in the Texas house, ran down the stairs from the hurricane roof and along the boiler-deck guards to the cabin entrance.

A pair of black cabin boys, their eyes white and starting, came tumbling into him at the door. It would have been comical, this terror of theirs, had its cause been less real; but no one knew better than the river negroes how quickly the serene white boat could turn to an inferno of shrivelling heat.

Huston blocked the way. As the negroes gathered themselves to rush past him he would have smashed out at their black faces with his fists. But they stopped and cowered in front of him, their eyes rolling as if for other means of escape. Already the deck was growing hot under their bare feet. A great purl of dry smoke bellied up from below and rolled over them, past the cabin windows.

He must have been a terrible figure to them in that moment, this half-naked white man, to hold them so. Below, the turmoil had subsided as suddenly as it had begun; but they heard the crack of black snake whips and the smothered, gasping yell of a fireman against an impersonal silence more terrible than the clamor of fear. The chill mist that bounded their world took on a pale efflorescence of light.

"Wake the passengers!"

Huston's lips were thin, and drew away easily from his strong teeth when he laughed; he seemed to be laughing now, but savagely, green-eyed and demoniac. The negroes stumbled away from him toward the long lamplit passage between the rows of stateroom doors.

The thin captain disappeared from the entrance and for a moment flattened himself against the bulkhead beside it. One of the slaves made a break for the smoky outer air, and Huston, swinging with all his strength, smashed the black's face with his fist. Huston wore a shoulder-holstered gun which he would have used without hesitation, but the man went reeling and staggering back. And after that they did their work, pounding on the white-paneled doors with frantic palms—"Git up, masses, git up, git up, 'e bu'nin', 'e bu'nin' fo' sho'!"

Below on the main deck the cotton was already wrapped in blue sheaths of flame. There was no fighting the fire; there were no facilities to fight it.

Against the weaving blaze in the open deck room the stanchions stood black. The fire lighted brilliantly the lower deck, showed the ripples of the oily black water slipping along just below the chocks of the guards; and beyond, the everlasting fog, intangible, black, folding them in from the outside world.

Forward on the forecastle, in the tilted deck-space between the bows, half a hundred slaves were herded against the circular sweep of the chocks, staring-eyed, silent, huddling as far as they could from the increasing heat. They cowered, their jungle spirits terrorized by the black depths of the river, the ghostly fog, and the merciless fire-demon that pressed them against unknown deaths. There were a score of slave women and pickaninnies there; and of the thirty or forty brute-muscled roustabouts less than half could swim.

Huston's mate, a man with bowed, powerful shoulders, had fought his way among them, seeking his leadsmen; and now the sounding calls rose again in despairing wails: "Quarter twain! Quarter twain!"

The captain raced aft along the deserted guards through heat that crisped his naked shoulders as he ran; to the fireroom, where the steaming blacks should be stoking the boilers. The firemen on numbers five and six were gone from the narrow fire alley; but the other four were working frantically, the sheen of their sweat outlining them in burning red from the fire doors.

The second mate was already there, a little wizened man with whiskers like smoked cotton; his trousers and shirt shone white against the wood pile on which he stood. His limber whip ran here and there among the firemen like a snake, its slithering threat spurring them to their work.

A weird shape scraped along the lip of the chocks. Huston recognized the great crooked finger of a snag that thrust four feet above the surface, a hazard that had groped for the steamboat's last moments of life and missed. By this remembered sign he knew that they were half a mile from shore, a long half mile, a half mile that they would hardly make.

The last of the passengers were tumbling down the stairway as Huston regained the forward deck. They mingled with the fear-crazed negroes, clinging together in little groups, white faced, half clad. There were only eleven of them this trip, thank Christ. A baby was crying pitifully; some darkies were singing some wild, outlandish hymn—"Come *now,* Marse Jedus, come now, come soon. *Oh,* Marse Jedus, come soon!" Two foolish lines over and over, with the ghastly sincerity of the fear of death.

Stronger than these minor things, stronger than the low mutter of the boat herself, spoke the ugly flapping crackle of the flames, not loud but softly inescapable, reducing all other sounds to a background of silence. The heavy smoke billowed forward, blinding them; with it came the strangling cotton gas, so torturing that it seemed drawing their lungs out through their throats. When the smoke turned away it revealed the huddled group stricken. A third of the people were down, yet in the respite from the smoke there sounded again, diminished, the wild swing of that primitive hymn.

The people were crushed together now along the curve of the forward chocks, drawing away from the reaching heat of the blaze. A mad scream, instantly checked by the closing water, was heard as someone was jammed overboard and disappeared under the great boat. "Ma-ark twain! Mark twain!" Twelve feet of water. . . . More than a quarter mile to go. . . .

A section of the boiler deck fell into the blaze, letting the flames pour roaring upward into the cabin itself. The intense heat on the forecastle just above the water became intolerable, scorching. A stanchion twelve feet from the nearest fire burst into flame. Pickaninnies hid their faces in their mothers' skirts; the little ones screamed and pled. The mass of the darkies crouched jibbering and praying in the smoke.

"Quarter less twain!"—a tortured cry of despair. Huston set his teeth, his hands were at his sides in trembling claws. There was a bar to be passed just here. Already the broad hull seemed to hang back against the thrashing paddle wheel, as if the steamboat felt the reef ahead. "Come *now,* Marse Jedus—"

"Eight feet! Seven!" Then, after a long age, filled with the hungry roar of the flame—*"Mark one!"* One fathom, six feet! She couldn't make it, she couldn't—by God, she did!

A great roar of cheering voices went up in the fog ahead, and red streaming eyes turned wonderingly toward the unseen shore. She was in free water again. Only a furlong now, only a furlong more. The flames rippled over the light woodwork of the cabin. They had made a flue through the hurricane roof. A great shower of golden sparks flung upward against that vast silent ghost of fog. . . . Half a furlong more. . . . The pilot house must go soon. It was certain that the pilot at the great wheel would die there, now. . . .

The mate was marshalling his negroes to throw out the stage plank, shouting savagely, his whistling blacksnake biting deep wherever it fell. A yellow bank loomed over them. Suddenly the boat nosed into the wet clay with a great laboring groan and a swift sickening check of speed; and the *Peter Swain* disgorged her human life. . . .

CHAPTER II

ARNOLD HUSTON was a man toward whom violence naturally gravitated. He seemed marked as a center of storm, as if born under turbulent stars.

At twenty-seven he was slender as a stanchion, bony, and of no more than ordinary height. His thin lips drew away easily from his teeth, as easily as the chuckling, free-running laughter welled out of his throat, for he laughed both readily and well. The creases that result from much grinning already carved his lean cheeks; but in repose his face was harsh, giving the illusion that vicissitudes, not humor, had carved those bracketing lines about his mouth. Above his forehead stood a stiff, often tangled roach of tawny hair.

On the river he was not widely known. At a time when owners of great lines numbering scores of ships were struggling for mastery of the Mississippi trade, a single personality, however individual, made little mark.

At that time—the year 1858, three years before the civil conflict—the river trade was not only at the flood tide of power, but seemed only in the infancy of that power. Great white packets, ever greater, faster, more luxurious, were being launched by the score. Million upon million was invested in the fragily towering craft, at a time when a million represented untold wealth. And still the full-bodied river trade, growing lustily, was calling for more. No boat lacked a cargo, none its quota of passengers. The Mississippi seemed to be coming swiftly into its own as the very heart stream of the nation's trade.

St. Louis, Cairo, Memphis, Vicksburg, Natchez, Baton Rouge—above all, New Orleans, the gateway to the sea—teemed with river-men of every rank, from the lowly raftsman and the vanishing flatboatmen to the affluent owner, and the long pilot to whom all looked with respect as the man without whom no keel could move. Hard-shelled slave traders brushed shoulders with the strolling, light-fingered gentry of the card packs—professional gamblers whose harvests were never lean. Wealthy planters, gentlemen bred and born, rode the river unaffected by its restless tone, too constantly immured, perhaps, in the plantation atmosphere of their own making to be susceptible to the seethe and drag of trade. Rough back-country men of the Louisiana bayous, Texas cattlemen, travelling salesmen from the north, men wanted by the law—all appeared on the river, all contributed something to the fiber of its life.

Men of ambition held their ears to the ground; the river's future, immediate and ultimate, was perpetually first in the minds of its lords. Jealously each watched the growth of competing lines, the most recent departures in speed, the newest standards of elegance in cabin accommodations. Rumors of late achievements and bold projected plans ran up and down the great stream, almost outracing the fast packets themselves.

Nor were men lacking to look farther, to feel the pulse of foreign trade, shrewdly calculating its relationship to the trade of the Mississippi, alert for means to extend river power overseas. Their eyes, too, turned constantly to the north, where were rumbling with increasing menace the first thunders of the storm that was to destroy the old south; and with it the life of the river itself.

For the river trade had its roots in the soil of the southern bottomlands. Advancing to the river's very margin, closely enfolding the hell-roaring steamboat towns, lay the great plantations, leisurely, wealthy, sustaining a life of their own that differed from anything else the world could show. The black soil of the deltas, cheaply worked by herd labor, blossomed into the limitless tonnage of cotton that supplied the globe. It was the plantation that gave the steamboat its mountainous loads of bales, filled its staterooms with the grace of aristocracy, and its cargo decks with sinewy blacks.

"If you are going to hunt turmoil all the time," said Arnold Huston's father, "turmoil is going to begin hunting you."

That was when Arnold was eighteen. At that time he had already been four years on the river.

Turmoil was a common word with old Anastasius Huston, tossed out repeatedly like a poker chip until it was well worn with use. It represented to him the very epitome of the undesirable. He lived in an unpainted house on the outskirts of Natchez, a house that had once been beautiful and grand. He owned some land, somewhere, and some rented-out slaves some place else; but until his death Arnold knew neither the extent nor the exact source of his father's income. In his last years Anastasius Huston had the thin-carved cheek that his son had inherited; but his lips were long and full. They seemed to stroke over and mould out the slow words that he spoke.

Anastasius believed that he was of the oldest of the old southern aristocracy. The discrepancy between this inherited position and the slight attention accorded him made him wonder with an increasing dim bitterness what the world was coming to; and he hid his mortification behind a grim half-smile that looked cynical where cynicism played no part.

But the strength of his forebears did not appear in Anastasius. The rich black mucklands that they had spent their lives to win dribbled away, and their magnificent potentialities passed into other hands.

There was a mouldiness about Anastasius in his later years, and the ruined lineaments of strength behind the mould seemed hollow, as if the man were vacated by all significant things. His son Arnold, born of an Irish mother—what eccentric madness made Anastasius choose her?—found nothing in his father to hold him, nothing at all.

At twelve, three years after his mother's death, Arnold Huston was haunting the river front; at fourteen, he had left home for good. In the next four years the river took him past recall, shaping him into what he was always going to be. Cabin boy, engine room striker, pilot's cub, second mate at eighteen—by the time he stood uncomfortably before his father again he was part and parcel of the river roughage that Anastasius Huston so loathed.

"If you are going to hunt turmoil all the time, turmoil is going to begin hunting you."

Well, it seemed to be so. If Anastasius Huston had never accomplished any other thing in his life, he had at least mouthed out one virulent truth.

It was almost their last conversation. If there had been more, if Arnold had sought to know his father better, other curious and hard-carved things might have been dug up. But he was not interested; and when his father died, eight years later, Arnold was left with a memory full of sharp cluttery detail—the odd ruffled black tie that went with Anastasius Huston to the grave, the agate buttons that had appeared on each succeeding vest, the fatuously systematic manner in which his father had always folded his napkin in a certain way. But the actual shape of his father's mind remained forever hidden. It had been a thing too cloudily passive, as it lurked in its misty silences, to have left any definite impress.

The fortune which Arnold had expected to inherit no longer existed. When five months of liquidation had dragged through there were no slaves, money, or lands; only a small remaining debt, which he promptly paid out of his pocket. He saved, however, the house in Natchez where he had been born, which he had abandoned for the river in his earliest youth.

By that time Arnold Huston had some money of his own. Pilots had then been ruling the river for some time; five hundred dollars a month was no uncommon wage. When he had clapped every obtainable mortgage onto the Natchez home, borrowed what he could, and stretched his credit to the cracking point, he found that he was able to consummate the initial ambition of his life. He equipped a small sort of stern-wheeler, and plunged headlong into the river trade.

Thus Anastasius Huston in death achieved for his son what in life he would have bitterly deplored. And the last wealth of the Hustons took to the coffee-colored water in a freshly painted veteran of a boat.

THE fog had cleared; beyond the bright wreckage of the *Peter Swain* the breeze burnished the dark water in slow-winding rings and lines, returning the firelight like water snakes of molten gold.

For an hour the night had been troubled by the screaming hiss of the *Swain*'s escape valve, flung open as the last act of her engineer; and her whistle, fouled by falling wreckage, had bellowed for a time, a long, hoarse roar heard for miles up and down the river. But the steam had exhausted itself at last; and with its passing the whistle had subsided into a choking moan, and so fallen silent forever.

The *Swain*'s superstructure was gone, collapsed sideways in a welter of fire from which slender timberings still thrust up, flag staffs crowded with pennons of flame; and though her heaven-soaring blaze had died away, the guts of her still burned like a floating chunk of hell. Somewhere in the horrid crackling of the fire mass was whatever remained of Tom Cole, the *Peter Swain*'s pilot. No one had been able to find the boy who was Cole's cub. Probably he was there, too, claimed by destruction along with the man he had idolized.

A broad slab of mahogany from the cabin trim, thrown into the water by some freak of the cabin's collapse, floated past in the back-wash; on it in great raised letters of gold showed the motto, "In God We Trust."

Over the crowd ashore rolled a great billowing cloud of cotton gas and smoke, herding them roughly back from the edge of the bluff; and Huston, his face and torso grotesquely painted by the singe of heat and soot, stumbled after the rest. A hairy, sweat-drenched arm fell across his burnt shoulders, but he was hardly aware of the pain. The mate was walking at his side.

"Our luck," the mate was muttering. "There she goes—rip, snort, and to hell. . . ." The man had owned some small share in the *Peter Swain.* "First and last boat. . . . All over. . . . End of the Huston Line. . . ."

To himself Huston was saying, "No, no, by God, no! It's only the beginning. . . ." But he could say nothing aloud; and the wet corded arm fell away.

CHAPTER III

TWO nights later, in Natchez.

A cold weight was upon him as he topped the long climb up Natchez bluff. One foot after the other in the dust was a plodding way of motion to him, unlike that of the boats that glided smoothly upstream, or swung down-river on the back of the current, New Orleans bound.

He turned and looked back over the bush-fringed, switchback road; it hugged the face of the bluff so closely that he could spit to its very foot. Beyond the broad light-trimmed blotch of Natchez-under-the-hill, the Mississippi lay gray in the night, lighter in color than the black woods of its towhead islands, lighter, even, than the faintly starred sky. Huston never saw it without feeling the strong pull and draw of that current that could drown a horse or a man, swing a great steamboat to break her rudder against the bank, or, by Gargantuan caprice, devour a whole farm in a night.

Far up the river, in the broadening bend, a tiny thing like a bright match box afloat was a steamboat bound upstream. He could make out the red and green flecks of running lights on her smoke stacks. She might have been going great guns; perhaps her band was rippling off some swinging air, and her decks were gay with people. But far off there, seen from the somber Natchez bluff, she seemed as motionless as any other bright fragment, dwarfed to insignificance by the broad waters on which she rode.

The great silver-gray reaches, empty of traffic but for the single boat, flowed undisturbed, desolate, vastly lonesome. Yet the aged river remained to Huston the artery of life itself. On the dusty bluff, where his best strides were a poor poking trudge, he was no better than a rooted thing. It was different on the river, on the hurricane roof of a broad white boat, with the shores sliding past and the churning paddle wheels putting the waters behind them all night long. . . .

He was trying not to think of the disaster hardly seventy hours gone. The funeral of his pilot had been an inadequate thing, considering the labors the man had performed in his river years, but it was over with. Tonight, Huston reflected, he owed nothing to himself nor to the world. He hung suspended in a silent interim of inactivity between the achievements that were gone and the reconstruction that must presently begin.

The oiled bandages beneath his shirt pulled at his scorched skin, hard to forget. Now, if ever, he needed something to blot the past, push the future a little farther away. Below, Natchez-under-the-hill was diverting a thousand others; it could not divert him. Steamboat men, raftsmen, flatboatmen, knockabouts, loafers, wharf rats, river wreckage—they all found their places there, drinking, brawling, gambling, hunting out the red lights. There was nothing for Huston there.

He had wandered through Natchez-under-the-hill, drinking here and there. As he walked, an erect, slim figure, his eyes red in a harsh gray face, swaggering men had brushed his raw shoulders, jostled him at the bars and in the streets. He could have had a dozen fights for the asking; yet for all his ragged nerves his swift temper had not once risen, and within himself he was apart, and cold. Then presently the close reek of the bars had sickened him, and he had left them, sober still.

A single muscle of his face had tightened with the heady rise of the liquor; it gave his cheek a weary feel. Also there was a curious aspect about the lights as he looked down over the moil under the hill, as if they floated obscurely in limpid water. Otherwise he was as cold sober as before, and the liquor had brought him none of the benefit he had craved.

He strolled on along the road at the top of the bluff. Trees stood over him, close and brooding as he walked, their heavy-foliaged masses against the sky making him feel small, and more than ever bound to the dust. The town was different here; on the tree-shaded heights stately houses were set in wooded lawns. Their tall pillars gleamed austerely, cool in the faint starlight. Planters had their town houses here, and retired rich men, those who controlled the river, and those who owned the most successful of the gambling dives and bars. The brawling wave of the river roughage broke at the foot of the bluff, permitting the pillared dwellings to gaze out from above, unnoticing and serene.

He told himself that he was wandering aimlessly, that he neither knew where he was going nor cared. But even as he pressed this reassurance through his mind his feet were slowing, as if reluctant to advance in the direction he took. Some sinister sort of fascination pulled him on, preventing him, in his present flotsam mood, from turning aside.

Thus he presently approached the end of the bluff road. He had been walking with averted eyes, but he raised them now; and from a hundred yards away stood staring at the great ghost of a house that barred the way.

The house at the end of the road was immensely tall, with lean columns pillaring the height of its narrow façade like bars. It had once stood upon a swelling knoll, but the bluff had caved away so that the building overlooked a breath-taking drop on the river side. Its owners had sold the land before it for city lots to its very lintel, and the right-angled road under the door had been graded down until a ten-foot wall was necessary to sustain the earth that thinly protected the foundations of the house from the street.

The effect of these workings of time was ghostly in the extreme, accentuating the building's already narrow height, leaving it singularly desolate and suggestive of vanished things. It loomed monstrously above the river and the town; and its flat-hipped roof, as if its builders were dissatisfied with the great height it already possessed, supported a thin pillar of a watch tower, empty and dark, and showing the sky through the glass that panelled its six sides.

The tall parallel columns gleamed pallidly, lighter than the silver-gray river and the sky. No light showed within; the facade seemed the death mask of a house long dead, mournfully sinister in the slight glow of the stars.

It was the early established home of Dennison Huston, the brother of Arnold's father. For twenty-nine years, a period of time terminated only by the death of the one, the brothers had not spoken. Each had watched the other's fortunes with hatred that could have been founded on nothing less real than a significant wrong. Though the younger was now dead, the brotherly hatred lived on, one-sided and without means of expression, but implacable still.

Somewhere within that ghostly tower of a house was the study where Dennison Huston worked, a many-doored inner room, lighted by lamps even on the brightest days. Through the years that Anastasius Huston sat alone with his vest buttons, twiddling his thumbs and silently reproaching his waning stars, a constant stream of visitors had made their way to the tall house on the bluff, always business-like and always male, for Dennison Huston never entertained.

Lately the visitors were fewer, but individually more important; Dennison Huston had not become a palsied, chair-bound old man without gathering into his hands certain strings, at the ends of which figures danced to the twitch of his age-blotched hands.

Of this man Arnold Huston could obtain nothing,

wanted nothing; yet in the contrast between the fortunes of the Dennison Huston branch of the family and his own he found a morbid fascination. He was aware of a new jealousy that repudiated the cool disinterest he had felt toward the uneventful feud as a child. Like Anastasius, Dennison had but one son: Will Huston, two years older than Arnold. To his hands the weapons forged by Dennison Huston were now all but resigned. Will Huston found himself fingering, at his leisure, the handles of such powerful tools as he probably never would have the courage to wield boldly; while Arnold, leaning with sagging frame against a tree before the house of his uncle, gazed bitterly at the stronghold of Dennison.

He cursed softly as he realized what his mood had led him into, and turned away. There was but one other spot in Natchez that could faintly interest him to-night. He started along the brick-paved walks in its direction.

Suddenly he stopped and pivoted on the balls of his feet, arrested by a single brief sound from the mask of the tall house. It had been at once sharp and muffled, like the sound of a heavy fall; Huston knew it for the report of a pistol. For an instant a window rattled in response; then silence again, more desolate, more deathly enigmatic than before.

Huston suppressed a swift impulse to rush up the narrow steps, crash through one of the low-silled windows behind the pillars, and learn for himself what weird thing had happened in the inner depths of that inhuman place. But a chilled thoughtfulness came over him, and as suddenly as he had stopped he turned and went away, cat-footed in the darkness under the trees.

During the six years prior to the death of Anastasius, Huston had not set eyes on the house in which he had been born. It had held nothing for him in those years, and could offer nothing now; yet he found himself turning toward it, urged by an inner restlessness that called no place friendly, yet sought perpetually for something toward which to move.

Like that of Dennison, the house of his father had been a plantation home, overtaken by the growth of the town. A city street, distinguished from a road only by its brick walk, now ran past its gate. Its lawn, however, remained to it, a rank, weed-grown acre darkened by trees that withered with age, yet were able, with their interlocked arms, to hold out the starlight still.

Huston's steps grew slower as he drew opposite the dwelling in which he had once lived; his feet were silent in the turf beside the walk. He could make out the face of the building now, darkly gray behind the trees. Its checker-paned windows were as black as if cut in coal. Only one or two of the panes, set less squarely in the warping frames than the rest, showed a sad gray gleam, a reflection of the dim sky. Except for these the house was of a piece with the night.

Staring across at it, he almost ran into a group of three or four negroes. They were standing close together, motionless and silent, their gaze so steadily fixed upon the still house that they failed to notice

Huston's approach. He was about to brush past them, but paused, swaying on his tired legs, made curious by the fixety of their gaze. He was still feeling the unusual effects of his liquor; and while his sight was abnormally clear he seemed to find an odd aspect in the huddled group of slaves, as if there had been some intangible deformity about them all.

" 'E show, 'e show!" said one in a husky whisper; "I seen 'e shinin' on the stai'. Jes' you wait—'e show!"

"Ah gwine home," said another. "Ah doan' *wanta* see nuffin'. Dis ain't no good place fo' niggas at night."

"No, man, sho' ain't; I'se heahed the death-rattle comin' out o' that house—"

"Jes' you wait—'e show!"

Huston turned his eyes to the old house, and saw no movement, nothing out of the way; only the broad weathered front, dismal in the dark, of a house that would never see good days again. Then, as he looked, a little square third-floor window made itself visible in the dark, as if behind it the dimmest sort of glow had been lit. It strengthened until it was a tawny block, only dimly luminous, but so definitely alight that no trick of the eyes could explain it.

"Dar 'e! Dar 'e!" chattered a negro with an aged voice.

"Ah, Lo' Jedus, it's 'em!"

Huston drew in his breath in spite of himself. Then instantly he was angry with himself for the start the light had given him.

"What you talkin' about?" he suddenly demanded of

the negroes.

"Ah, Jedus!"

There was a gasp, a scamper of broad bare feet. Huston watched a diminishing silhouette of bobbing heads; then the negroes turned the corner of the street and he was quite alone.

For a moment Huston stood looking strangely at the lighted window in the old house. Then he strode directly across the street and vaulted the rotting picket gate. Beneath the trees the night was utterly black, but his feet were sure enough on the once-accustomed ground. From the rank grass and weeds under the trees came a cool dank breath, as if frogs should be living there, though from no place in the vicinity of the house came voice or sound of a living thing.

From time to time as he approached through the long dark of the trees he could glimpse the light in the high window on the third floor. The tired muscle of his cheek tautened perceptibly; but he shoved his hands into his pockets and advanced steadily.

The steps were close ahead, steps so broad that twelve could have walked up them abreast. There were sixteen of them, bridging the blackness under the gallery that crossed the breadth of the house. Above the gallery he could not see, until suddenly he emerged from among the trees and the house rose before him, sad and old in the faint grayness of the stars.

CHAPTER IV

LIKE the high-pillared home of Dennison Huston, the façade of the aging dwelling looked like a deathly mask; but this one was broad and sunken instead of whitely tall and austere. And while the mask of the house of Dennison still shielded a place where people lived as they had always lived, this covered only a dusty moulder of remains from which all animate things that had belonged there had gone.

He suddenly stopped and stood motionless; the light in the third-story window was gone.

Seeking the unknown in a labyrinth of silent dark was different from merely climbing the stairs to enter a lighted room. He stood uncertainly.

"Some tramp bedded down," he told himself; but was not reassured.

His reluctance to enter the house was replaced by a less negative sensation, a conviction that, unseeing, he was seen. The unrevealing upper windows seemed staring with empty eyes; behind them, he thought, someone was watching who had perceived his approach and destroyed the dim light. Huston's position before the house became intolerable to him. It did not occur to him that he could turn back. He went forward, and silently climbed the decaying steps.

Instinct made the light balls of his feet soundless as he crossed the broad gallery to the door. So little did the starlight penetrate the damp gallery that he could not perceive that the door was open until his hand sought its panels and found that they were not there. Unimpeded he stepped into the inner dark.

A thin cold odor of must and rotting carpets was in his nostrils. He could see nothing; a glance over his shoulder to the dim starlight he had left made the darkness about him seem the more impenetrable. He stood quiet for a time halfway down the length of the great central hall, listening and trying to accustom his eyes. At first he could hear only the irregular coming and going of his own breath. Then, gradually becoming clear to his straining ears, the thin, steady, scraping sound of a gnawing rat, emphasizing the desolation of the dark and the long absence of human life.

He moved impatiently, then instantly checked again with a swift contraction of the heart. He was certain that something had moved ahead of him, a figure as tall as himself, blacker than the dark behind. For an instant he stood motionless, seeking to disregard the shock that the movement had brought him. Then as suddenly he relaxed, swearing softly; he remembered now the cheval glass that stood at the end of the hall, so placed as to startle him by no deadlier thing than the shadow of himself.

In two strides he verified this solution; and, made suddenly nonchalant by his disgust with himself, he sought the rail of the broad curved stairway that led to the second floor. He found it by memory alone, and went softly up the carpeted treads two at a time, his fingers gathering a soft, mouldy accretion of dust as they brushed the rail. On the second floor, beyond the turn of the long stair, he paused to listen once more.

From where he stood not even a window was visible. If it had been dark in the lower hall, it was darker here, without the open door to let in even the reflection of the starlight. Yet he knew where he was as well as if he could have seen.

He had hated that dark upper hall as a child; to-night, as he listened in the mouldy dark, he hated it still. It was long and narrow, its high ceiling distant. On either side of it were spaced white doors, some of which he had never seen opened. He had often run past them as a child, imagining them full of phantom shapes. There was not a one of them behind which some one or other had not died; people whom he had neither loved nor known, an assemblage of mysterious old names. Huston had neither credulity nor patience for superstitious belief. Yet to-night the chill of the upper hall seemed thronged with the people of another world, cold and hostile, striving with their ghostly hands to press him down the stairs and away.

A swift chill coursed over his back and shoulders, and the bandaged skin of his back twinged as suddenly as at the touch of fingers. But the silence was complete save for the faint distant gnawing of the rat; and Huston shook himself free of the unseen hands and went on.

The stair to the third floor turned and narrowed, climbing a windowless well. Like the lower stair, it had been carpeted once, but the carpeting was threadbare and thin; his light footfalls were distinct on the treads. He was less careful now, in haste to get the matter over with and return to the outer air.

At the top he once more stood and listened. He could see a dim square of checkered window, its cobwebbed panes admitting no more than enough light to show where it was. But no sound came.

It only remained to examine the room in which he had seen the light. He walked softly to its door, a memory that he had not been aware of showing his feet the way. Again the panels that his groping fingers sought were not where he expected them to be, for the door stood slightly ajar. Without hesitation he pushed it partly open and went in. The hinges emitted a rusty moan, repeated as the released door swung back to its previous position. In the silence the brief metallic sound seemed to scream through the house.

Alone in the room in which he had seen the light, with the door returning behind him, Huston again felt the chill of suppressed cowardice ripple the length of his spine. Then the match that was ready in his fingers blazed sputtering; and when the blindness of the sudden flare had left his eyes he could see about him for the first time since he had entered the door two floors beneath.

The room was large, low-ceilinged. Although it had been unfurnished ever since he could remember, it had for some reason never been allowed to accumulate the forest of discarded things that filled some of the other third-floor rooms. The dust lay thick upon the floor; in the light of the match he could not see whether or not it were disordered.

In a corner stood a packing case and two old trunks.

When his match burned out he walked to these in the dark, and struck a second match to look behind them. It was a move of ostentatious thoroughness, for he knew as he did it that he would find nothing there.

The chills coursed repeatedly in his back, making his scorched shoulders burn. It seemed to him now that the descent of the long stairs, turning his back upon the mystery that he had sought in this high room, would be infinitely harder than his silent climb into the dark. For some reason he particularly dreaded passing the black hall of the second floor; but the only excuse for delay would have been a more thorough search of the third floor, and this he was more than willing to forego.

He waited a moment, balancing in the dark with his fingers against the wall.

"Slow and steady," he told himself. "Slow and steady. . . . One quick step and it's all off. . . ."

He remembered the story of another riverman, who, like himself, had witnessed the burning of his boat with the loss of certain of those aboard; who, also like himself, had gone wandering sleepless in the night, and had somehow shut himself into an empty house which he had had no sane reason for entering. And how that man had been taken from the place the next day, jibbering insane.

"Slow and steady. . . ." Huston whispered. . . . "Let's go. . . ."

He took a single step forward, then stopped, rigid. And as he listened the chills played in great surges in his back, making his muscles crawl. On the stair between the second and third floor he had heard a step. Then another, and a third.

There followed a little pause, and desperately Huston listened. He had even begun to convince himself that the sound had been a fiction of his overstressed nerves, when it came again. The faint footfalls came up steadily now, though so deliberately that between each and the one that followed there was the suggestion of a pause. So slow were they that they seemed to climb forever, approaching always up such a number of stairs as had never existed there. At last they reached the top, and once more paused.

He could not deceive himself as to what he had heard, for his fingertips on the wall had felt the tremor of weight upon the stairs. The prickle of sweat ran across Huston's forehead. With a great effort he broke his rigidity and fumbled for a match. He drew it out of his pocket with stiff fingers, leaned against the wall, and set the head of the match against the plaster. It rattled there with a tiny dull chatter until he pressed it to stillness.

The sound of steps began again, slower now, at once stealthy and deliberately firm. They came steadily to the door of the room in which he waited. They stopped there; and for a long time there was silence.

It seemed to Huston that he could bear the suspense no more. He determined to rush the door, fling it open, assail whatever stood there with fists and hands. Yet when he had decided this he could not bring himself to move. His knees were as brittly inert as ice, and the match head remained fast to the wall.

Across the room from him the door moved; not steadily as he had moved it before, but slowly, so that its rusty moan was reduced to a series of small ticking complaints. It seemed to him at last that he could see a black blotch that protruded itself into the room, yet he knew that this must be impossible in the thickness of the dark. His eyes had strained until he could withstand their madness no more; he closed them, and concentrated all his senses in his ears.

There was a step within the room; a long pause; a second; a third. Sound had ceased in the middle of the floor. The time had come for him to strike his match, and still he was unable to move. The moments passed. With a great effort he ripped the match along the plaster, and opened his eyes in its instant flare.

Facing him from half across the room, tight lipped and staring eyed, stood his cousin, Will Huston.

The man was immaculately groomed; his black cutaway set faultlessly; his curly dark hair was meticulously brushed and pomaded. But Arnold saw only the pallid terror of his cousin's face. His frilled shirt front and the high collar whose points flared on either side of his jaw were no whiter, it seemed, than Will Huston's mouth.

Arnold laughed harshly.

"Well, you ass?" He had a hard, even voice, slurred by the drawl of the lower river. The match scorched his fingers, and he let it drop.

"Gad, man," said Will in the dark, "what a scare you gave me!"

"You must have been in the house when I came in.

Didn't you hear me on that last flight of stairs?" By the light of a fresh match Arnold could see that the color was returning to the other's cheeks.

"I was on the second floor," Will admitted. "In fact, I saw you standing in front of the house before you came in. But—"

"But what?"

"You were reported dead."

"Would I be standin' in front of the house, dead?"

"Gad, you should've seen yourself. You stood there still as a corpse, with a face like a death's head."

The match died. In the dark Arnold chuckled. It was always difficult for him to realize that he was probably the only one of his family who did not believe, at heart, the superstitions that their negro mammies had instilled in their formative years.

"You thought I was dead, and you followed me up here to see what my ghost was after?"

"Something like that," said Will shortly.

"In God's name why?" Huston laughed.

"What would you think?" said the other testily. "D'you think I'd go plunging out of the house for *your* ghost?"

"Well," said Arnold, grinning, "you've got more guts than I gave you credit for."

"Can it be possible!" Will returned.

"Let's get out of here."

On the lower gallery they paused, and in the comparative warmth of the outer night they stood for a moment, regarding each other awkwardly. Their curious experience in the old house had not changed them. They remained aloof, unfriendly as they always had been, linked remotely by a bond of relationship resented by both.

Will Huston chose to affect an ironic formality. "I regret that I failed to receive you at the door."

"Oh, you do?" said Arnold, his annoyance flaming at the other's tone. "Well, I ain't accustomed to being received at my door. To what am I indebted—"

"I am sorry to disillusion you," said Will sarcastically. "But it doesn't happen to be your door."

"I beg your pardon!"

"Why simulate stupidity?" said Will. "Your mortgage is foreclosed." The formality of his diction was elaborate.

"I got no notice," Arnold declared hotly.

"That was due to no omission of mine."

Arnold, now recollecting clearly enough that the mortgage in question must have expired, saw no reason to doubt his cousin's statement. Knowing the real source of Will Huston's bitter hostility toward him, as he had known also the reason for Dennison Huston's enmity for his father, Arnold's attitude toward it was ordinarily tolerant. Now, however, his cousin's cool sarcasms whipped him to a consuming blaze of passion.

"Seems like you're even more offensive than usual to-night," he said.

In the faint starlight he could see the pale oval of Will's face, plumply expressionless, with short eyebrows and insolent eyes.

"Still quite the little ruffian," Will murmured.

Lord, thought Arnold, the man might lack brains or sense of humor, but he had the Huston brass! Aloud he said harshly, "Will you repeat that?"

"I said," returned Will with sudden unnecessary loudness, " 'Still the little ruffian!' "

Arnold's fist smashed into his cousin's face. To his surprise the man pitched backward, lit on his back halfway down the gallery steps, and rolled to the bottom. Huston was not accustomed to men that fell as easily as that. With his hands on his hips he watched Will slowly gain his feet, perfunctorily dusting his clothes with his hands. He laughed, praying for fresh opportunity.

Will Huston's face was white again as he raised his head. A slender trickle of blood from his mouth traced a crooked line on his smooth chin.

"Of course you'll have to fight for this," he said, his voice quivering with a rage he tried to conceal.

Arnold went down the steps. "I'm waitin'," he said.

"I suppose a rough-and-tumble brawl would suit you," said Will. "It doesn't suit me."

"No?"

"The choice of weapons is your privilege, but they must be weapons."

Arnold was disgusted by what he took to be a cowardly evasion. "Oh, jump in the river," he suggested.

"So you're a coward as well as a ruffian, are you?"

"What the devil are you talking about?"

"Pistols, of course."

Arnold was honestly mystified. "Well," he answered, "I'm sorry I can't shoot you. But I don't carry a gun ashore. If you call on me to-morrow—"

"To-morrow is impossible. Let me suggest Saturday morning in New Orleans."

"You damn fool," said Arnold, "do you know what year this is?"

"Certainly."

"It's 1858," Arnold told him. "Do you get it? Not thirty-eight, *fifty*-eight. Duelling is as out o' date as knee pants."

"I think not," Will contradicted. "One was fought last week on the Carson plantation, and two the month before at—"

"Oh, rubbish!"

"—Lovell's point. I know that in your class the practice is to hit your enemy when he is not looking for it, and then judge the matter closed. I suppose—"

The anger that had sent the hot blood to Arnold's head was ebbing away now, leaving him prey to the weariness of his shattered nerves. He was sickly dizzy, and his raw back and shoulders were surging with fresh flame under the bandages. A roar was in his ears like that of the fire that had taken his boat.

"Oh, all right," he said. "I'll shoot you, if that's what you want."

"Name a second, please."

"Well—Mark Wallace, I guess."

"I'll send my second to him."

Arnold stood, smiling sardonically, while the other went up the steps and locked the door of the old house. Will passed him on the way to the gate without looking back. Arnold watched him as he picked his way meticulously through the weeds, and so disappeared into the dark.

CHAPTER V

THE room in which Huston found Mark Wallace was small, occupying hardly more than a dormer of a house on the Rue Royale in New Orleans. The single checker-paned window, curtainless, looked across the narrow street into the neighboring balconies. Within, the walls were lined from floor to ceiling with books. Books had entirely taken the place; they were piled among the loose papers on the table, they were in rows and stacks on the floor, they struggled to displace a dusty bust of Rosaro on a mantelpiece that could hardly spare them room.

Huston stood for a little staring wearily about at the familiar buttresses of books. Mark Wallace was sitting before an empty fireplace hardly larger than a cigar box, and Huston, in an effort to be casual, avoided meeting his eye. Then Wallace sprang up, shook him by the wrists, and pressed him into the better of his two chairs.

"How are you feeling, Arn?" Wallace was nonchalant, and Huston felt himself relax.

"Rotten, thanks." Wearily he contemplated the familiar features of his friend who in turn regarded the plaster face of Rosaro through smoke rings provided by his cigar.

The face of Mark Wallace was regular but distinguished by a delicate sensitiveness so marked as almost to place him outside of both his surroundings and his time. His slender moustache was well-kept, but his hair, dark brown as a seal, was in tousled disarray.

"You know," he said presently, his voice casually modulated, "when I heard the *Peter Swain* had burned, I said 'Thank God!' "

"What!"

"I thought that would get to you," Wallace smiled. "You came in here with a face as hard and gray as cement. No ray of light—nothing mattered. But now that I've got your attention, as they say from the soapbox—"

"Tom Cole burned to death with the *Peter Swain*," said Huston harshly. "He stayed with the wheel; deliberately gave his life to land my burning boat. So you sit there and say—"

"I didn't know that, Arn."

"Hs cub stuck with him," Huston went on, his voice bitter. "He's dead, too. Maybe you remember him; a curly-headed youngster of about fourteen, who sometimes tagged about with me, when he couldn't be with Tom. And you—"

"I didn't know that, either, Arn."

"—you sit there and blow smoke rings and say 'Thank God!' Good Christ, anyone would think you'd never been outside this room in your life!"

"I didn't mean it that way, Arn—"

"Well, what did you mean?"

Mark Wallace opened his lips to reply, but thought better of it. Instead, he dug a pinch-bottle out of a cabinet lost in the books, and poured drinks. Arnold selected a lean cigar from the box offered him.

By settling himself into the cushions with care, Huston found that he could lean back without too much troubling his healing shoulders. His deep draught of wine was mellowing, and the lean cigar was good. They sat silently, contemplating by habit the empty fireplace.

"I've named you as my second in a duel," said Huston at last.

"A duel? With whom?"

"Will Huston—that numb skull cousin of mine."

"Oh," said Wallace, relaxing. "He can't shoot. He's never fought before in his life. It won't be serious. Someone fights a duel nearly every month."

"Oh, nonsense!"

"Of course it doesn't get much publicity nowadays, but they do, anyway. This one will be only a waste of time."

"Yes?"

"He'll miss. How many times do I have to—"

"I won't miss," said Arnold flatly.

"Why?"

"Because I can shoot. I can hunt possum with my pistol. How can I miss in broad daylight?"

"Point at him; he'll fire and miss. Then you let go into the air."

"No, Mark."

"I tell you, Arn, you'll regret it, if someone is actually hit."

"If I go out there to shoot a man," said Huston dully,

"I aim to shoot him."

Mark Wallace sat bolt upright, and his fine eyes rested on Huston with a gleam of humor.

"Oh, all right," he said, relaxing. "Shoot him then! Make everything just as messy as possible. If you can manage to plant the ball in the middle of his face the affair will be especially gratifying. I recommend the bridge of his nose."

"I can hit it, too," said Huston sullenly.

"Oh, Lord! . . . Do you know when he wants to fight?"

"Saturday, here. He's challenging, and I want navy pistols, not an old tiddlywink of a duelling set."

"Won't cannon do?"

"His second will look you up; I don't know who he is."

"To-night's Wednesday—isn't it? Well, will you have whisky, or chocolate, before? And where?"

"I'll have coffee, here," said Huston.

"Worst thing you could do. 'Captain Huston, crazed with java, calmly emptied his gun in all directions, and was forced to brain his opponent with the butt.' "

"Coffee," Huston growled.

"Oh, very well. . . . They'll probably hang you, you know, if you insist on hitting him."

"But only once," said Huston.

"Once is commonly fatal."

"I am depending on it."

"I tell you, Arn, it's no joking matter!"

"Then why are you joking?"

Wallace gestured impatiently, and fell silent. When

Arnold at last looked up he found the other studying him.

"Where are you going, Arn?"

"No place; why?"

"You've shaved two days under the skin."

"I always shave that way."

"I can tell you where we're going; we're going to a place you've never been before, a place—"

"No place," said Huston shortly.

"—where no one else could possibly take you. It's a privilege, let me tell you. If there is another like it in New Orleans, in the world—Of course, it may appear commonplace to you; people look at things differently. Only, you and I are so much alike—"

"Alike?"

Huston's dark-circled gray eyes observed the other incuriously. Though his life had been untroubled by introspection, he knew himself clearly enough for what he was as he sat there beside Mark Wallace's empty grate: a weather-hardened riverman with a colorless roach of hair above a face now harsh-lined and haggard; a man with corded wrists and cold eyes, skillful only in devices for beating the river game. Little similar, he thought, to this other young man of the books and the town, with his suave hands and sensitive mind, and a face that was close to being beautiful.

"Oh, what are you talking about?"

They smoked for a while in silence before Wallace spoke again.

"Do you feel like sleeping?"

"Good God, no! I haven't slept two hours since the *Swain* burned. When I lie down in the dark I hear the fire, and it like to drives me crazy. I can see it plain—that awful mass of fire, with the body of Tom Cole in it— You should 'a' heard those niggers hollerin', Mark. I never heard anythin' so ghastly in my life. It'd *give* you somethin' to say 'Thank God' about."

Mark Wallace said nothing. Presently he rose.

"Come on."

"Where you going?"

"Out."

"I'll sit here, I guess."

"Look here, Arn—do you care a damn about anything to-night?"

"Nothing in the world, Mark."

"Then humor me and come along," he said with an air of conclusion, and opened the door.

Almost reeling with his nerve-wrecked fatigue, Huston followed him away.

Wallace led him down the Rue Royale. At Père Antoine's Garden, the little grassy plot behind the St. Louis Cathedral, they turned into Orleans alley; and, traversing its tremendous flags, passed between the close-rising walls of the Cathedral and the buildings beside it, past the black mouth of le Petite Exchange, past the iron-bound door of the Spanish arsenal, where showed the deep grooves that wheels of old cannon had left in the lintel stone, past the massive Cabildo; until the old Place d'Armes opened before them, its new statue of Jackson lonely in the light of a sinking moon.

It was impossible for Mark Wallace to pass this place by night without imagining that he saw mistily the black moving bulk of the Spanish Guard, the rakish parallel lines of matchlock muskets, the bellying swing of Spanish officers' capes. Huston, observing rather the twin stacks of the huddled steamboats on the levee beyond, saw none of these things; yet saw many things of more immediate interest to the times.

They turned downstream on Chartres, picking their way along the narrow banquette of the narrow street; and paused presently before the arched carriage way of an old house. The building rose sheer from the street, as did all the buildings in the old quarter of New Orleans, jutting upward so vertically that the balconies above made them seem to overhang. Wallace rattled the latch of a lock so massive that its keyhole could have received his hand, and in answer a little grilled wicket opened in the timbers of the gate.

"Who dah?"

"Wallace."

An entrance more like a window than a door swung inward in the frontlet of the great gate, after much audible fumbling with bolts and bars within. Ducking their heads, they stepped high over the twelve-inch barrier of the sill into a flagged and vaulted passage of proportions designed to receive a coach and six. Beyond the last great arch of the passage the yellow radiance of a coach lantern showed an inner court, and beyond, the dark arches of a cloister garth that must have been a stable, once.

The bald and withered slave who had admitted them went bobbing ahead, his slippers flapping on the flags; and so they were led up a broad and curving stair, and through a dark passage to a white door, elaborately decorated with a raised design; and admitted, at last, into a spacious chamber.

The furnishings of the room were few, and included little not in common use at that time; yet some curious turn of mind, half primitive, half austere, of the person who had selected them had given the room an effect barbaric and exotic. A single lighted lamp shed a bright yellow disc at its feet; the rest of its light was diffused through a shade of Indian red, leaving the room deep in warm shadow. Three walls of the room were of plain sea-gray, unadorned except for wall candelabra of brass; but the fourth wall was taken by tall French windows, now swathed in straight hanging mulberry drapes. Just below the ceiling ran a broad frieze the color of clean ivory, its bas-relief figures dim in the stained light.

"Whose place is this?" Huston asked without interest.

"A friend's," said Mark. . . . "Sit down, Arn. Use this settee—it's very comfortable, really."

Huston turned impatiently, as if to speak to the negro, but he had disappeared. He remained standing obdurately by the door, his lower lids sagging, his face grayer and harsher than before.

"Come, come! Sit down."

"Nope. I'm leaving." He turned slow eyes on Wallace in a gaze implacable in its black distaste. But the fine eyes in the sensitive face did not flinch; they seemed disinterested, rather, and studiously contemplative.

"Where are you going? Will you turn in?"

"No, and I don't know where I'm going, and I care less," Huston said. His jaded body, flayed by a haunted restlessness that would not let it sleep, was turning him savage. The room looked odd to him, as if he were in liquor when he was not. A ragged, sawing pain was drawing at intervals across the base of his skull, his legs were weak with fatigue, and all sensations were alike his enemies. He would have given a thousand to relax into genuine sleep; yet was kept from it, more than anything else, by his conviction that he could not. He must sleep soon, he knew; yet he knew no other way of hastening that end than to yield perpetually to his restlessness until that restlessness was borne down by utter exhaustion.

"You shouldn't have brought me here." As he snarled at Mark the red smoulder in his eyes seemed to break into flame. "Learn now. I ain't an exhibit, to show your friends. . . ."

He stood swaying drunkenly on his legs, trying to steady himself enough to break from the room: and in this condition first set eyes on Jacqueline DuMoyne.

She appeared so quietly that he hardly knew at just what moment she entered the room. He had noticed the door opposite him, through which she entered, for it was hung with tapestried folds in tone with the wall. She seemed to take form uncertainly before his fever-blurred eyes; he was unaware that she was there until he found himself staring at her. He realized vaguely that Mark Wallace was pursuing the formalities of introduction. He failed to catch her name, and stood confusedly trying to gather his shattered forces into something like a mannerly front.

He remembered afterward that he had not thought her beautiful, then. But he was surprised, and ashamed: ashamed of that angry speech, which she must have overheard. As she stood before him, a slender, relaxed figure with her hands quiet at her sides, it seemed that it was she who had been dragged out for him to look at, rather than the reverse.

He could not, though, ever remember what sort of thing she had worn. Something black, he guessed, that came up about her throat; for he recalled only the curiously pale oval of her face with the close dark hair about it, and eyes so dark against the pallor of her skin that they seemed drawn in with charcoal, or with india ink; and her slender hands.

She came slowly across to him as they were introduced, looking rather wonderingly at him, he thought; had he been able to see his own haggard face he would not have been surprised. She seemed to hold his eyes with her own; and she gave him her hand, which he certainly did not expect. It was a cool hand, at once thin and soft, yet very steady, as if there might have been strength there that she had never found it necessary to use.

"Madame," he murmured in acknowledgment, and bowed rather lower over her hand than he usually did or had meant to. But still his eyes did not leave hers.

"Captain is weary," she said. There was the suggestion of a trill in the "r," as if she had first learned a Latin tongue; but her voice came from low in her throat.

Again he was surprised, for he heard himself say, "Yes; damn well corked."

She flashed a glance at Mark Wallace, who murmured in apology, "He hasn't slept for three nights."

"I—I must excuse myself," Huston faltered. "I really have to—to get along."

"Please don't go," she said gently; and his objections died on his lips. "Mark, turn the settee to the windows, so; his river is better for the captain to look at than my unlovely room."

Huston stepped forward to swing the settee, but Mark was before him. Jacqueline DuMoyne's slender pale hands arranged cushions in the corners of the seat. Then she pulled a cord that drew back the mulberry draperies from one great window, unlatched the French casements, and let them swing wide. Into the room came the mild fragrance of the outer air.

Huston's eyes sought the open dark beyond the balcony's wrought-iron lace. Over the French roofs of the one-story dwellings below he could see the darkly huddled buildings of the levee; and beyond these the river, black now that the moon had set, reflecting in broken weaving bits the riding lights of sea-going ships. He could count the steamboats, where they lay ranked close against the levee, by their tall twin stacks, by their pilot houses that showed white over the roofs even in the night.

For several minutes Huston stood looking out at the port. Then he drew his breath slowly, and said: "This is a good place."

He noted curiously, when she had made him sit beside her on the broad settee, how luxuriously she reclined among its cushions, her knees crossed, her body relaxed. He was accustomed to think that "ladies" sat upright, with spines like pokers; yet the serene poise of her head would not permit him to consider her as anything else. She was so suavely matter-of-fact that he also relaxed, and let himself settle into the cushions.

The settee was deep, the cushions gentle to the bandage under his coat. He could lean back his head and look out over the dark river where the little sternwheeler *Belle Marie* was passing, touched here and there with pins of light: she was drifting with the current, her idling paddle buckets languidly bathing themselves in the black water.

"She's little," said Jacqueline DuMoyne, "but she handles prettily."

Huston turned his head to look at her. For once, he was thinking, a woman had said something sensible, something he could understand. He studied her profile until her dark eyes turned on him; then he returned his gaze to the river, for now his only desire was for rest.

For a long time they sat in a silence that held neither search for words nor sense of constraint. He was aware at last that she was talking to him, though he hardly knew what she said. He realized that she was talking about the river, and the bayou country; but her casual low voice did not seem to demand that he either listen closely or reply.

The sawing pain at the base of his skull was diminishing now. About him the stained lamplight was mellow; before him lay the river and the illimitable depths of the dark.

"A hundred miles of night," he thought. "This is a good place. . . ."

CHAPTER VI

HUSTON woke to find the sunlight pouring over the clean sheet under which he had slept. He stretched luxuriously, and found that the skin on his back and shoulders felt whole again, his head was clear, and his mind at peace. Mark Wallace was sitting with his feet on the table in the middle of Huston's bare little room, and now snapped shut his book.

"It was a great night for sleep," said Huston lazily.

"Which one?" asked Wallace.

"Which one?"

"You've slept two nights and a day," Wallace told him. "I compute that you've slept better than thirty-five hours."

Huston looked dazed. "When's the duel?"

"To-morrow morning."

"This Friday?"

"Positively, Arn."

Huston's easy smile drew his lips back from his teeth. "Well!" he ejaculated. He sat up and looked about him; and Wallace saw that though his eyes were puffy with sleep they were clear again. "My laundry should've come yesterday."

"It's here."

The riverman swung to his feet. "Lord, I could eat a wolf!"

"Breakfast will be up in a few minutes. I ordered it as I came up."

"That's certainly a coincidence. After sleepin' for thirty-five hours, I come to life just as breakfast is bein' brought up."

"No coincidence," said Wallace; "I set the head of your cot on a chair."

While Huston sponged and put on fresh clothes a mulatto boy was laying a white cloth and a steaming breakfast. He noticed with satisfaction that though the food was plain there appeared to be a great quantity of it.

"If there's anything appeals to me," said Wallace, "it's to see you overeat, and then complain about it."

While the other dressed he explained the various arrangements he had made for the affair with Arnold's cousin. There would be navy revolvers as requested; a secluded site had been agreed upon; at the last moment Mark Wallace had had misgivings about Will's marksmanship, and had got the distance increased from twenty paces to thirty-five. Arnold remained unenthusiastic.

"I almost think I won't shoot him, after all," he offered.

"You certainly will not shoot him," said Wallace crisply.

"Why?"

"Because I have other plans for you."

"Let's hear some of 'em!"

"Get something into you first."

He fell silent. Toward the end of a long breakfast Huston spoke through a mouthful of hot grits.

"Mark, who was that girl?"

"What girl? Oh, that one. Just a family friend."

"Never mind the family—who?"

"I don't want to talk about her now. I—"

"But I do!"

"Well, then, she is Madame DuMoyne."

"Madame."

"Mrs., then."

"Mrs!"

"Certainly." With an air more of disinterest than secretiveness, Mark Wallace pressed on to other subjects before this could sink in. "Arn, would you mind telling me just what your plans were before the *Peter Swain* burned?"

"What plans?"

"Financial; business; on the river."

The question was one Huston had answered for himself often enough so that he was able to reply to it succinctly; and black coffee had made him communicative. The haggard grayness was out of his face, and the smile that had seemed permanently frozen was now ready, deepening the grin creases in his thin cheeks.

"The *Swain* was just clearin' herself, Mark. You have no idea how little I begun with. Even with that old wreck of a boat, I was loaded to the guards with mortgages—all the paper I could carry. I made money, plenty of it—a steamboat can't help it, hardly. But I put it back into the boat, to make a pretty packet of her. Then she had to have new boilers, and she went into dry dock for caulkin' and patchin'—that's expensive. And her cabin was all done over; and I stuck twenty feet on her stern because her transom was ridin' too low; and finally put in new engines altogether.

"Oh, she was gettin' to be a fast boat, Mark," he grinned; the pain of his loss apparently had left him entirely. "As sweet a little job as you'd want to see. And her mortgages were lifted—nearly. But she only got in a few trips before she burned. So I'm sunk." He grinned again, wholeheartedly enough for a man who had lost the first stage of a fortune in one night's disaster.

"But—" he interrupted himself—"you asked what I *meant* to do, didn't you? A second boat, of course. A third, a fourth, and a fifth. Small boats for the way landin's, relay warehouses, city offices at Memphis, Natchez, Vicksburg, St. Louis; the biggest boats the river has seen yet for the through runs; feeder lines up the tributaries, and as far up as St. Paul. Then the Pittsburg trade—"

"And now that you're flat—what about it?"

"Begin again."

"Are there many claims against the *Peter Swain*—financial claims that can be carried through the courts?"

"Oh, Lord, I'll bet there'll be a hundred! They'll

come out now like worms after a rain."

"We'll sidestep all that. Put the total assets in the hands of a receiver, and let the claimants fight it out."

"We?"

"It's the only thing to do, Arn. Absolves the boat, clears your skirts forever, beats the man whose five-dollar mule is worth three hundred now that it is dead—"

"Oh, yes, of course, but—"

"I said 'we'," explained Wallace, his fine eyes studying the lean face of his friend intently, "because you're taking me into partnership now."

"Oh, what are you talkin' about?" Arnold swallowed a chuckle.

"That is what I intend to demonstrate." Wallace's patient smile would have been sarcastic on the face of another, but Mark's sensitive features made any sort of smile beautiful.

"I don't doubt in the least, Mark, that you have money—and I reckon you're offerin' to throw some into the breach, and it's mighty fine of you and all that; but—"

"But I'm a hopeless ignoramus about steamboating."

"Well—put it that you don't know the hazards of the river."

"Just by way of curiosity, Arn," Mark digressed, "how many trips did the *Willis K. Humphrey* make to St. Louis last year?"

"Nine or ten."

"Eight. What was the second biggest item, in dollars, that she carried? What was the cargo, I mean?"

"Sugar."

"Jute!"

"Oh, nonsense."

"It's not nonsense, it's a fact."

Huston forked his eleventh slice of bacon and glanced at the other sharply.

"Who owns the Demerest Line?" he asked.

"Not a syndicate, as you suppose. That's just another of your mistaken ideas. Mordecai Leonard, of Pittsburg."

"That's news to me," said Huston skeptically.

"Naturally," returned Mark suavely.

Amused by Wallace's undisguised attempt, but a little exasperated by its success, Huston fished up a question from the obscurities of the field he knew best. "How much water was there in Cat's Head Cut-off last week, at the shoalest point?" he demanded.

"Nine feet," said Mark, "when Jeff Morton took the *Samson* through."

"Great Scott," cried Arnold. "What manner of man is this?"

"I cheated you on that one," Wallace chuckled. "I only happened to overhear that. Now answer a sensible question. Tell me all you know about the *Frontier City*."

"Old Captain Pumpernickel's boat?" asked Huston, stifling his chuckle with toast. "Well, she had a fast keel. But her upper works made her top heavy. She was under-engined, for economy, so she was slow, and the engines were old, so she wasted her steam. Somethin' killed her as a passenger boat—"

"Fleas," put in Wallace.

"Say," said Huston, sitting back again, "I guess you know everythin', don't you?" He raised his brows in mock admiration.

"No, no, go ahead."

"Well, her rudders were hung wrong, and Pumpernickel was too cheap—"

"Too poor."

"—too cheap to change 'em, so the pilots wore themselves out sweatin' at the wheel, and the whole affair had a very poor name. And crabbiness from havin' a little authority—"

"Anxiety," Mark corrected.

"—lost the big end of her trade, and she went broke. And she's now lyin' in a bayou up the Teche. And he wants a fortune for her, which he won't get, because her timbers are rotten as cork."

"I beg your pardon," said Mark, "but all your later statements were incorrect. For instance, she can be bought, by proper handling, for less than five thousand."

"He's come down, then. Anyway, you can build the beat of her for fifteen."

"Where'll you get the fifteen? And her timbers are not rotten, but sound as the day she was made."

"I can poke my fist through her!"

"You can go see for yourself, Arn; that's what I did."

"I haven't five thousand, and—"

"I have!"

"—it'd cost ten thousand to put her in shape,

engines and all—"

"Too high, by half! But I have it, Arn."

"Huh? You have?"

"Yes, yes!"

"Look here, Mark, I know you're all steamed up over the idea of our floatin' this old wreck of a boat, and all; and there's nothing in the world I'd like better. But—damn it, Mark, you don't see what we're up against. Just to get the boat is only a start. Five thousand runnin' money has to come in, before she pays. Anyway that much. I *know* this game, Mark—haven't I sweat night after night tryin' to make a dollar work for four, with my whole stake in it? I've played that game, and beat it—and where am I now? One unlucky night, and—whoof! Broke. I've beat this before, and I'll beat it again, by God, but don't you get into it. You put your money where it's safe, Mark, and leave the river run. You don't like that, I know, but a poor friend I'd be if I told you anythin' else. God help the man the river gets—it'll make you old faster than any game in the world; and for every man it makes, it breaks fifty more, so help me God if I'm lyin' to you!"

Mark was unperturbed in manner and in tone; but the flush over his cheek bones and the surface light in his eyes betrayed the quiver behind the suavity of his mask.

"I could get twenty captains to-morrow—" he began.

"Go ahead if you want to, but you'll never get trimmed on account of me, Mark, that's all I can say."

"—but as it happens," Mark went on as if he had not

heard, “it won’t be necessary, because I’ve decided upon you. As for—”

“You’re no more built for the river, Mark, than I’m built for plantin’. You’ve—”

“That’s why I need you. As for the money, it’s mostly raised capital, it’ll have to be protected by insurance, and it’ll have to be turned. So there’s no use talking about keeping it safe.”

Huston looked at him for a long time, hardly knowing what to say. “What in the world have you been about?” he asked at last.

“Just looking around, Arn.”

They let that soak in for a while. “Are you offerin’ me a job, Mark?” Huston presently asked in a tone between curiosity and something else that Mark could not have named.

“No; I’m asking for a part in a project.”

“I’ll have to know where the money is comin’ from.”

“You will.” Mark Wallace yawned and rose. “You have a letter,” he said. “I didn’t mention it, because I wanted your attention. You can have it now, though.” He handed Huston an envelope, and prepared to leave. “Think over what I’ve said.”

“Wait, Mark!”

“No, I’m going home to bed. Come around to my room any time of night—but day is for sleep.”

He was gone. Important as his statements had appeared to be to Huston’s interests, he temporarily forgot them as soon as Mark had left. The envelope before him was addressed in a hand he had seldom seen, yet was unlikely to forget. He ripped open the envelope; then smiled as he studied the single line of writing which the enclosed sheet contained.

"Come to Mandeville."

It was written in uneven copybook characters, as by the hand of a child. There was no signature; but he knew its source well enough; and by the very brevity of the message he was able to perceive the attenuated struggle, the prolonged embarrassed uncertainty that had mothered those words.

CHAPTER VII

DUSK had settled again as Huston dismounted from his sleek borrowed mare by the shore of Lake Pontchartrain. The ride from the city had been a pleasant one, along the seven miles of shaded road beside the Bayou St. John; the evening was cool, and the saddle mare peppery and soft-footed. Now, leaving the animal tied to a post, he walked along the landings at the mouth of the bayou, seeking the mooring of a certain oyster boat in which he had often crossed Lake Pontchartrain before.

Under the proud straightness of their light masts the little snub-nosed oyster luggers lay squat, broad of beam and bulging of bow. A reek of fish rose from the litter of disordered tackle and rigging on their decks; they did not run to trimness nor to paint, yet they had an air of impudent hardiness. They carried heavy loads in any weather, and, like nonchalant floating corks, were game to take the open sea, never caring that they were more like big pirogues than little ships.

Huston found the lugger he sought, one whose tip-tilted bowsprit thrust up rakishly from a sway-backed hull. At his hail there was a stir in the little rat-box of a cabin in her stern, and out popped the head of a man who must have been on his hands and knees, in order to exist in so small a space. It was the head of a Sicilian with a face so ostentatiously villainous with its close-bound red handkerchief and sweeping moustache that Huston grinned.

"Como ce va, Giuseppe?"

"Buono, signore! Git in."

"My horse, Giuseppe."

"Ah! Si."

When the saddle mare had been secured in a rude shanty near by, Huston sprang down into the lugger, and together they poled her into open water. Giuseppe shook out a remarkable quantity of sail with a thundering rattle of canvas that would have done credit to a boat triple her size; and they began to draw away under the impulse of a breeze so faint that it hardly rippled the smooth yellow waters of the lake.

The lugger was slow in the faint breeze, for all the smoothness with which she glided over the shallows with hardly a rippling purl along the bulge of her bows. It was night, with a moon like a great gold plate, by the time Huston left the oyster boat at the Mandeville landing.

He walked along the shaded avenues of the little old town, a place where houses with pillared galleries, their first floors built high above the damp ground, lounged among moss-draped live oaks with an air of infinite leisure; and so presently came to the rambling house, set back among its trees, from which had come the three mandatory words in the childlike hand.

He was shown into an ornate parlor by a black butler, a Congo slave whose starched shirt emphasized rather than concealed his likeness to some animal of the jungle swamps. He had a great shapeless roll of a body, with short skinny arms and legs, and sharp, contracted raccoon face in which not even the gleam of teeth nor eyeballs was permitted to break a flawless blackness.

The room was a familiar one. He felt again the curious, slightly disquieting inward pressure of the walls, which were papered with a minutely complicated panorama of mediæval Europe. The crowded pieces of furniture, too—the whatnots, the rococo carved mahogany upholstered in horsehair, the gilt framed cheval glass, the crystal-hung chandeliers—all of which he considered very elegant, were things alien to himself which association had made friendly. They were in truth subordinate members of a family whose head was hostile to him, but who themselves were glad to smile and wink at him, while pretending to receive him coldly.

The stuffy parlor was lit by a plenitude of candles. They beamed and twinkled in all quarters of the room from their many-armed glass candelabra, making the pendent crystals flash like polished ice.

Huston settled himself and waited with a sense of lassitude that was strange to him here. The house in which he sat was one into which his family name admitted him without being sufficient to make him entirely welcome. It had been built as the winter home of the Shepherds, who were upriver cotton planters; and it had become the more and more frequent retreat of Earl Shepherd, the fussy old man who, having been born and raised in a cotton patch, was sick of cotton and all its means of cultivation.

Land was the adequate support of the Shepherds' pretension, and land was their gauge of the pretensions of others, ranking hardly second to that other time-honored measuring stick—length of tenure. For Earl Shepherd, Huston had no particular use, but in Caroline Shepherd he had heretofore discerned no resemblance to her progenitors. During the three years in which he had courted her awkwardly in the face of heavy chaperonage, he had fancied that she was his real goal, the ultimate reason for his uphill battle for success on the river.

She would be with him in a moment, having sent for him for the first time in her life. But beyond a certain curiosity as to why she had done so, Huston found himself indifferent. During his sail across the lake he had been thinking of little besides boats; while he walked through the avenues of Mandeville he had been thinking of how pleasant it would be to own a house, and what manner of place he would build, if he ever had the money and the leisure; and now as he sat in the elaborately crowded parlor his mind was turning absently to steamboats and to Mark Wallace.

The thought of Mark Wallace made him think of the

house on the Rue Chartres; of a face in which the eyes were singularly dark, like charcoal smudges on pale ivory silk; of delicate slender hands. . . .

When a step on the carpet made him glance up to find that Caroline Shepherd was before him he sprang to his feet in confusion.

In comparison to the slender figure of which Arnold Huston had been thinking, Caroline seemed short and plump. Her face was gently featured, smoothly contoured, as aloof from worldly travails as the girl's life had been in her closely sheltered rearing. Huston blamed only himself for the impression that came to him now—that it also seemed free from any indication of thought.

She gave him her hand, a cool small hand in his long fingers.

"We heard about your terrible disaster," she said. "I wanted to tell you that I think it is perfectly terrible."

"Tough," he agreed, his voice sounding a little lighter than he thought, critically, was fitting to the occasion.

"I just had to tell you," she said, withdrawing her hand, "how terrible I think it is."

She was looking at him rather impersonally, he felt, though a faint flush had appeared over her cheek bones. It was Caroline Shepherd's misfortune that however sympathetic she might feel, the constraint of inexperience prevented her from looking anything but detached, aloof.

"You don't know," he said, "how much I appreciate your sayin' that."

"Won't you sit down?" She perched herself on the edge of a chair; and sat there daintily erect, a small figure with her skirts billowing about her.

He sat down, and was silent. It seemed to him that he missed an element in the usual situation here. "Where is your mother?" he asked suddenly.

"She's away. Papa is playing cards with some men in his library; he doesn't know you're here." The impersonal look in the eyes of this girl who had sent for him remained unmarred.

Huston felt as a dog looks who, having barked hysterically at another from behind an impassable fence, suddenly finds that the gate is open between them. How often he had desired only this much opportunity! How eagerly he had contrived complicated devices to be alone with this girl, and now—something was lacking. He thrust his hands into his pockets, slumped in his chair, stared moodily at his crossed boot-tips.

"I'm so worried about Will," she said suddenly.

"Will?"

"Your cousin, you know." The identification was superfluous; they had been bitter rivals here long enough for him to know whom she meant by Will. "The death of his father was so sudden. It's upset him terribly. Arnold—how did Will Huston's father die? Will only said he had an accident. People are saying he shot himself!"

"I don't know," said Huston. He was thinking of his night in Natchez, and the sound of a shot from the house of Dennison Huston.

"Will was in a terrible state," she went on, leaning

toward him. "He said—he said I might never see him again—alive."

"That ass," thought Huston. He said aloud, "What seemed to be botherin' him?"

"Oh, Arnold, he's—I promised him to tell no one, and I haven't; but I do want to tell you, because maybe you can do something about it—he's going to fight a duel!"

"Oh, my God!"

"Arnold!"

"I beg your pardon," he said, immediately serious again. "Who's he fightin'?"

"He said it was someone of our own class, yet not in our own class; a terrible somebody who was used to fighting all up and down the river, who'd shoot to kill without winking an eyelash. Isn't it terrible?"

"Awful," said Huston profoundly, his face like stone.

"Oh, Arnold, he'll be killed, I know he will! He's so reckless, and brave—people say he plays at the gaming tables to any amount, and he'll risk a thousand on the turn of a card!"

"So I'm told."

"Isn't there something we can do?"

"What, Caroline?"

"Take it to the authorities, or something like that?"

"I—I'll give the matter my best thought, Caroline, and—and my closest attention."

He was studying her face, noticing the contour of her lips, the deep blue of her eyes. Her hair had hardly more color than his own, but it was soft and fine, and the candlelight behind it brightened its outline like a nimbus of saffron light. He felt a little guilty that this girl did not stir him now as she always had stirred him. It was as if the purgatory of the burning *Swain* had left him old.

"Won't you play for me?"

Her fingers were gentle on the keys of the big square piano; he stood beside her making a pretence of turning the leaves of the music, though she seldom glanced at it, and he had no idea when the sheets should be turned. He had often stood this way before, happy to be near her and looking at her without being observed.

She played for a long time, seemingly forgetful that he was there; and he felt, as he always did, that her playing brought them closer together than anything else could. Though he would not have admitted it, her music moved him deeply, with a primitive strength. It filled him with nameless longings, making him feel like a caged animal, like a dog who wanted to howl at the moon.

He stood looking down at the profile, beautiful in the candlelight, of the girl he had loved so long; and he knew that she was beautiful still, perhaps more beautiful than she had ever been. She had sent for him, and they were alone; the spell of the rippling keys wrapped around them like an intangible veil, separating them from the world. . . . The faintest tremor of her lashes told him that she, like himself, was altered by the voices of the singing strings.

Now, he knew as well as he had ever known anything in his life, he had only to extend his hand, and she would have been his. A stillness came over him, and his hands were cold.

The song stopped, the hum of the strings died away; she turned her face upward, looking into his. The motionless quiet remained upon him as he met her eyes.

"Arnold."

"Yes?"

"You'll leave the river now—won't you?"

For a moment he looked down at her blankly; then the spell broke, as he straightened up and laughed. The strong surge and draw of the Mississippi caught him in its current again; and no nonchalant raft ever whirled zooming downstream on the flood waters more swiftly than Huston was ripped out of the sphere of the magnetism of Caroline Shepherd, out of the spell of her music, out of her life. . . .

CHAPTER VIII

THE mare was returned to her stable shortly after midnight; and Huston strode under the balconies of the Rue Royale toward the narrow building under whose eaves was the room of his friend.

He found Mark Wallace up, of course; he was smiling over the pages of Machiavelli, which he was reading from the Italian. His dark hair was rumpled twistily, but he was otherwise as immaculate as if he were starting for a ball, instead of reading away the night alone.

Wallace snapped the book shut—it sent up a small puff of dust—and offered Huston cigars. As for himself, he was smoking a long clay pipe. Huston sprawled upon Wallace's cot in the corner and blew long threads of smoke.

"I was looking for you," said Mark. "I want to go a little more fully into our plans—"

"In the first place," Huston interrupted, "who is DuMoyne?"

Some sort of a spark twinkled in Wallace's eye.

"A dead man," he said shortly. "There's every reason, you'll agree with me, for pressing our project along as quickly as we can—if we are going to engage ourselves in a project. Now to begin with—"

"Dead, is he?"

"Why, yes. That is, I guess he is. But as I was saying—"

"You *guess* he's dead?"

"Well—of course, when circumstances are so shadowy as they were in DuMoyne's case, you can't exactly be certain, I suppose. But it's the generally accepted opinion. I've no reason for doubting."

"But *what* shadowy circumstances?"

"Somebody was found in a bayou—and DuMoyne was missing. By putting two and two together—"

"Do you mean to say no one tried to identify this somebody from the bayou—"

"Now, Arnold, there are certain factors, such as alligators; together with certain other natural processes, which, working in conjunction with each other, or separately, are capable of rendering unrecognizable practically anything. I will be more specific. The—"

"Where was DuMoyne seen last?"

"That," said Wallace, pulling at his pipe with relish, "is the very thing that makes people think he is dead. Very odd situation! Sometimes I'm moved to think—"

"Mark! Will you answer me, sir?"

"He was seen, my friend, standing in the corner of an empty room. In his left hand was a candle, lighted, it being night; in his right hand was an eight-inch knife. He was seen to snub the flame of the candle against the wall—and was not thereafter seen; unless, as I have said, the—"

"Gad, Mark, you deliberately madden a man. Who saw him?"

"Since the windows were battened, he was only seen by the man who faced him from the opposite corner—also equipped with an eight-inch knife. His name was Jean Fouchet."

"Never heard of him. Who was he?"

"Oh, that's a long story, Arn. Do I have to go into all—"

"You most certainly do."

"Do you realize you are going to fight a duel in the morning?"

"So I understand."

"Once and for all, Arn, are you going to shoot this cousin of yours, or not? Because if you intend to, you'll have to have rest. If you don't intend to, I don't see that it makes much difference in what condition you face him."

"I suppose I'll let him off, Mark."

"Do you mean you'll deliberately miss?"

"I didn't say that. Do you guarantee that *he* will deliberately miss?"

"Certainly not."

"Then what are you talkin' about?"

"I think," said Mark, "that everything considered you'd better go to bed. In the morning you may want to make a fight of it. And a fine second I would be if—"

"I'm not goin' to bed until I find out what I want to know."

"And I surely am not going to be a party to keeping you up." Mark reached for his book.

"Oh, be reasonable! I don't mean to hit the fellow."

"Is that a promise?"

"No!"

"Then I'm not going to—"

"Oh, yes, you are!"

"Well," said Mark wearily, "what is it you want to know?"

"First, who was DuMoyne; and who was Jacqueline?"

With a steady insistence, though without finesse—Wallace had all the finesse of those two!—Huston got out of Wallace everything that he knew about Jacqueline or Andrea DuMoyne—almost. He did not realize the existence of that "almost" at the time, felicitating himself as he did that nothing Mark knew was concealed from him.

The story was somewhat irregular and disordered, considering the natural clarity of Mark's mind. As if some inner urge were pressing Wallace to talk of things which his upper judgment preferred he should not discuss. But Huston was able to arrange the fragments into an ordered comprehension in his own mind.

Andrea DuMoyne, he learned presently, was of blood that was old upon the American continent. The name DuMoyne was not truly representative of his stock, for he was of Spanish origin, rather than French.

As a descendant of old families, DuMoyne was more or less remotely related to certain well-considered contemporaries; but his own particular line had run its course, and none was particularly eager to claim him. At the age of twenty-two he had already become a rather dissolute young rake, of no distinction other than a wild recklessness and a curiously perpetual luck at cards that did nothing to place his character on firmer ground.

It was about then, Mark thought, that DuMoyne had executed his first disappearance. There was nothing particularly mysterious about this one. He had been a heavy winner for some weeks, and when he was presently missed from the gaming tables it was assumed that he had chosen to go travelling—an assumption which later proved correct.

He was gone two years. Where those two years were spent, no one was certain. DuMoyne bored no one with accounts of his travels. This was an omission which his friends would doubtless have regarded as a boon, had not a curiosity arisen as to where the man had got himself so cultured and distinguished-appearing a wife.

"Jacqueline?" Huston demanded.

"Your perspicuity," said Wallace, "astounds me."

"Well—where *did* she come from?"

Mark Wallace submitted that he did not know. Andrea DuMoyne, he pointed out, had been regarded as an exceedingly handsome young man. His stature was not what it might have been, but he made up for that with a certain dash and swagger of bearing that was admired by people who cared for that sort of thing. His family was sufficiently distinguished surely; and he had a certain amount of money. Though Mark was ready enough to agree that these observations did not entirely explain Jacqueline.

For a time, after his reappearance with his bride, it seemed that DuMoyne was of a purpose to mend his ways. For some months he was seen at the gaming tables no more. Andrea and Jacqueline were frequently together at social functions, apparently having won to a reinstatement in the social estimation of the city. During this period they were undoubtedly, said Mark, the happiest looking people he had ever seen.

This new way of life did not last with Andrea DuMoyne. Perhaps he became bored with his comparatively orderly manner of living. More likely, thought Wallace, it was need of funds that first sent him to the gaming tables again.

"You will agree," Mark offered, "that respectable means of livelihood, for young men of the upper families, are decidedly difficult to discover in New

Orleans, without sacrifice of all social position."

"Bah!" said Huston. "There never has been so much opportunity in the world before."

"That's all rubbish," Wallace averred, "from the standpoint of this particular type of young man."

"My family is as good as the next," Huston retorted. "But I'm not ashamed to work on that account."

"What type of job would you suggest," Mark asked, "for an educated but untrained young man who finds it necessary to support a wife elaborately?"

Huston made an impatient gesture, and pressed on with his questioning.

DuMoyne's luck at cards had declined during his absence. He managed to piece along, though, and his absorption in what now appeared to be his chosen profession soon became a nightly affair. Jacqueline was seen at social functions more and more rarely; and at last no more at all. Except that in a handsome house on Rue Chartres there existed a Madame DuMoyne, it was as if Andrea had never been away.

It was no more than a year after the return of Andrea to New Orleans with Jacqueline, that he disappeared again. He was gone something like two months; and returned in such a petulant mood that, so far as Mark knew, polite questions as to where he had been never elicited anything from him but thinly disguised savagery of temper.

There was a third absence on his part, then a fourth, and at last a final one that, so far, had remained conclusive. No one thought of associating the "disused article hauled out of the bayou" with Andrea

DuMoyne, until the curious confession of Jean Fouchet.

Fouchet was a proud-faced man, very stern of expression and deportment, of perhaps thirty-five years. He came to New Orleans from San Domingo, or some such place, not long after the first return of DuMoyne. He had letters of introduction, Mark believed, that gave him entrance about wherever he chose; but he took little advantage of this. He was lame, and leaned on a cane that he made as inconspicuous as he could but bore heavily upon nevertheless.

One day Fouchet and DuMoyne were separated forcibly in the drawing room of a club. There was, however, no talk of a duel; and both remained silent upon the affair. And when DuMoyne disappeared, a fortnight later, no one thought of questioning Fouchet.

A year after DuMoyne's disappearance, Fouchet left New Orleans for ports unknown. He left behind him, in the hands of a friend, an odd document, beginning, "To All Whom It May Concern, Greetings: Known by these presents, that I, Jean Jacques Fouchet—"

"And that sort of thing, you know," said Mark Wallace.

In his communication Fouchet attested that he had had a quarrel with Andrea DuMoyne, the cause of which he did not name; that DuMoyne had challenged; that he, Fouchet, had thought he detected a strain of cowardice in the man; that, not wishing to fight DuMoyne, he had named weapons calculated to cause DuMoyne, if he were cowardly, to withdraw. Accordingly, he stipulated that they should fight without seconds, and that the weapons should be knives, without light, in a closed room.

Fouchet's estimate of DuMoyne's character appears to have been a mistaken one, for DuMoyne did not withdraw. They met as Fouchet had stipulated, in a locked room in a deserted house which Fouchet had named in his representation. Each with a lighted candle and a knife, they faced each other from opposite corners of the room. Fouchet was first to strike out his candle. DuMoyne instantly did the same.

For a long time, he said, there was no sound or movement in the dark; until suddenly, guided by premonition rather than sound, Fouchet struck out with all his strength—and the knife went home.

At this point, with an admirable frankness, Fouchet's document admitted that he was overwhelmed by the same cowardice with which he had impugned the character of Andrea DuMoyne. For the first time in his life he was terror-stricken by the circumstances in which he stood. He flung his knife away, and rushed from the house.

He made his way toward town, and for perhaps an hour wandered lost in the swamp groves, having attempted a short cut. By this time he had recovered himself, and instead of continuing to town for help as he had intended he returned alone to the house where, he believed, lay the body of DuMoyne. It was his intention to give to his enemy that aid which would have been his first thought previously had he not been set beside himself by sheer fear of the dark.

It had been a late hour when they entered the house.

The sky was graying with the morning light as he again reached the scene of the duel. He went directly into the room where DuMoyne had fallen—and found that he was gone.

He could not believe, Fouchet said, that his adversary had gone far; so that he was at considerable pains to discover which way he had gone. The task was no harder than that of following "any other wounded beast"—the words were his own—and he believed he was successful. He stopped following the trail at the edge of a bayou, into which he believed DuMoyne, probably fatally wounded, had stumbled and met his death. . . .

"Who was the friend?"

"What friend?"

"That he left the statement with?"

Mark hesitated. "I was."

"How does she live?" demanded Huston presently.

"She appears to have means."

"A sinister background, I should say," Huston commented.

Mark nodded. "It isn't that a man was killed so much," he said, "as that there was such a pall of mystery and uncertainty about it all; that ghastly duel in that black room was so typical of the whole business. But five years have gone by now since he disappeared; and it seems to me that the circumstances of his death are just a little more agreeable to regard than the previous circumstances—of his possession of her."

"She must be older than I thought, Mark."

"She is twenty-four; nearly twenty-five now."

Huston looked surprised. "But if five years—"

"Jacqueline was eighteen when he brought her here."

During the time that they were silent Mark Wallace devised a dark-looking drink that burnt its way through the throat but had a pleasant warm fragrance once it was swallowed. They had begun to notice the coolness of the deep night, and Wallace laid a charcoal fire. When the little grate was filled with bright flame-colored coals the book-walled room took on a new aspect: as if the unpleasant tale Wallace had told were now kicked out like a night-prowling cat that had got in where it did not belong.

They relaxed into more comfortable positions. And presently, warmed by the fireglow and the warmth of the drink within, Wallace smiled more pleasantly, and with his head tilted back began to talk in a different vein.

"When I first saw Jacqueline," he said, "I thought she looked like a child; you wouldn't think so now, would you?"

"Nope."

"But then she was just a tall little girl. It was at a ball; all I remember about it was that she was there. I wondered why such a child should be at a ball. Then I found my eyes following her about; and presently I began to ask who she was, and where she could have come from, that I had never noticed her before. And when I found out that she was married to that young rake I was furious. I sulked all night, and had the very devil of a time apologizing for the dances I cut."

"How old are you, Mark?"

"Twenty-eight. I was twenty-one then." His fine dark eyes regarded Huston languidly.

"She was poised enough," he added presently. "Her bearing was better than half the matrons in the hall. But she was just a little girl, all the same. There was a draught in the ballroom; I wanted to put my cloak over her shoulders to save her from it; then pick her up in my arms and carry her away from there. . . ."

"When I first saw her," said Huston, as reminiscently as if it had been ten years before, instead of two days, "there was a roaring in my ears like that hellish fire; and damn me if I could scarcely see her at all."

"But do you think you'll ever forget her?"

"Lord, Mark, I should certainly hope so!"

"That," said Wallace, "is my idea of a hell of a hope."

They talked very little after that, but sat smoking by the light of the little fire, after the lamp had burned itself out, each moodily comfortable in his own way. And before they expected it the graying of the checkered panes told them that morning was seeping up through the river mists, the eternal cool gray mists of the Mississippi's dawns.

CHAPTER IX

ON the coping of the building opposite, silhouetted against the graying sky, a lank cat trotted, head and tail low, hurrying home from a night of prowling over the huddled roofs. Below in the street the big wheels of a cart rolled over the muddy cobbles with a slow-paced rattle and a shrill hub-whine. An early milk-huckster was sending up occasional wailing shouts: " 'Eel', hi-ho-o-o!"

Mark Wallace stirred, roused himself, and consulted a watch as bulbous as an apple.

"Well, Arnold . . ."

The motionless figure on the couch did not answer.

"Show life, Arn!" Wallace shook his friend.

"Whazzamatter?"

"Come on, get up! You've got to fight, you know!"

Huston turned his head away sleepily. "Don' wanta fight yuh."

"Get up, I say! You've got a duel on!"

"Oh." He opened his eyes and sat up drowsily. At Mark's insistence he got to his feet and stretched. "What time is it?"

"Nearly five o'clock. Your cousin is expecting you at six. Now you go take yourself a bath. And don't dawdle. If there's anything I won't allow around here, it's dawdling. And another thing—"

The door shut behind Huston. When he had returned from his chilly tub and had borrowed clean linen from Wallace he looked considerably fresher.

"Did you get the pistols ready, Mark?"

"Why, certainly."

Wallace produced a duelling box, and Huston frowned. "I thought I told you—"

"You told me navy revolvers."

"But these are—"

“Navy revolvers.”

“They’re no such thing! That’s a fumidididdle of a duelling set. When I said—”

“I meant,” said Wallace, “the navy of twenty years ago. You didn’t say, my friend, what navy, or when. These are of exactly the navy type of officer’s pistols of that time. Only the workmanship is vastly better—look at that silver chasing! And they’re star-gauged. They don’t make guns like that to-day.”

“Let’s see how far they can sink a ball into the door frame,” Huston challenged.

“All right.”

A heavy roaring shock rocked them back onto their heels as Wallace fired. A splintered hole as big as a man’s finger appeared in the white poplar at the side of the door, and such a reek of smoke drifted back over them that they could hardly see each other.

Out in the hall there was a clattering bump, followed by a scurry of bare feet.

“What the—” Wallace dashed out into the hall, the smoking gun still in his hand. He almost stumbled over a tray of dishes—but there was no one in sight, and the scurry of feet had died away. A look of consternation came into his face. “Oh, lord! I bet we’ve made Jeff spill our coffee!”

“We? You did.”

“You told me to.” Together they stooped to examine the tray on the floor of the hall.

“It isn’t spilled! It’s only slopped a little onto the napkin.”

They stood up and gravely shook hands.

When they had taken their coffee and argued over the cleaning of the fired gun they made their way to a stable in Decatur Street, where saddled horses were waiting. The levee road that they took down-river was soft but fairly dry; their mounts liked the going and stepped off at a brisk trot.

The river beside them lay silver in the clear light that floods the Mississippi just before the first rays of the sun. Across the river the skyline of trees lay smooth, for the ragged skeletons of dead trees, which usually gave it a look wildly forlorn, were not visible as yet. The smell of the river was in the air, moist and cool; Huston drank it in great lungfuls, feeling as refreshed as if he had slept all night, instead of sitting in an atmosphere of wine and smoke.

"See those coach tracks?" said Wallace. "Those are Will Huston's: he started half an hour ago. I learned that at the stable." He shifted the polished pistol case to his other arm and consulted his watch again. "We've about two miles more to go—and it's getting on toward that time."

"Get along then!"

They let out their saddlers to a hand gallop. The animals were good, seeming to sail over the ground as smoothly as boats. With the rhythm of the gallop Huston's spirits rose and soared.

"It seems to me," he shouted, "I never saw so fine a mornin'!"

"For a murder?"

"Oh, I'm not goin' to hit him."

"He may not be so liberal."

They went on in silence; and so turned, presently, into a grove of live oaks into which the morning light had hardly penetrated at all. From the thick twisted arms of the oaks the moss hung in long trailing beards of slimsy gray, overhanging avenues between the massive trunks, avenues so apparently deserted that at first they thought they were alone. Then they sighted the black hulk of Will Huston's coach, and approached it at a light trot.

As they swung down Will Huston himself appeared accompanied by a slight young man of so formal and correct a bearing that Huston compared him to a figure from a stiff old print. The two parties approached each other silently until they were almost face to face. Arnold Huston was first to speak.

"Well, you ass?" he accosted his cousin.

The hard round eyes of the slight man became a shade more coldly formal. "It is my understanding, Mr. Wallace," he said, "that the principals do not ordinarily address each other."

"Oh, of course not, Mr. Bateman," said Wallace flamboyantly. "Most incorrect!"

"Perhaps my ears deceive me," Bateman offered.

"Oh, undoubtedly," Mark rejoined.

"Mr. Huston instructs me," said Bateman, "to present his compliments, and state that he is ready."

"Captain Huston," said Wallace, "thanks Mr. Huston for his compliments, and intimates that he is equally so."

"I do no such thing," said Arnold.

The slight young man looked shocked, the effect of

this emotion being to make his axe-like nose appear a little more prominent than it had before.

"What are we to suppose?" he inquired.

The smooth oval of Will Huston's face was gradually suffused with an angry flush. "Be so good as to inform Mr. Wallace that we are not here to be trifled with," he said.

"I impart that information," said Bateman, bowing.

"The hell you do!" said Arnold, with mock astonishment.

"Captain Huston asks me to say," Mark said, "that such was by no means his intention."

"I said nothin' like that at all," said Arnold.

"It seems to me, Mr. Wallace," said Bateman, "that a certain discrepancy exists between your own attitude and that of your principal."

"Sir!" blazed Mark with a remarkable show of suppressed fury, "will you force me to suspect you of eavesdropping?"

"What do you mean, sir!"

"How could you find a discrepancy between myself and my principal without deliberately overhearing our conversation?"

"It seems to me, Mr. Wallace," said Bateman, "that Captain Huston forces himself upon us."

"Are you challenging Captain Huston?"

"Oh, certainly not, sir, I only—"

"Then have a care, sir!"

"I assure you, Mr. Wallace, sir, I have no other desire than to carry this affair through with politeness and despatch."

"Then," said Wallace more equably, "let's proceed to the examination of the weapons."

They drew a little apart; and with elaborate care began to draw the loads of the weapons, which Bateman studied minutely.

"Well, Will," said Arnold to his cousin, "still angry with yourself?"

"I have nothing," returned Will Huston, "to say to you, sir."

"I can hardly expect you to realize," Arnold told him, "that everythin' about this business is highly ridiculous."

"I can hardly expect," Will said after him, "you to realize that there is nothing about your behavior suggesting that of a gentleman."

"How would you like a punch in the nose?" Arnold asked.

Will Huston turned his back. "Still quite the little ruffian," he murmured audibly.

Bateman and Wallace were pacing off the distance. An elaborately polite argument ensued, Bateman protesting that Wallace's strides were more than normal. A slight delay was occasioned on this head, but the disagreement was adjusted at last; and Will and Arnold were led to their places.

"The guns will be held down, at the sides, until the handkerchief falls," Mark Wallace told Arnold. "I shall say 'ready'—but do nothing; that's only a warning. Bateman will then give the signal to fire. As soon as the handkerchief drops, make a great show of aiming; that's to make him miss. When he has fired, send your shot good and high over his head, and we'll go back to town."

"All right," said Huston.

The two seconds walked toward each other, met between the duellists, and took up a position to one side.

"Are you ready, Captain Huston?" called Bateman.

"Mr. Huston, are you ready?" Mark called to Arnold's cousin.

"Why, certainly," Arnold answered.

Will Huston answered slowly and gravely: "I am."

Bateman raised his silk handkerchief above his head.

"Ready!" cried Mark Wallace.

Instantly the silk handkerchief swept downward. Huston raised his pistol to cover his cousin. Slowly, with equal deliberation, Will raised his own weapon. Even at the firing distance Huston could see the nervous tremor of his cousin's hand.

"Steady, now," Arnold called. "You can't hit anythin' like that!"

Will let the pistol down, and for a moment held it in both hands; and though he pretended to examine the lock, it was apparent to all that he sought only to quiet the trembling of the barrel.

Arnold Huston lowered his own gun. "Well, you ass?" he sung out. "Are you goin' to kill me or not?"

As if he had not heard, Will Huston again raised his gun, a little more quickly, yet with deliberation; and this time no tremor was visible. Arnold waited until the pointing gun was almost levelled upon him, then jerked his own arm up, as if he would have fired.

One gun crashed mightily, belching smoke; it was Will Huston's. The watching seconds saw a look of astonishment turn Arnold Huston's face gray. He took one faltering step backward, then recovered himself and stood erect. Then as suddenly as if he had been struck across the face with a whip, a contorting blaze of fury appeared there. His strong teeth gleamed bare, his arm swung up; and Will Huston collapsed grotesquely, like a dropped puppet, as the second pistol roared. He lay there unattended for a moment under those great twisted oaks, a curiously awkward sprawl of arms and legs, face down in the leaves. . . . .

Mark Wallace cried out: "Arn! Arn! You've hit him!"

And Huston said, "I've killed him, Mark."

In those moments in which they believed that Will Huston was dead, Arnold experienced a curious detached calmness. His high pitch of cold excitement, as recorded by the heavy beating of his heart, gave him the sensation of physical drunkenness, but his mind was quietly, almost indifferently, observant. Wallace applied cotton to the bullet scratch on Arnold's side, the sting of which had spurred him to unplanned murder.

From the shelter of this state of mind he perceived a thing that even then he thought surprising. After the first look of dismay had passed over Mark Wallace's face, Huston saw that expression replaced by one of strange satisfaction, as if, in spite of the disarrangement to his plans, Wallace enjoyed the destruction of the fallen man. This Huston soon forgot in the distraction of a second and more consuming phase of the unexpected.

They walked to where Will Huston lay. Bateman was already bending over him, searching for the wound with nervous hands. When they had turned the unconscious man upon his back his second's examination was minute, yet—discovered nothing. After a more studied examination, and a conference with Mark Wallace, Bateman was reluctantly forced to the admission that his principal had fainted. Wallace went further, and discovered the mark of Huston's bullet in the trunk of a tree. Huston had missed by at least five feet.

Bateman now expressed a fear that Will Huston had been attacked by heart failure. This, too, was confuted by Will himself, who returned to consciousness in response to cold water poured on him by Mark Wallace. And Bateman was reduced to reiteration of his opinion that it was extraordinary.

It was hard for Huston to believe that he had missed; it was harder for him to believe that his cousin had lost consciousness at the mere sound of his gun. These things worked their way into his comprehension at last, however, and he joined the laughter of Mark Wallace. Bateman assured Wallace that they could be of no further assistance; and when Will Huston had been lifted into his carriage, Mark and Arnold mounted and rode off, chuckling over the fiasco to which their affair of honor had been reduced. One ceremony had been omitted: the principals had, at the last, neglected to shake hands.

CHAPTER X

THE chocolaty, mile-wide river curved in a vast S, fifteen miles from tip to tip; the smooth waters wheeled around the great bends with a strong swing and pull, incomprehensibly racing out the longest way to the Gulf. In the curve where the river bent northward lay the smudgy huddle of New Orleans, dwarfed by the giant river, dwarfed by the open sweep of the sky, belittled by the vast flatness of swamp and brake and bottomland in which it lay.

Its smallness, though, was only for the eyes of the still-floating turkey buzzards who could see at once the great patchwork of the up-river plantations and the faraway blue sparkle of salt water. Men, with their feet on the ground, saw greatness, rather, in the spreading intricacy of her deep-etched streets, in the crowds that thronged the long reach of her river front like flies.

At the feet of the low-built city, thickly clustered along the margin of the stream, the white packets lay; hundreds of them side by side, a mile and a half of close-ranked white boats. Behind them, not daring to nudge the levee as the steamboats could, the deep-sea shipping lay scattered, bound fast to lighters or wharf-boats, or anchored free in the stream with the current purling brownly along the bulge of their bows.

The tall, delicate masts of the sea-going ships reached upward like needles in floating corks, trailing cobwebs of rigging. Great rakish schooners were there, and proud square-rigged clippers, squat luggers, ancient brigs and brigantines; but for every one of these there was a dozen, a score of the double-funnelled river boats, the beloved "floating palaces" of the Mississippi trade.

Down the tilt of the cobbled levee, tumbling and bounding over the round-polished loaves of stone, came a constant cascade of thumping bales, booming kegs, complaining crates, hazed by blacks with big hands and feet flat as ducks'. Up the tilt of the cobbled levee, laboriously dragged or carried, came other files of crates and boxes and bales reluctantly, as if holding back, unwilling to leave the surface of the flood.

The seven o'clock sun from beyond the river was just touching the gray stones of the levee with dull dust of gold. Over the cobbles the strangely long blue shadows of men slipped and fled, weaving together. The sun brightened the sky with the greenish tinge of robins' eggs, tipped the tall masts with gilt, and pointed up with Chinese white the fragile woodwork of rail and paddlebox. Over the levee and the city a flat-layered cloud drifted in the still air, the smoke from the twin stacks of the river steamboats.

Among the toiling negroes, above them on the levee's crest, strolled the men of the river, the town, the ships, the plantations. Nondescript sailors with bold-angled, unshaved faces; big-handed Swedes, swaggering Cockneys, swart Spanish, Portuguese, Italians. Merchants and men of finance from the town; slender suave Creoles in blue coats and buff waistcoats, portly men clamping full-blown moustaches over fat cigars, sallow-cheeked oldlings trimmed down by fever, barrel-bodied gentlemen with fancy vests. Bronzed planters, broad-hatted, neatly whiskered. Assured pilots, swaggering cubs who were pilots in the making. Whiskered steamboat captains, burly-voiced captains' mates. Shaggy, booted men of the swamp country. Lank flatboatmen and raftsmen. Sleek slavetraders. Gamblers who looked like anything that they were not. . . . To each the levee was a different levee, to each the river, the town, the people, had a different significance.

Arnold Huston and Mark Wallace strolled, light-footed, among the hustled shipping, enjoying the sun that poured a new warmth upon the river's drifting eddies. To Huston almost every steamboat within the reach of his eye was a known personality; there a good full-bodied cargo-carrier, there a stubborn little wretch, here a handy boat easy to land, there a hard boat to beat in the open stream. And there was the berth, crowded by others now, where the *Peter Swain* docked last trip, and was loaded so handily and quickly in the charge of Nate Miller. . . .

"This project of putting a steamboat on the river," said Mark, "hinges on two things. First, myself; I can raise a little better than fifteen thousand."

"That's because you never tried to borrow any money," said Huston. Then sharply: "I thought you said that was arranged already?"

"I have the promise," said Wallace, "of the endorsement of my notes. Family connections made that possible. After all, Arn, there are only two things to be considered in lending a man money: can he pay if he will, and will he if he can. I have certain properties—they aren't making me anything; but they are enough to make it possible for me to pay if it comes to that. And certain of my relatives, with ample backing of their own, feel equal to endorsing my willingness."

"Well?"

"We will negotiate with the owner of the *Frontier City* for a small cash payment, and delayed settlement. Certain other concessions will be made to us in regard to supplies, some of them. In short, the *Frontier City* will be enabled to float. That's my end of it."

"And the other hinge?"

"Yourself. You must get credit for fuel for the first few runs. You should be well enough known on the river by this time to be able to swing that little item."

"I think," smiled Huston, "that somethin' can be arranged."

"You'll also," Mark went on, "have to see about the necessary hands—firemen, roustabouts, cooks, cabin crew—"

"And that," Arnold answered, "is absolutely impossible."

"Not necessarily. You have perhaps heard of a swamp-rat named Walt Gunn."

"I've unloaded at his landin'; I don't know the fellow."

"He knows you."

"Do you know him?"

"Indirectly. I have reason to believe that he will provide the slaves, taking our debt in return. He is the only one I know, just now, who would listen to a mortgage on the boat. This man will."

"You sound foggy," said Huston.

"Walt Gunn knows nothing about me. My name is some help in the town, but yours will have to answer on the river. You are the lad who must pry the slaves away from Walt Gunn."

"Likely chance, Mark."

"You had better try."

"So far," said Huston, "it seems to me that there had been a minimum of actual money brought into this thing."

"There will be a minimum of actual money, Arn. But we'll want no more partners by the time we extend to the open sea."

"Sea?"

"The river trade and the sea trade, my friend, are not two things, but one."

"Nonsense."

"Don't think for a minute," said Mark with sudden intensity, "that I'm interested in your river trade alone. I'm not. It's picayunish!"

"It's what?"

"It's trifling. Look here—don't you see the tremendous advantage of offering rates from St. Louis to Liverpool, Pittsburg to Madrid, Hongkong to Minneapolis—"

"That's open-sea stuff, you ass."

"Certainly it is. D'you see what we have here, Arn? The main channel of transportation for a continent—all the land between the Alleghenies and the Rockies, with a bigger volume of trade every year. A good grip on the river trade means vast fortunes. But add that to overseas transportation. D'you see what it is? A floating empire, a vast growing thing that reaches to every part of the globe, with its roots in the heart stream of American trade—"

"Mark, you're mad!"

"—a means of taking advantage of every turn of trade, every new demand; a thing that has no limit in possibility. And—"

"You're talkin' about somethin' you know less than nothin' about."

"Maybe; but look: if we had twenty packets, I don't suppose you'd object to running a clipper or two around to New York? By way of a feeder to the river line?"

"No; that'd be a good idea. I've thought of that before. But—"

"But nothing. That is just what I'm looking ahead to."

"But the first thing is a packet."

"Arn, that's just what I'm trying to get at. We've got to have a packet. The longer we delay the more we're the losers. I grant you that this is something of a shoestring proposition—"

Huston laughed. "I never saw a slimmer piece of business in my life. For a man with five thousand you've got the biggest notions I ever—"

"—but it may work. Don't you think so?"

"This packet? With management, and luck, it might possibly just squeeze through."

"If I'm willing to gamble, why shouldn't you be?"

They walked in silence for a while, Huston unenthusiastic, Wallace waiting. At the foot of the levee the *Elton McGregor* sounded her final bells, snored steam; struggling negroes hauled her stage plank home. Her high-piled cargo made her look like a great square shoe box, majestically moving off over the surface of the coffee-colored flood. Great rolls of good gray smoke piled upward out of her funnels, dropping gentle showers of soot and wood ash over the broad back of her hurricane roof. Tiny figures stood along the rail of her high boiler deck; here and there a small flutter indicated a handkerchief waved to a friend. "Up—river," whoofed her slow engines as she backed away, "up—river; up—river—"

The moving *Elton McGregor* stirred in Arnold Huston an imagination which Mark Wallace's fantastic dreams of empire had not aroused. He suddenly was eager to believe that there might be a way for him to take to the river again in a boat at least partially his own.

"Just what is my position in this scheme?" he demanded.

"Well—" Mark pressed his lips together as if he were bracing himself for a stiff climb—"you give me a note for seventy-five hundred, and take a half interest."

"I don't see why you should—"

"Do you think I know the practical side of the river?"

"No!"

"I agree with you. That should answer your question."

"It hardly sounds substantial, Mark."
"No. Will you gamble on it?"
"Yes!"

CHAPTER XI

WHEN the *Mary Christopher* had hauled in the stage plank that had landed Arnold Huston, he stood for a few moments looking across the broad moonlit gray of the river, reluctant to leave it.

"When you're ashore," an obscure old steamboat man named Bilgus Magruder once said, "you're in jest one fixed spot, like a old cow, or a tree. When you're on a boat you're jest boomin' along to some place else. I never was ashore that I didn't feel like I was stuck down."

Arnold Huston, who never knew Bilgus, felt the same way as he now turned his back on the Mississippi and took the dusty wagon track that led inland from Gunn's landing. The track led through a dense grove of cottonwoods that the neighboring woodyard had not yet eaten away. Through the upper mass of the leaves the moonlight hardly struck at all; the patches of light where the moon did find a way in were scattered blotches. Seen distantly through the pillaring trunks the light spots looked like mysterious painted things, unnaturally radiant in contrast to the prevailing dark.

The wagon path presently emerged from the cottonwoods and ran along the edge of a planted field;

twisted obscurely across a dry meadow, and on directly through another broad acreage of planted cotton. Here the night jars were calling overhead, invisible voices somewhere in the upper air: "Chuck! Will's widow, Chuck!" It was a good three miles to Walt Gunn's cabins; they had once been on the brink of the river, but that had changed. Huston was tired of tramping in the dust by the time the downward dip of the wagon road told him that he had not much farther to go.

The last half mile of the way led through a jungled bottom land, an old bed of the always shifting river, where the water still came during times of flood. Through the cypress tangle a network of small bayous, equal to floating a pirogue, but nothing more, crawled twisting over the bottoms; the wagon road crossed these on rude bridges.

It was black in this half mile of swamp. It was such a place as the silent alligators love to inhabit. The darkness had a deep, velvety quality here, as if it were misty with black damp. There was a trill and chug of frogs; and the high thin hum of mosquitoes was incessant.

Following the twisting road Huston at last climbed the swell of land that marked the old bank of the river, and saw a huddle of cabins ahead. Although it was not long after eight o'clock, only one of the cabins showed a gleam of light, an orange streak in the purple dark. By its position, as well as by its size—slightly larger than the slave quarters close at hand—Huston knew it for the dwelling of Walt Gunn himself.

A tremendous bellowing of hound dogs now set up, a clamor of barking and canine hallooing, as Huston went up the path. A lean-to confronted him, and he stepped directly into its black mouth, intending to knock on the inner door.

Something hard jabbed his middle so suddenly that he almost doubled up. Then, recovering himself, he quietly put up his hands.

"Git back out—slow," a twanging voice drawled; and Huston stepped out backward into the path.

A yard or so of gun barrel followed him out, its muzzle still pressing into his stomach. It was followed by a figure so lank that Huston's slender build was heavily muscled by comparison. By the light of the moon he made out dingy overalls and a ragged shirt from which thrust up a long corded neck. The face of the man was pinched and hard, a sharp, triangular face expressive of a harsh shrewdness, shut in from the world by an inbred suspicion.

"Wha' ye want?" The thin nasal voice was muffled by a mouthful of tobacco.

"I'll talk to Walt Gunn," said Huston harshly. He lowered his hands. "Take that gun away!"

"Mebbe I will, an' mebbe I won't. Who air ye?"

"Captain Huston."

"Wha' ye want with Walt Gunn?"

Huston held his temper and slipped into the other's drawling tone of speech.

"Aim to make a trade with him."

"Air ye Arnold Huston?"

"That's right."

The lean man of the swamps seemed uncertain; there was a long pause, while from within the cabin came a low, continuous muttering, uninterrupted by the contention without. Then: "Air ye alone?"

"Why, of course I am."

"Well—" the close-set eyes bored him speculatively—"I reckon the dogs is sayin' ye be. I guess it's all right. Come 'long in."

When he had motioned Huston into a dimly lighted doorway, the bony man lurked in the lean-to for a time, peering around the edge of the door; but presently he went out into the moonlight, and Huston saw no more of him.

The log-walled room which Huston entered was small yet unspeakably bare and forlorn. A chest stood near a lop-sided fireplace that gaped blackly like a distorted mouth; some old clothes hung from nails like Spanish moss—and that was all the furnishings. There was a pervasive smell of coffee grounds, old food, rats' nests, and sweat.

At a scarred table sat a massive man, his shaggy head bent over a great book that Huston presently recognized as a Bible, bound in heavy leather and hasped with brass. A big blunt finger, dirty-nailed, was tracing the lines by the wavering light of a candle stuck in a whisky bottle. The man was droning through his beard, a slow, painful reading of the words, accompanied by spelling aloud. Huston interrupted him.

"Walt Gunn?"

The big tousled brown head swung up, and Gunn blinked at his visitor through incongruously small square-lensed glasses. Then suddenly he surged to his feet with a movement like an animal.

Walt Gunn was a man like a bear; and when he had pulled off his glasses with a sweep of one big hairy paw his eyes were like those of a bear, small and pig-like, wide-set beneath the heavy slope of his brow. The shag of his beard bristled downward to collar bones like axe handles. His body was long and barrel-like, his legs short and twisted; and all over the man were great balls and swells of muscle, lumpy under his clothes.

"What ye want?" The voice boomed deeply yet carried a sharp edge.

"Want to make a trade," said Huston again. "Arnold Huston is my name, and I'm a steamboat man. If you don't want to trade with me, I'll get out."

They stood studying each other for a moment, and Huston noted the heavy shoulder holster beneath Gunn's left arm. There was a shoulder holster under Huston's arm, too—but his was within his shirt and his light seersucker coat.

"Set down," said Gunn finally, with an air less of invitation than of command; and Huston, pulling up a chair with a broken back, seated himself across the table from Walt Gunn.

They did not come to business at once. Gunn first had to finish the reading of the Biblical chapter in which he was engrossed. Huston sat for a long time, he thought, listening to the chanting mutter of Gunn's voice, slowly spelling out words many of which he mispronounced and palpably misunderstood. It was not clear to the riverman whether he was being read to, or whether he was merely a silent spectator to Gunn's studies. But he sat patiently enough, waiting for the end, and watching the wax of the candle gutter down over the squat whisky bottle in tortured shapes.

The long reading was finished at last. Gunn was in a perspiration by the time he was through; his flimsy shirt lay like damp cobwebs over the muscles of his shoulders. He discarded the little square spectacles and studied Huston slantwise as he filled a blackened corncob pipe. Huston held his silence.

"Niggers?" suggested Walt Gunn at last.

"Yes."

There was a long silence, in which the little pig eyes seemed to look through him shrewdly, yet without seeing him, as if looking at something beyond. Huston looked the man between the eyes and waited.

"Yo' boat bu'ned," Gunn offered.

"Yes."

The conference got under way slowly, with a sort of bafflement on Huston's side and some unfathomable cross between suspicion and purpose on the other. Occasionally Huston tried to take the lead, and thus a certain amount of time was wasted. Walt Gunn's brain worked its way ahead slowly and steadily, like a plodding ox; quick explanations passed over his head without leaving a trace, and had to be gone over again, point by point, as Gunn slowly trudged up. Finally Huston abandoned the lead altogether, and confined himself to brief answers to Gunn's briefer questions.

So they sat for half the night in a silence punctuated

by short communications; Gunn sucking at his black pipe, Huston smoking his thin cigars. And it at last became apparent that a certain progress was being made. Gunn was drawing out Huston's plans in his own way; and once he had satisfied himself as to a given fact it did not have to be returned to.

Somewhere out in the sticks there presently began a chanting of negroes, accompanied by the dull beat of a club upon a hollow log. What wild ceremony the blacks were going through Huston did not know, but he knew that the songs were neither ballads nor hymns. The distant wailing chant lasted for two hours, sometimes thinned to a single voice, sometimes swelled by many. At last it stopped, but within the cabin Walt Gunn and Arnold Huston were still sitting, lounging on either side of the scarred table, slowly working their way toward the trade for which Huston had come.

Huston had plenty of time to think, in the interims between Gunn's queries. He was aware throughout the hours of the conference of certain comings and goings outside, the meanings of which he could not make out. Aware, too, more sharply, of the repeated clamorings of the dogs, of which there must have been more than a dozen; he wondered how Walt Gunn and the lean man ever got any sleep.

But most of all he was conscious of the great river, three miles away at his back, and of the boat that he had left. By this time she would be far upstream, sliding smoothly over the surface to the thrust of her churning paddles. He realized now that without his boat he was only partly himself, as if he were a brain without hands or feet to work with. The ownership of a steamboat was less a means of livelihood to him than a necessity of his life.

The project that Mark Wallace made possible was a fragile one, rockily beset by obstacles at every turn. But now, as he chafed at the delays of Gunn's slow brain, the objections that had made him wary before seemed only to challenge the resources of his strength. A gleam came into his eyes, and presently, when Walt Gunn went into another prolonged fit of staring at him, he looked back into the pig eyes with such clarity that they dropped.

The long conference came to an end at last; Walt Gunn, in his stoically ponderous way, had learned what he wanted to know, and, apparently, had judged his man. What Huston wanted and on exactly what terms he wanted it was finally clear to them both. Walt Gunn meditated, sucking the black pipe; and the hound dogs clamored twice more before he spoke.

"Huston, our sins are heavy upon us," he said irrelevantly in his hoarse bass, and heaved a mighty groaning sigh.

The steamboat captain sat relaxed, with only his eyes showing a faintly humorous gleam of combat that betrayed his tension. Here, in Walt Gunn's decision, was the first skirmish of the long struggle that was ahead. He knew instinctively, as certainly as if the whole affair were past, that what Walt Gunn said when he finally answered would be conclusive, beyond further argument or persuasion. The man was a monolith, movable only with the greatest effort, and when once he had arrived at his position there would be no changing it.

The great bear of a man surged up with that animal movement, went to the door and looked out, paced back across the room with his shaggy brown beard tangling with the coarse hair of his chest. Then for a long time he stood looking apparently at an old pair of overalls hanging on its nail six inches before his nose, as if he had discovered in them something that altered his whole conception of life. He sat down—he was almost as tall sitting as he was erect, by reason of the short crookedness of his legs—and with his big hands clamped all over the massive Bible, sat staring at the book from under lowering brows, like an animal contemplating an enemy destroyed. There seemed no end to the man's ponderous gyrations of thought.

Huston, sitting cross-kneed on the broken chair, watched Gunn's extraordinary struggles; and he looked like a man who, having offered a handsomely generous thing, waits with good-humored indifference for its acceptance. But within he was saying to himself, "That man has my boat in his hands. . . ."

Gunn was shaking his head in slow swings, more than ever like a bear; he raised his big fist, and brought it slowly down on the table in a deliberate blow that made the floor boarding quiver. Then he suddenly looked up, and regarded Huston with a curious air of abstraction. He leaned forward.

"I'll do it!" Gunn said suddenly in a curious small voice hardly above a whisper; and immediately the man's shaggy jaw dropped open, and he stared at Huston as if he had heard some utterly astounding bit of information.

Huston tramped the three miles back to the river-bank with a light heart. Throughout the dim cool hour in which he paced the shore, waiting for an opportunity to hail a boat, his mind was racing ahead. The feel of his next boat was already under his feet, and the throbbing thrust of her engines was in his blood.

CHAPTER XII

THOUGH it was but nine in the evening a faint mist from the Mississippi blurred the air, giving a blue depth to shadows already deep and softening the glow of the occasional street lights. In the river beyond the levee the perpetual steamboats bellowed at irregular intervals; day or night, at New Orleans, their hoarse reverberations were never silent for long.

Huston had been back from his visit to Walt Gunn two days. As always, his strides turned toward the levee; but to-night, for a hidden reason which he instinctively refrained from seeking out, he bent aside and sauntered down Chartres Street, a lean figure in gray stovepipe hat and long black coat. The Rue Chartres was not pleasant to him, in comparison to the breezy levee where he usually walked. Thick reeking water moved stagnantly in the gutter beside the narrow banquette. Above, the intricately grilled balconies hung darkly, making the narrow street so much narrower that it seemed a man could reach across and brush with his fingertips the smooth plastered wall of the buildings on the other side.

But he sauntered on, knowing well enough where he was going, yet concealing his purpose from himself as a man sometimes will; and so paused presently before the massively timbered door to which he had first been led by Mark Wallace. As if on a sudden impulse he hammered on the door with his fist. He immediately doubted that he would be admitted, and more than half hoped that he would not. But he waited calmly, and in a moment the little iron door behind the barred wicket swung open, and he could see a hidden light reflected on the old negro's bald head.

"Who dah?"

"Huston."

"Yas, Captain."

He heard the muffled fumbling with bolts and bars within; then the window-like door within the door swung open to let him in.

Once more the bald and withered slave went bobbing ahead, his slippers flapping on the flags of the high-vaulted passage; and presently Huston found himself in the sea-gray room with the mulberry drapes and the broad ivory frieze. This time the objects in the room about him seemed incisive, brightly distinct; perhaps because he had remembered them as he had seen them before, through eyes blurred by fatigue.

He was wandering nervously about the room, wondering whether or not she would really appear, when, with a shock of surprise, he found himself confronting a mirror. All evening he had been thinking of himself as a comparatively old man, one who looked down upon the youthful fancies of Mark Wallace with the understanding that mature experience has for youth; only to find that the face looking back at him from the mirror was a boyish face, smoothly untroubled for all its thinness when those deep grin lines were not creasing the cheeks. The gray eyes were alert and hopeful, not cynical as he had supposed. And the upstanding stiffness of the mane above the smooth forehead had a youthfully tousled look.

He was trying to correct this with his fingers when Jacqueline came in.

She came across to him light-footed, her full-billowing skirt emphasizing her slenderness, and she, like the things in the room, surprised him a little that she could be seen so distinctly, instead of being of the blurred stuff of dreams. She was again dressed in black, but this time in an evening affair that left her shoulders bare; and in her pale face the eyes were intensely dark, as if her face were of paper, with the eyes brushed in with ink. In some dim way he had felt that he might be called upon to explain why he had come here; and when she smiled pleasantly he was suffused with relief.

They spoke at first in conventional phrases. She said she was glad he came, he said it was a great privilege to be there. She said the weather was warm for that time of year, and he offered that the river was rising. But though his old-south courtesy was handy enough, he was not thinking of what he said.

He was studying her face, which was as delicately modelled as that of a child; and wondering why she seemed so much older than he was, when he knew that she was the younger of the two. It was a cool face, regularly featured, but undistinguished had it not been for those disturbing long eyes, so dark in contrast to her paleness.

They sat on the settee again, this time speaking conventional words. He seemed to recall that when he had last seen her here she had relaxed luxuriously in the depths of the settee; she was not so now. The calm of her pale face, the poise of her head, her quiet hands folded in the lap of her billowing skirt—these gave her an effect of singular distance, as if he were no nearer her, here beside her, than as if he had been up the river on a boat.

As for Huston, he felt by no means relaxed, but vaguely disturbed. The moments when she met his eyes were disquieting, like electric sparks in an experience otherwise of a vacuous gray. The sensation of disquiet within him grew and grew, until it was recognizable to him as the stirring of a hidden fear.

At first he thought this a recurrence of a youthful worry he had once known: an alarm felt when conversing with a woman, that he should run out of things to say and so be made to look idiotic. But all this time he was talking freely enough, in the casual way that conversation of no consequence suggests. And presently he understood that the stealthily stirring fear within him had its source in no immediate embarrassment of his own, but in some mysterious latent quality in the woman with whom he spoke.

To Huston, Jacqueline DuMoyne was an inexplicable oddity. She was different, certainly, from the daughters of the plantation aristocracy with whom he had some general acquaintance. She was not of their type, nor yet of any other; neither aristocrat nor common-run, but herself—as if she were of a race apart. She did not hesitate, apparently, to receive men, unchaperoned, at night in her home; yet she was as coolly aloof as a grande dame, and with infinitely greater subtlety. He did not think her beautiful, yet she held his eyes.

He wondered if he was making a fool of himself by believing she was really so aloof as she seemed. He thought of taking her hand, as an experiment, to see what she would do; then that deep-stirring fear moved upward with a chill that was not to be denied, as the damp creeps up Louisiana walls; and he was checked.

So, presently, he turned his eyes toward the river, through that tall French window at which he had sat before; and sought across those low roofs below for the lights of the levee and the smooth expanse of the Mississippi beyond. At first he could see nothing but a dimness of mist, with the roofs arranged in geometrical patterns of flat color in the foreground. But in a moment his eyes accustomed themselves to the outer dark, and the faint river scene came into clarity as a developing photograph comes onto sensitized paper in response to the light.

He could make out the pilot houses of the steamboats, the riding lights of the ships beyond, and the smoothly parading lights of a boat nosing downstream to her berth. Beyond these, receding illimitably into the dark, lay the pale surface of the river. The Mississippi looked as motionless under the moonlit mist as if it were of locked ice; but he instinctively sensed the giant current under the mist, dangerous in its stealth. Beneath the faint thin blanket of vapor the river was still tugging at its steamboats with the same strong swing and pull, trying to take them down with it to the Nirvana of the sea. The presence of the river made Huston feel like himself, so that he became discouraged with the triviality of the conversation he had been making. He slumped in his seat, thrust his hands into his pockets, and let the small talk lag, more like a man lounging on some cotton bale than like one in the drawing room of a woman whom he had come to see.

"This window is everything to me," said Jacqueline DuMoyne presently. So well had the river held him that he had not realized, until she spoke, that they had been silent for some little time. "So many hours I've sat here, watching the steamboats and the ships, and wondering who was on them and where they were going."

Huston looked along his shoulder at her, now that he was brought to the necessity of saying something again, with an attitude almost comically like that of an animal at bay. He bent forward in the act of rising to take his leave; but her next remark held him.

"I've never been on a steamboat," she told him.

"What? Never in your life?"

"Never."

He held the belief that anyone who had never set foot on a steamboat was a person incomplete, a curious recluse who could have very little idea of what the world was like.

"But—you haven't always lived here, have you? How did you come here without travelling on a boat?"

"I came on a ship."

"Oh." He contemplated the curious state of her ignorance with an air of abstraction.

"It seems to me," she said, "that for years I've been wanting to go down to the levee and take a boat."

Her voice came from low in her throat, yet with the faintly audible trace of some almost forgotten Latin inflection. There was in it a quality that held his ear, as animals are made to stop and listen by certain notes. It was as if some hidden string vibrated in answer to her voice, as a violin string sometimes answers the softest murmur of an organ tone.

"You want to go back to—to your home?"

"Santo Domingo," she said, answering his implied question. "It is a beautiful place; I suppose there is no place like it in the world. But I don't want to go back there. I'd rather go on."

His knowledge of geography apart from the river was blurred; yet the name of Santo Domingo, which he vaguely thought was in the Virgin Islands somewhere, had some dim association in his mind. On the Rue Chartres, so near at hand that he could have seen its tiled roof if he had cared to lean forward, stood an old café, the Café des Refugiés. It was a small place, uncommonly secretive when the moonlight sometimes for a short space penetrated the narrow cleft of the street. The name of Santo Domingo had at one time been whispered so often within those old courtyard walls that it must have penetrated them with the damp and become twisted into the stems of the aged vines.

He had heard old men speak of the motley company that gathered there, French and Spanish, bleak-eyed or superficially gay; men with resolute, brooding faces, and others of lesser fibre who gesticulated and gibbered in whispers, all but shedding tears into their drinks. They were refugees from some Dominican trouble to which Huston had no clue, aloofly sorrowing exiles from the land which they had chosen to call home.

Huston had no idea whether Santo Domingo was a state, an island, or a town; he pictured it as a sort of combination of all three. He thought it had probably been a humble mud-walled colony at the time of the row; but he knew that when its exiles spoke of it they must have made it sound like a land of extraordinary beauty, a gleaming white city, rising tower upon tower from a luxuriance of palms. "Santo Domingo . . ." The name carried some of that same implication of mysterious beauty when Jacqueline DuMoyne said it in her low, faintly exotic voice, with its hidden ability to stir a man.

It made her seem even more of a stranger to him than before; as if she were some curious tropic bird from palmed jungles. Yet when he looked at her again she seemed less aloof. She was looking at the river;

and her mouth was wistful, in spite of the cool quiet of her eyes. There was almost the quality of an impulsive appeal in her voice when she spoke again.

"Tell me about your river!"

"Why"—he floundered a little—"what about it would you like to know?"

"What do you do when you are away upstream? What is the country like?"

"Why—just country, you know—plantations and things—"

She looked at him blankly. "How would you like to leave the river?" she demanded suddenly. "For good?"

"Oh, I'll always be a riverman!"

"Yet you see nothing in it you like—nothing that is worth telling about at all!"

He was silent for many minutes, despairing of her ignorance, wondering how to put into words of one syllable a definition of the river's hold upon him. It never occurred to him that he did not himself know what it was. He was turning over in his mind various inconsequential phases of river life that were vivid enough to give him nostalgia when he thought of them; but not one of them could be advanced as a source of appeal.

He was thinking of coffee and sandwiches in the dark hours after midnight, during a night watch at the wheel; how good the coffee tasted then; how satisfyingly the engines throbbed, down there below, as they drove the boat that you were guiding upriver through the dark. But how could he tell her of the delights of a damp sandwich in the lonely dark of the pilot house, in a night made interesting by a sort of chugging noise going on some place?

He was thinking of the meals in the lighted cabin, among a gay company that was forever changing; how enjoyable a dinner was with the boat stepping off her distances strongly while you took your ease; and how good the food was after being on your feet all afternoon in a cool river breeze. But how could he tell her that he certainly enjoyed eating regularly among strangers, provided he had worked up an appetite in the course of the afternoon?

He thought, too, of the snug comfort of his cabin when the northern reaches of the river were bitter cold and a man was glad to wrap himself in his blankets fully clothed, to snatch an hour or two of delicious sleep before the next emergency came up. How could he explain that he appreciated getting exhausted and half frozen, because it was so pleasant to get over it again? Everything he liked on the river was ordinary, or else had a disagreeable string tied to it some place.

"I don't know exactly," he said at last.

It had taken him so long to arrive at this feeble conclusion that Jacqueline DuMoyne had abandoned hope of intelligence from him, and had for some time been pursuing thoughts of her own.

"Don't know what, Captain?"

"I don't know why I like the river."

"Do you really know the river?" The question was so casually pleasant that if the words had been in another tongue he could not possibly have detected any hint of irony in her tone.

He smiled at the futility of his own speech, and murmured an evasion. "I knew it last week; it changes its channel every trip, of course."

"What are you saying?"

"Why, you see, the river is crookeder than a shoelace, and the current is strong, as you'd expect in a river a mile wide that can rise and fall a good thirty feet. The current chews away at the banks at the foot of every bend. Then perhaps it cuts through and eliminates a bend altogether; that shortens the river. But the current is thrown just that much harder against the next bend, so the bend deepens; and that lengthens the river again. And that goes on forever, with the channel shortenin' and lengthenin', swingin' from side to side. To look at it out there, it looks quiet, and tame. But the river is the most restless thing I know. It'll take this town some day, I wouldn't be a bit surprised. It's done harder things than that before now."

"Do you really think it could?"

"If that levee broke now, the Mississippi would have the streets under four feet of water as fast as it could pour in. It's risin' now; that means the flood would be whoopin' around the feet of these buildin's fit to cut the foundations from under them in no time. They're built on swamp land, anyway, you know. And the river comes higher every year; that's because of the levees they're always buildin', hundreds of miles upstream."

He would have let it go at that, but she pressed him with questions; and he talked for two hours, touching here and there on nearly every phase of the river life that he knew. He told her something about the river-bottom plantations and the northern towns from which the steamboats drew their cargoes; of the wild country near struggling St. Paul, almost a frontier town then; of river characters, and of others that sometimes rode the river—Texas plainsmen, forest runners and fur traders from Indian territory, planters, plantation overseers, slave traders, peddlers, river gamblers—a variegated throng enlivening the decks of boats so loaded with hustled freight that the water lapped the chocks. . . .

He talked rather badly, on the whole, but some of the pull and swing of the river got into his stories, nevertheless. Jacqueline listened with brightening eyes. To her he was as strange a type as she was to him. His peculiarly direct manner of speech had at first seemed brutal to her; afterward it impressed her with its genuineness. An education given entirely by the river had not polished Huston beyond reason. He had none of the facile pitter-patter to which she was accustomed. He had something else, though, a rough-cut originality of thought that was refreshing to her; and he was assuredly of the stuff of the river boats that she had grown to love distantly in two lonely years beside her window. But he was sinewy and straight, with a rugged head commandingly carried; and his eyes glowed when he talked of the river like steel that catches the glint of some external fire.

Arnold's narrative trailed off. She was no longer sitting rigidly erect as she had when he first came, but was relaxed luxuriously in the cushions. She was looking at the river, where the mist was rising from a surface of live ebony; her head was beautifully poised, her eyes radiant. In the half-barbaric light of the shaded lamp her shoulders took the sheen of warm satin.

She turned toward him and let her eyes rest upon him with an impersonal dreaminess, as if unaware that he was there; and he returned her gaze with a counterfeited air of absentmindedness, wondering how it was that he had not perceived at first that she was beautiful. The hidden dread that had puzzled him earlier in the evening now stirred again more insistently than before. It crept upward, this mysterious fear, stiffening his lips, turning his eyes cold. He groped confusedly for its cause, but came only to the clearer realization that when he looked into the dark quiet of her eyes it was as if a limitless abyss was opening at his feet.

He felt out of place, uprooted from the familiar footing of the boats, the river towns, and the plantations; as far from his Mississippi habitat as if he had been in the fanciful realm of Santo Domingo, instead of in the river's leading port. Yet there was the undeniable fascination of Jacqueline's appeal. . . .

He got to his feet, formal phrases coming readily enough to his tongue.

She said, "Do come again."

"Thank you, Madame."

"You will come, won't you?"

"With your permission, Madame," he said woodenly.

"You have it, Captain."

When he got out through the little door in the arched gate it was with a feeling of escape.

"I'll never go *there* again," he told himself. He repeated for his own reassurance: "No sir, never." But he said it with a curious sense of loss.

CHAPTER XIII

ARNOLD HUSTON never felt better in his life than the day that he first boarded the *Frontier City*. A fresh breath of autumn was in the air of the bayou country, pleasantly contrasting to the late hot spell in the narrow New Orleans streets from which he had come. Now Huston's star was conspicuously on the ascendant; he was eager to get his teeth into the labor ahead. His blood went through his arteries with a zing, making every muscle in his body enthusiastically alive.

A stubby little sternwheeler had brought him up the threading bayou beside which the *Frontier City* lay, six miles from the main channel of the Mississippi. The sluggish stream was so narrow that the overhanging branches of cottonwoods sometimes brushed both guards of the little steamboat. There had been an encouraging amount of water there, however; and as for the width of the channel, Huston presumed that if the *Frontier City* had got up there once she could get down again, given an equal stage of the river.

"How long has the *Frontier City* been up here?" he asked the pilot once.

"Only 'bout eighteen months."

"River pretty high when she went up?"

"Oh, middlin' high." The man at the wheel considered for a time. "Well—heavy middlin', I reckon. She'll float next month, I sh'd say."

Huston craned for the first glimpse of his prospective boat as the puffing sternwheeler at last opened the mouth of the tributary bayou where the *Frontier City* lay. His first glimpse of her was disappointing, she looked so definitely decayed. She was bigger than he remembered her though, measuring two hundred forty feet from deadpost to transom; and now she looked larger than she really was, squatting broadly in the mud, completely bottling up the mouth of the inlet she had chosen for her interment. Her three decks towered imposingly, ancient and gray, behind the leafy screen.

Huston leaped to the bank without need of the stage plank; and the fussing sternwheeler pompously shoved its way on up the bayou in a trickle of water that looked as if it would hardly bear up a duck.

"Hi! Captain Pumpernickel!"

After an interval of alternate hailing and chewing at bits of grass, both without result, Huston impatiently boarded and ran up the leaf-drifted main stairway to the boiler deck. A curious figure met him at the cabin's entrance.

"Captain Pumpernickel, I'm Arnold Huston."

The captain of the *Frontier City* was struggling into a rusty old coat; but he now paused halfway in the process, looking more like a man taking off his coat to fight than one dressing to receive guests.

"Who?" Pumpernickel was aged, it appeared, beyond all reckoning, but he retained the pinkness of skin of an over-washed child. His cheeks were drooping, rounded folds, his nose a shorter and more bulbous fold, but equally drooping, laid in the middle. Beneath the apparently boneless nose his mouth was an almost circular pucker. He was the only man Huston had ever seen that held a cigar straight out under his nose as he smoked: the shape of the man's mouth seemed to explain that he could have smoked no other way.

"Captain Arnold Huston," the riverman repeated.

"Well," said the old man, still poised in the suspended struggle with his coat, "you don't look it." His voice was as dry as the windrowed leaves with which the deck was cluttered, but his eyes were of a piercing blue, round and shiny as glass marbles. He inspected Huston from the shoe laces upward, so that beneath the brim of his hat only the flabby old face was visible; until as they travelled upward those round blue eyes seemed to pop from under the rim of the hat with an effect that was startling.

"No?" said Arnold.

"You're a boy," the old man averred dogmatically. "You got a face like a boy. Anyways," he added uncertainly, "you have until y'start grinnin'." He slowly drew his arms out of the coat sleeves again, and the garment collapsed to the deck as if overwhelmingly relieved. Captain Pumpernickel let it lie. "What boat was y'captain on?"

"My own boat," said Huston, "the *Peter Swain.* She burned."

"That so? Well, I'm glad to see you. A captain's a captain. Even if he is on'y a boy. Y'gimme a start at first. I thought y'was one o' the capitalists. I been expectin' 'em to come see about buyin' my boat." He gave Huston a hand like a skeleton pasted over with parchment.

"Were they comin' to-day?"

"How?"

"I say, were the buyers comin' to-day?"

"I dunno if they was comin' to-day. Mebbe they ain't comin'. Hope they don't. I jest said I was expectin' 'em."

"How long have you been expectin' 'em?" Huston inquired disinterestedly, peering past him into the cabin of the boat.

"How? Oh. About a year."

Huston was surprised into shooting a quick glance at him. At this point there appeared from the dark interior of the cabin a lank, high-hipped, long-striding cat of extraordinary size. The animal rubbed a bony small head with enormously long ears against the cabin timbers; emitted two purrs so loudly that Huston looked down to see what had broken loose; and disappeared around the corner of the cabin, striding.

"Who's that?" Huston demanded.

"How?" Conversation with Captain Pumpernickel required perpetual repetition. "That's just a cat. No partic'lar cat. Come with the boat. Always been with the boat. You're fidgety. Askin' who is a cat. Glad to see y'though."

Pumpernickel shook hands with Huston again in an undecided way, as if uncertain whether he had done so before or not.

"Expectin' to sell. That's why I ain't keepin' her up better. Don't want to go throwin' good money after bad. Don't know whether them capitalists is comin' or not. Leave 'em stay away. Want to make a beggar out of a man. Won't pay nothin'. Hurtin' no one but their-selfs." Here Captain Pumpernickel mumbled off into a procession of virulent blasphemies that sometimes made his dry voice crack like a whip, and sometimes seemed to be choking him with their invisible bulk. "Have a drink," he concluded.

He had led the way inside to the cabin's best state-room, a compartment equipped with a dresser and four-poster bed instead of the usual bunks. Here a stupendous confusion prevailed. The drawers of the dresser were half out, disgorging unlaundered linen; old suits and overalls were wrestling among themselves on the floor, on the bed, and on the single chair; the doors of the wardrobe stood open, but only one or two things were hung up inside. A tray of dirty dishes stood on the dresser, and on the floor near the door was a second over which Captain Pumpernickel stumbled with a great clatter and spluttering of oaths.

"Eat breakfast in bed," he explained in his dry voice. "Cook it night before. Wake up in mornin', there she is by the bed. Cold, of course. Better'n gettin' up, though. Man has to use his head. Pervide for himself."

Rummaging, he produced a squat bottle and a pair of glasses that he cleaned, after some thought, by wiping with the disordered bedspread.

"Well, here's how."

"Luck," responded Huston, tossing off two fingers

of brandy in a gulp.

"Place look like a torpoon struck it," Pumpernickel went on disconsolately. "Ain't cleaned up lately. Man gets tired cleanin' up. That's nigger work, anyway. I got better things t'do 'th my time 'n to do work a nigger should be doin'. Time's more valyble 'n that."

"Certainly," Huston agreed.

Pumpernickel brooded, his loosely folded features drooping over his glass. "Aim to live like a white man. Can't no one do that by doin' nigger work. Wasn't always this way. Times has gone to the dogs. I used to be captain of this boat. I'm captain yet. I'll take her out an' run her pretty soon, if times get better. Got to get capital first. If I don't I'll have to get a ladder to get into this room. Can't afford a nigger. All I got left is this boat. Little money. Not enough to rent a nigger. Good boat, though. Damn her, anyway. God help rivermen. Ain't nothin' but misery fer a man runnin' a boat."

"Look here," said Huston; and Captain Pumpernickel said, "How?"

"Why don't you," Huston almost shouted, "sell the old boat, and get you a little house, and a nigger, and live in comfort?"

"Can't get nothin' for it," Pumpernickel said testily. "Ain't goin' to sell fer a price that'll keep me four or five years, then leave me without a roof over my head. They want to make a beggar out of a man. Don't want to give nothin'. Jest as soon see the rightful captain of the boat settin' out in the rain. Make 'em laugh. Say it serves the old fool right. No, sir. I won't do it. Decided this ain't a boat no more. It's a house. Damn good house. Many a millionaire ain't got the ekal. This ain't the boiler deck no more, this is the second floor. That out there ain't the guards, it's the side gallery. The Texas house is the attic an' the pilot house is the look-around cupola. The galley—"

The old man seemed game to follow out the fancy indefinitely, but Huston, growing impatient, broke into the monologue.

"Captain, I often meet men that might be interested in buyin' a boat—an' payin' its full value, too. Why don't you let me look her over? Maybe I can find a buyer for you."

"How?" said Pumpernickel, cocking his head to one side; and Huston went over it all again. When he understood what Huston was getting at the captain of the *Frontier City* remained unenthusiastic. "Glad to show you the boat, though," he decided.

With this he fell into a reverie, his glass-marble eyes goggling moodily at Huston's knees; and he remained thus for so long that Huston almost lost hope. When loud throat-clearings failed to attract the old man's attention, he went out to look over the boat for himself.

Down the leaf-fouled stairs he went, feeling that the *Frontier City* was a house indeed, squatting so flatly in the mud, and made his way back through the rubbish of the deck-room to the hatchway of the hold. There was water in it, of course; the wonder to Huston, as he peered down into the blackness by the aid of a match, was that there was not more. He could tell nothing by looking in from above, so he stripped off his clothes; and retaining only his long-bladed knife, lowered himself into three feet of chill black water in the bottom.

The steamboat hold was, of necessity, a shallow affair; in the *Frontier City* there was hardly five feet of clearance between the flooring and the timbers of the deck above; and this flatly cramped space was such a forest of trunk-like uprights and diagonal bracing timbers that a man could hardly grope his way among them. The flooring went but a little way to either side of the central passageway, where the timbers of the bottom itself were exposed. For some little time he worked his way about, feeling the wet wood here and there with his knife; and he was both pleased and surprised by the result. Finally he struck the knife into the bottom timbers with a great chunking splash; and having broken the blade in the hard wood, was satisfied.

He turned back toward the dim light of the hatchway through the black under-water corridors, a labyrinth like a catacomb, its flatness making the boat seem, from this viewpoint, a vast leviathan; and was suddenly startled by the vision of Captain Pumpernickel's head, weirdly hanging skull downward through the hatch. The eyes were so glassy, and the flabby features—drooping the other way now—were so motionless that Huston thought the man had fallen dead in the act of leaning over the hatch. A thin strand of hair that Huston had not noticed before trailed downward from the top of the old man's inverted head like

Spanish moss.

The suspended head offered speech.

"Oh, there you are down in the cellar," said the desiccated voice. "Ain't you, huh?" Pumpernickel seemed anxious to assure himself that nothing malignantly mysterious was going on. "Hey! Where *are* you, anyway?"

"I'm here in the hold!" Huston shouted, suddenly fearful that the old man should clamp down the hatch upon him in some senile misconception. "Here in the hold!"

"Cellar," Pumpernickel amended abruptly, with an apparent loss of interest. The head disappeared, only to descend again a moment later. "Your clo'es is up here," said the head inanely.

"I know it!" yelled Huston.

Captain Pumpernickel withdrew; Huston could hear him mumbling to himself above in the deckroom. "What's he doin'? Clothes up here. Arnh. He put 'em here hisself. . . ."

As Huston had almost gained the hatchway again the flabby face was suddenly thrust down again not six inches from his own. The cracked old voice shouted mightily in Huston's ear, Pumpernickel evidently believing that his visitor was still in the distant depths of the hold.

"Be you takin' a bath?" he shouted.

"NO!" roared Huston, and the head was snatched away.

The riverman pursued the remainder of his examination swiftly and systematically. Captain Pumpernickel pattered after him, relating long irrelevancies in short sentences that alternately rose to an ear-piercing rasp and sunk to unintelligible mumbles. Before Huston put on his clothes he lowered himself from the chocks, and went diving and wallowing in the muck under the boat as far as he could reach in an examination of the outer sheathing. Pumpernickel was still talking each time Huston emerged from the mud, exactly as if he had never noticed his guest's submersion at all.

Later, as he bathed in a clear pool of water a hundred yards aft the *Frontier City*, Huston studied the lines of the idle boat with an increasing appreciation. At first sight she was homely enough; but her timbers were true as the day she was made, and he reflected with satisfaction how trim she could look with her Texas house reduced by half, her boiler deck lengthened forward, and fresh paint over every inch of her dingy gray. By the time he had completed his inspection he knew what he was going to do.

"How would you like a job as mate on a boat?" he asked tentatively.

"How? . . . No, sir!" Pumpernickel's vehemence might have been surprising, had not Huston understood that the old man's proposal to return to the river had no grounding in actual intent. "Never!" said Pumpernickel again. "I don't want nothin' to do with runnin' no boat. Misery. Not me. I been through the mill. I got a good residence here. I know when I'm well off. If I was offered a thousand dollars a day I'd not—"

Huston tried a new tack. "When I quit the river," he said, "I'm goin' to live on somebody else's boat. I'll take it easy, and I'll have everythin' a man could want. Cabin niggers to clean out my room, the best meals in the country, breakfast in bed—"

"Yes, you will!" Pumpernickel burst out. His drooping features quivered with a suggestion of rage, but his sharp blue eyes, being perfectly round and glassy, could of course express nothing. "When you get old you'll be like me. You'll turn your boat into a house, because nobody'll give you nothin' for it. Takes money to be a cabin passenger. Rivermen make money. I've made plenty. But what does it get you? All gets away. Leaves you where you started from. Show me the riverman that ever got anywhere? Every damn one dies broke."

Huston could have named an unlimited number of rivermen that had got somewhere, but he did not trouble himself. "If you got enough money for your boat to ride the river as a cabin passenger the rest of your life, would you sell?"

"D'you think I'm crazy?"

"How much do you ask?" Huston demanded abruptly.

"Seventeen thousand," said the dry voice.

"You're three times higher than you'll ever get," Huston told him.

Captain Pumpernickel stared at him while he developed himself to a state of complete enragement. It took the greater part of a minute for the old man to achieve this, but when it was accomplished he fairly jiggled.

"You're jest like the rest," he shrilled. "Want to cheat me. Won't give nothin'. Don't care if—"

"Come down a little!" Huston shouted back at him. "Come down within reason!"

"Not a damn cent! Not a damn cent! I won't hear—"

Huston could hear the fussing sternwheeler poking her way back down the bayou. In not so many minutes her stage plank would be out for him, and he would have the opportunity of leaving his business unfinished or staying with old Pumpernickel until next day.

"Listen!" said Huston so harshly that the old man's tirade ceased. "I'll give you two hundred dollars a year for life. And—"

"I won't hear it! I won't—" Pumpernickel bounced up and down on the balls of his feet.

"Listen!" Huston checked him again. "If you sell me the boat on those terms I'll put her on the river; and I'll give you free cabin passage for as long as you live. I'll sign a contract for that."

Pumpernickel was given pause. His drooping features relaxed from their temporary distortion. "How?" he said presently.

Huston explained it again. The proposition soaked in slowly, but when it had penetrated it was plain that most of the wind was out of the old man's sails. "You'll have to come higher," he contended querulously. "Don't think you can come it over me! You're only a boy. I know what I'm about. I—"

"Three hundred dollars a year," said Huston. "And that's my last word."

The whistle of the sternwheeler was shrieking for

her landing, with a volume of sound suggesting that a mighty five-decker was going to emerge from the willows instead of a scant two decks with a pill box of a pilot house on top.

"I'm leaving on that boat," said Huston. "Are you interested or not?"

"Don't push me," Pumpernickel warned him. "Because I ain't to be pushed. I—"

"All right. I'll buy another boat. Sorry we can't come to terms." He thrust out his hand.

The old captain shook hands dazedly, and Huston turned to the stairs.

"Where y'goin'?" demanded Pumpernickel, coming to life. "Let's talk this over! Mebbe we can—"

"Shall I bring the contract to-morrow?"

"Well—Stay over, Captain! We got to talk this thing out. I don't want to—"

The bayou steamboat was sagging to a stop at the mouth of the inlet. A hail came from her hurricane roof: "Cap'n Huston! Yuh comin'?"

"Yes!" he roared back. Then to Pumpernickel, "Good-bye, Captain!"

He ran down the stair and sprang across the grass-grown stage plank. A cry that was like a shout of despair hailed him from the boiler deck of the *Frontier City*, checking Huston on the path. Captain Pumpernickel had come to the rail. He looked a pathetic figure, standing there outworn and old by the bleared woodwork of his boat. He seemed to be vainly pulling up against the droop of his whole frame; as if the tentacles of the years were climbing up to gather him in, as the long stems of the woodvines were creeping up from the shore to cover the *Frontier City.* And there were the marks of a long despair in the loosely folded face with the puckered lips, as if the man might be ghost-ridden by night.

"Bring the contract," he shouted. The cracked voice was almost conciliating. "Bring it to-morrow! Won't do no harm. Have a look an' see what it is."

"All right!" Huston shouted back. He grinned as he ran down the path.

CHAPTER XIV

HUSTON and Wallace had bought the *Frontier City* in early December. As Christmas drew near, Arnold's plans for his new boat were already taking visible form.

These days were the happiest that Huston had known since he first had taken possession of the ill-fated *Peter Swain.* The Mississippi River, at once the background and the lifestream of their project, was at this season teeming with a renewed life. The cotton crop was just beginning to bear down upon all means of transportation with the full weight of its mass; and under their towering loads the steamboats plied the great waterway rejoicing. Parties of planters and their families travelled the river to St. Louis, to Memphis, to Vicksburg, or to New Orleans, hastening to brighten the holidays by expending some part of the wealth promised by the crop. On the bigger boats bands played, and there was gayety and dancing every night.

Down in New Orleans, the second port of the nation, the winter weather alternated between periods of relenting sunshine, when it seemed to be midsummer once more, and intervals of rawness, in which it rained every day. At the same time reports came down-river that the steamboat *Cally Mandarin*, in attempting a final run to St. Paul, had become locked in the ice, and was indefinitely delayed, waiting for a thaw.

The river was running high, swelled by the periodically thawing northern snows. But ultimate high water would come two months later, so that the fullest flood was still well ahead. Similarly, the high flood of river trade was also ahead, giving the steamboat men reason to look forward to prosperity still greater than that they already enjoyed. Christmas was coming, high water was coming, the boom days of the crop were on their way; and the steamboats rushed at their work with a song. You could scarcely step out onto the bank of the broad Mississippi, in those days, without sighting a steamboat; at no part of the river were their bellowing whistles silent for long. Their good gray smoke was almost always visible some place to the people of the river-bottom plantations, encouraging them with their implications of thriving trade and the bright beckoning of prosperous towns.

Through these days Huston and Mark Wallace worked in a frenzy of enthusiasm, each in his own way. The articles of incorporation had been drawn up to their satisfaction at last, Huston insisting upon and obtaining a wide latitude of control. Each of them had found his work and his place.

Mark Wallace was proving himself a business manager of no mean ability. He had grown haggard under the eyes before those loans that he had arranged were finally consummated. But, to Huston's cynical surprise, he eventually delivered all he had promised; though it was doubtful if he could have turned up a dollar more, had it been essential. In the interim between the floating of the loans and the launching of the boat he was acting as a purchasing agent, in which rôle he was proving himself equally efficient.

Meantime, the *Frontier City* still squatted in the mud, for the high water that was necessary for her extraction from the bayou would hasten for no man nor moderate itself for any when it came. Until she could be floated out and taken to dry dock they could do little to repair her hull; they kept her pumped dry within to discourage rot, but the caulking had to wait. There was much, however, that could be done where she lay. Huston, eager to have her ready in time to get the benefit of the boom days of the crop, pressed the work forward with unceasing energy.

Since the *Frontier City* could not go to the yards for repairs, men and materials were brought to her remote retreat. Cooks came first. Next, two young men appeared with drafting outfits. For some days they worked long hours under Huston's direction, making measurements and drawing plans. Here matters seemed to pause for a bit. But Huston labored with unflagging haste, and the final plans for the *Frontier City*'s alterations appeared in his hands at last.

Now the peace of the deep-hidden bayou was disturbed in good earnest. Great stacks of lumber were thrown thundering onto her forecastle, and the next boat after its arrival brought a crew of carpenters and their assisting slaves. Thirty negroes, each burdened with his personal supply of sowbelly, cornmeal, molasses, and black-eyed peas, now arrived, the first allotment of the slaves arranged for by Huston on his visit to that old bear of the bayous, Walt Gunn. The boat swarmed with life, and the huge galley range was not again allowed to grow cold.

All day long the clatter of hammers sounded in the bayou in accompaniment to the screech of drawn nails. Down came the pilot house, and the whole huge, overbalancing structure of the Texas. Off came the whole front works of the upper decks and cabin, whose stubbiness had always given the boat a peculiar sawed-off, repulsed appearance. Stacks of rubbish beside the boat began to grow. The guards were piled with nail kegs, tool lockers, rope coils, tackle rigging, mill work, straw-packed cases of glass.

The framework of the extended cabin and upper decks appeared, giving in a single day an entirely different swing to the boat's lines. A new long, low Texas house took form on the hurricane roof where the disproportionate one had once caught the wind. It was surmounted in turn by a new pilot house, long and commodious, in place of the extraordinary spindling tower that had served before.

The slaves from Walt Gunn were set to work with scouring bricks, holystone, and sandpaper, dressing down the decks and cleaning the scaling paint from the main structure that was to remain. They sanded down the white and mahogany woodwork of the cabin, levelled the warping narrow boards of the decks, made every inch of her wood ready for new paint.

Through the reign of commotion Captain Pumpernickel survived in a daze. Occasionally he offered an ineffectual suggestion; but for the most part he kept out of the way nearly as well, though with less equanimity, than that lank, high-hipped cat, whose detached poise bore a touch of genius.

But by far most important of all to the destiny of the *Frontier City* was the advent of Arthur MacMaugh.

MacMaugh was a steamboat engineer—an engine-room engineer. In figure he was singularly tall, and bony in the extreme; he was not noticeably well proportioned, running to too great prominence of wrists and knees. But his hands, from which the engine-oil grime never quite disappeared, were at once powerfully and delicately strong, giving the impression that they could with equal ease bend a horseshoe out of shape or adjust the mechanism of a watch.

He had a great rock of a head covered with a shock of unkempt hair the color of mud. It was commonly in need of a cut, for MacMaugh was accustomed to forget about those things. His big face was irregularly lined into lumpy sections, as if he had carved it out himself from the original rock with one of his own cold-chisels, probably, and without the aid of a mirror. It was a strong face, though, with prominent thin lips and eyes at once kindly and very hard-bearing. And he was no more Scotch in soul than the bagpipes of Auchtermuchtie.

MacMaugh had not accepted the berth on the *Frontier City* unqualifiedly. Huston had been at pains to seek him immediately upon his definite acquisition of the boat. He had tracked him down at last in the engine room of a sea-going tug, sitting with the engines after the hours of his watch, absently feeding himself a stick of cornbread with one hand and making small figures in a notebook with the other. He had listened to Huston's story solemnly.

"It's my own private belief," Huston told him, "that this boat has one of the fastest hulls on the river. She's not much, otherwise, so I expect to make the most of that. I'll do anythin' within reason to give her speed."

"I'm no great hand on specifications," said MacMaugh in his low, rather thick-tongued voice.

"It isn't specifications I want," Huston returned, "but an engineer."

"And are there none idle?" MacMaugh asked.

"There are idle men in every profession," said Huston. "I've had enough of idle engineers."

MacMaugh smiled; and in the end he agreed to come and have a look. More than that he would not say.

As they rode the river to the place where the *Frontier City* lay, Huston was at pains to reveal to the engineer the exact state of the finances of the boat, together with a somewhat modified version of his own plans.

"Why do you tell me this?" MacMaugh asked.

"Because it is of interest to you."

"It is not."

"Then you are not the man for the job," Huston said.

"Of that we shall see," said MacMaugh.

When they at last arrived at the location of the boat it was four o'clock in the afternoon, but Arthur MacMaugh nevertheless slowly changed into overalls and disappeared into the engine room. He was submerged nine hours and seventeen minutes by Huston's watch, during which time they had to send him his supper, as he did not come out in answer either to the bell or to personal hails. Huston left him undisturbed during this period, judging as well as he could by the occasional noises from the engine room what MacMaugh was about.

At one time a loud prolonged battering was heard, as if the Scotch engineer had decided to wreck the entire equipment with a sledge hammer. Again, a call came for firemen; and for an hour and a half thick twin columns of smoke poured from the stacks. Just before the last of Captain Pumpernickel's wood supply was exhausted the fires were drawn; and thereafter there was such a long silence in the engine room that Huston was of the opinion that the tall engineer had gone to sleep. A little after one o'clock in the morning, however, some time after Huston had sent midnight coffee down, MacMaugh appeared on the boiler deck, and came to slump into a chair beside Huston. There was a silence.

"What do you think of her?" Huston asked at last.

"Hopeless," said MacMaugh.

"What seems to be the matter with her?"

"Everything."

"What are you goin' to do?"

"Go back to my tug. When you have decided what you are willing to put into her, you might let me know."

"That's for you to decide," said Huston disinterestedly.

"What is?"

"What to put into her."

"But you are the owner," drawled MacMaugh.

"You are the engineer. I want to put in an entirely different kind of hook-up down there. Of course, if you don't feel equal—"

"Why didn't you say so in the first place?" MacMaugh demanded. "I have spent the greater part of a night examining those engines!"

Huston grinned. "I thought you might be interested in findin' out what made her slow before."

"Ugh!" said MacMaugh.

"I want you to see to the purchase, installation, and management of the *Frontier City*'s new power," Huston told him. "If you're not the man for it, say so."

"And if I wish to spend—"

"I will affix my name to the checks."

"But if I spend too much—"

"You will break the company, and the boat will come back to her bayou. You know just what means we have, for I've told you. I want a fast boat. I think the *Frontier City* has the makings of one of the fastest on the river."

"Aye?" said MacMaugh sourly.

"Yes," said Huston.

MacMaugh knocked out his pipe upon the rail. "I'll think it over in the morning," he growled, and stumped off to his stateroom.

Huston, sleeplessly pacing the deck with a headful of ambitious dreams, nevertheless perceived, presently, that there was a light going in the engine room again; and, peering down the well of the precipitous stairway, was entertained by the sight of Arthur MacMaugh sitting at the engineer's station in a long white nightgown. It was almost three o'clock before the engine room was at last dark.

The ungainly engineer was at his renewed investigations early the next day; and for four days he appeared only at meals. Sometimes he smoked for hours, his eyes apparently absorbed by some inconsequential valve. At other times he made a great number of measurements. He was known to have spent a mysterious hour and a half in the starboard paddle box; again, he prowled for an entire forenoon in the flat black galleries of the hold. One day he spent several hours with two gangs of negroes, who hauled a heavy rope from stem to stern under the keel. And he used up all the stationery on the boat by covering it with algebra. It was apparent to Huston that MacMaugh already knew so much more about the *Frontier City* than he ever would that he was made to feel he had bought a pig in a poke.

Through it all MacMaugh preserved an attitude of the deepest gloom.

At eleven o'clock at night, following the fourth day of his obscure investigations, MacMaugh sought out Huston. For a time he sat facing the young captain, his hands slowly rubbing his knees. He appeared to be engaged in the deepest thought. At last he addressed Huston with the air of one imparting a most singular discovery.

"My friend," he said with surprising conviction, "you have the makings of a very fast boat."

The suggestion of a spark glowed deep under the brows of the steel-gray eyes; for the first time since Huston had known MacMaugh the man seemed brightened by an actively living interest. He was deeply gratified; so much so that he did not even smile at the solemn restatement of what he had told MacMaugh in the first place.

"Well?" said Huston.

"Well?" said MacMaugh.

"Will you undertake to power this boat?"

"I will, sir, under the arrangement that you suggested."

"Send me the checks to be signed, with just a notation of what the main expenditures were for."

"I'll start at once."

He left the mud-grounded *Frontier City* the next morning. Once thereafter, in the next six weeks, he conferred with Huston as to the dry docking of the boat. Otherwise he did not appear either at the boat or at the pigeon-hole of an office that Mark Wallace had set up in Decatur Street. From time to time word came from him by messenger or by mail; it invariably consisted of a long list of expenditures made out in MacMaugh's small, neat hand, the account detailed down to the last penny's worth of washers or bit of waste.

Arnold Huston read these lists with avidity, partly because their very completeness assured him of the care MacMaugh was taking that no time nor means should be lost once the *Frontier City* was afloat, but chiefly because the lists told him graphically of the progress made toward powering his boat. Slowly, he read, from week to week, of the assembling of the engines through the acquisition of an extraordinary number of individual parts found in divers places. It appeared that MacMaugh intended to assemble his engines from the greatest possible number of old wrecks. Huston's faith in the Scotchman, however, was unshaken. And Mark Wallace was elated at the smallness of the checks that were clipped to each list for them to sign.

So time passed. The carpentry and interior work on the *Frontier City* were done. She was ready to paint. She was painted. All was ready for the water to come to float her to her dry docks for hull work and the installation of her engines. They waited, it seemed, interminably.

Then at last, in the last few days of January, the old yellow-brown river rose and rose, breaking a levee here, ripping cross-country to shorten a bend there. All concerned lived on the *Frontier City* for three days, pacing restlessly, drinking much, praying for that last necessary foot of water. It came, and she floated! With MacMaugh's pumps singing, the brilliantly white boat took to the river again, floating high and proudly in spite of the ignominy of being towed by that stubby little sternwheeler.

"We'll be at 'em soon!" Huston said as they stood on the moving hurricane roof. "Oh, Lord, Mark! It's damned near time!"

CHAPTER XV

It was late in that long month during which the *Frontier City* lay in dock that Arnold was next sought out by his cousin. Will Huston found the riverman in a cabin of the *Frontier City*, of course; Arnold, now heart and soul in the service of his boat, was seldom away from her. He never slept except in the captain's cabin in the Texas, and though his thoughts sometimes turned, against his will, to the house on the Rue Chartres they for the most part followed the interests of the *Frontier City* as hounds follow a cottontail.

Will Huston came beautifully dressed in the rather distinguished planter's garb that he affected. He wore a long coat of gunmetal gray and a pleated shirt over which hung a tie, hardly wider than a shoestring, in long loops. The carriage of his head was proud, though naturally so; so that the flared points of his very high collar gave no appearance of discommoding him. But he was not so tall that he needed to take off his soft hat to go through doors, and he did not remove it as he entered Huston's neat cabin.

Mark Wallace and Arnold Huston were sitting at the

latter's narrow table, checking through certain lists of supplies. Mark rose and bowed slightly, and very coolly, as Arnold's erstwhile duelling antagonist came in; Arnold's nod was more genial, though suggestive of no respect.

"Well, say it," suggested Will Huston. It seemed to Arnold that the green-gray eyes in the pale smooth face were a little feverish above their dark circles.

"I beg your pardon?" said the riverman; and there the cousins stuck, staring at each other like two waiting dogs.

"I think your meaning eludes him," Mark suggested to Will.

"I think not," said Will Huston, regarding the lean man at the table with a sort of polite disgust.

"I beg to differ," said Arnold. "I haven't the remotest notion what you're standin' there gogglin' about."

"It is my cousin's gentlemanly custom," said Will Huston, "to invariably address me, wherever we may meet, by saying 'Well, you ass?' " He mimicked Arnold's voice more odiously than realistically, revealing the evil state of his temper. Mark Wallace was forced to conceal sudden laughter by choking in his handkerchief. Arnold showed only a slight flush of irritation.

"However," Will Huston went on, "if he is going to omit the usual formality, perhaps we may as well get on with the discussion for which I came."

"By all means," said Arnold, "let's proceed at once with the quarrellin'. What's the outrage this time?"

"That, I think, is a personal matter between the two

of us alone."

"Oh, rubbish," said Arnold with annoyance. "Mark Wallace is completely in my confidence. Now out with—"

"Oh, no," protested Mark, his fine dark eyes wandering sorrowfully from one to the other. "You'll most certainly excuse me, I am sure." They did not object further as he went out.

When the door had closed behind Mark, Will Huston drew a light chair near the table at which his cousin sat. He seated himself, crossed his legs, thrust his hands deep into his pockets, and for a time stared moodily at his knees.

"I hardly know how to make myself clear to a person like you," he said at last. He favored Arnold with the briefest upward flick of his green-gray eyes, then fell to contemplating his knees again.

"Regrettable," said Arnold cheerfully.

"You were born into a good enough family," Will Huston went on, affecting the air of the musing philosopher with a success which his nervousness marred. "I have heard that your father was a fellow without merit. It seems fairly apparent that this must be true."

The faintest suggestion of an ironical smile tightened the riverman's thin lips, and disappeared again. He watched Will Huston with an expression of concealed entertainment, eyes half-closed and mouth partly open: an expression so unusual to him that it came near giving Will the fidgets when he glanced up at him again.

"In any case, it is an indisputable fact that you have sacrificed your own social position."

"Ah," said Arnold noncommittally. "In what way?"

"You squandered your family fortune. You—"

"I?" Arnold interrupted. "Which one?"

"You and your father between you, then. You threw away your opportunity for an education. You degraded yourself to the level of a wharf rat. It's common knowledge that you killed a man with a chair in a Natchez gambling dive—"

"You astonish me," said Huston. "When was this?"

"Do you mean to deny it?"

"No. The incident may have slipped my memory."

"In any case, you've got to be pretty well known as a drunken brawler, consorting with the most disreputable associates—"

It was impossible for Will Huston to say these things to his cousin without a high degree of perturbation. He was attempting, Arnold could see, to give the iron-and-velvet impression, but his voice was less cold and hard than he must have wished it, and an occasional tremor in the muscles of his smooth face betrayed his tension. Arnold became curious.

"Well, what about it?"

"You persist in certain aspirations," Will answered, affecting the coldly precise, "which, under the circumstances, are necessarily odious to all concerned." He looked at his cousin squarely, and the malevolence in his green eyes was genuine.

Arnold was mystified. "If I want to launch boats," he said, "I'm goin' to launch boats. And the rest of the

Hustons can—"

"I consider myself," said Will, "to be speaking in the interests of the Shepherd family."

"So that's it!" Arnold sat back. "You're authorized to do so, I suppose?"

"You know as well as I do that Earl Shepherd is the last man to delegate anyone else to speak for him."

"Oh, you're self-elected then?"

"You can put it that way."

"A very pretty display of cheek," Arnold commented without heat.

Will Huston flushed. "You are very well aware," he said, "that Caroline Shepherd's father is a doddering old man, living nowadays entirely in the past. It's plain to anybody that he hardly has sense enough left to get himself fed and dressed, and probably wouldn't if it weren't for his servants. Let alone being competent to guard the interests of the young girl who happens to be his daughter."

"I certainly hope," said Arnold, "that Earl Shepherd will appreciate your puttin' in a word for him this way."

"Her mother," Will went on, biting down the resentment with which his cousin always inspired him, "is a most estimable woman, but—"

"Now you be careful," Arnold advised conversationally.

"—but has led a sheltered life, which has certainly not fitted her for coping with the schemings of unscrupulous rivermen."

"You make me sick," said Huston.

"You have seen fit," Will continued, forcing himself on through a situation that, though of his own making, was yet bitterly distasteful to him, "to take advantage of this circumstance to gain a singularly objectionable hold upon the mind of a virtually unprotected girl—"

Arnold suddenly exploded. "What do you mean, sir?"

"Exactly what I say—sir!" With a terrific effort Will Huston maintained his affectation of detached coldness, even forcing a tone of irony into the last word.

"If I understand you," said his cousin, "I have every right to shoot you where you sit."

"It would be becoming to your character to shoot an unarmed man, I have no doubt. On the other hand, if you wish to meet me again, any time or place will suit me. Last time you got off with a slight wound. I can't guarantee to be so lenient another time."

"We're not goin' through another long rigamarole for the purpose of seein' you faint with fright at the sound of my pistol," Arnold informed him. "Your last exhibition was sufficiently disgustin'."

Will Huston's face went scarlet with rage, his eyes blazed greenly. For a moment Arnold thought Will would fling himself bodily across the table. He partially recovered himself, however.

"I came here to warn you," Will got out at last, trying hard to bring his quivering voice back to a level of coldness. "I persist in my intention."

He paused, seeking to control himself, and Arnold said judicially: "Come on with the next insult."

"Your insolence may be monstrous," said Will

Huston, "but you nevertheless find yourself in a singularly precarious position." His voice was more successfully menacing than Huston had ever heard it. "I happen to know better than anyone else, perhaps, just what your ambitions are, and how much they mean to you. I also know exactly what you have been doing and how. For one thing, you have gone into bankruptcy, on the strength of the burning of the *Peter Swain.* Immediately on top of that you have formed another company. I know exactly where you got the capital for that, and how."

"Very clever, I must say."

"How you persuaded Mark Wallace is a mystery to me. I can only think that he is an idle-headed dreamer, easily overborne. Anyway, the mass of your resources came from him. More than that, I know just where he stands financially. I don't know whether you know it or not. But Wallace has put himself into a remarkably fragile financial position. Half his funds rest on call notes, and the other half are unstable."

"Your interest is flatterin'. But—"

"You may not realize it, but you are walking a singularly unsteady financial tight-rope."

"Well?"

"I don't think you are so badly informed that you don't know that I am now the controlling factor in very large financial interests."

"As nearly as I can judge," Arnold agreed, "your father's death slid you into a very soft thing. Hardly so big, though, as it seems to you when you have everythin' all muddled up."

"You are too poorly educated, of course," Will Huston went on insolently, "to know anything about the wheels within wheels that control the financial world. You'll have to take my word for it that I can personally be a considerable factor. You happen to be wrong in thinking the interests I'm handling are small. But even if you were right, a small cog in the situation can move the whole machine."

Will Huston had found opportunity to recover his mental balance before Arnold's relaxed air of interest. He went on coldly, with his eyes keen and narrow.

"You now have a chance for success. I hold nothing against you; I shall be glad to see you attain it. At the same time I consider that you are acting reprehensibly, and out of all proportion to your station, in aspiring to Caroline Shepherd."

Arnold Huston's increase of interest was sudden and unfeigned. "What did she say that threw you into this panic, Will?"

"She has never mentioned your name."

"You think my absence has depressed her, or somethin' like that?"

"She has been nothing at all but herself."

"You said a funny thing awhile ago," Arnold insisted. "Somethin' about some hold you thought I had on the girl. You'll have to explain that, I think."

"I am a student of character," said Will, according himself the most popular bit of self-flattery known to man. "I have an unusual faculty for reading people."

"Is *that* all you base your silly assumptions on?"

"Sufficient, I think," Will answered, flushing.

"In short," Arnold pursued, "you can't make any headway yourself, so naturally you blame me!"

Will's gorge was visibly rising again. "That's entirely outside the point," he declared.

"Well, then?"

Will Huston, with an heroic effort, whipped himself into the attack. "I mean to say this: you are entirely unfitted, by your own choices, to—to enter the Shepherd family. And I wish to propose—forcibly propose—that you withdraw from the situation, absolutely and entirely."

"Will, Will! You're outdoin' yourself!"

"Don't be in a hurry to laugh, my tight-rope walker!"

"What?"

Will Huston rushed on furiously in a stumbling torrent of words: "If you pertinaciously continue your intrusions—"

"Intrusions?"

"You don't deny that you are courting Caroline Shepherd—"

"I deny that it's any of your damned business if I am or not!"

"If you go on with that you are going to lose, and lose heavily! You were only a wharf rat to begin with, and you'll be just that and no more again, if you persist in thinking that your interests are separable from my assistance!"

"D'you mean you're offerin' a bribe?"

"Your financial predicament is a very perilous one. I'm certainly not offering a bribe. I'm calling your attention to a situation." Will was white-faced and trembling.

"A threat, then?"

"Call it that if you want to!"

Arnold sat back to study the spectacle that his cousin presented; and his chief emotion was that of mystified amazement. Looking at the other calmly, for all his annoyance with the man, Huston was at a loss, at first, to account for his cousin's extraordinary outbreak.

"He can't be so stupid," Arnold was thinking, "that he believes he can handle me that way!"

Will's smooth, rather round-cheeked face was paler than usual in his self-punishing wrath; but there was a quiver in the man's voice and a suppressed flame in his eyes that might have been madness, for all Arnold knew.

"In the first place," Arnold thought analytically, "he hates me; he has always hated me. When I look him in the eye I have the edge on him, and he hates me all the more for that. Now, he's gone out of his head over this girl. He leads himself to believe that I stand in the way. He frets and fumes, getting a little crazier each time he is checked. He persuades himself that I am doing the girl a wrong, in addition to discommoding him. Finally he comes here, wild-eyed, and makes a desperate silly play—"

But Arnold's logic was unconvincing to himself. Never having been out of his head over a girl, he could not comprehend Will's state, even when he had diagrammed it.

"What the devil's the matter with you?" he demanded suddenly.

"Not nearly as much as you might wish. I find myself in a dominating position, I think."

"I congratulate you!"

"By God," Will burst out, "I'll take the damned mockery out of you if it's my last act!" He got up so suddenly that his chair upset with a futile small clatter. His nostrils were white and trembling.

Arnold was angered by sheer contagion. A moment before he had pitied his cousin almost to the point of telling him that he had no further interest in Caroline Shepherd, and that she certainly had never had any interest in him. But the tension had become too much for him, and his temper broke.

"You fool," he cried, "d'you think you can?" He was grinning, the strong teeth and the thin creases of the cheeks taking the youth out of his face. His smile could be an ugly sort of thing.

"We'll damned well find out!"

Will Huston's anger was not explosive and destroying as was Arnold's. Like most of his other violent emotions it turned inward, tightening his muscles until he was racked with the tension. Thus the door did not slam after him as he went out, but closed uncertainly, with a shaking latch.

When he was gone Mark Wallace returned.

"You missed something," said Huston drily. "Your delicacy is too great for your own advantage."

"My delicacy did not prevent me from listening on the other side of the partition," said Mark with a faint smile. "What the devil do you want to have love affairs for? This is a fine time for it, I must say!"

"I haven't any love affair. Will and I have nothin' in common in that respect, nor in any other."

"But Will—"

"He doesn't know what he's talkin' about. As usual. As far as Caroline Shepherd is concerned, I'm out. Have been for a long time."

"Then why in Christ's name didn't you tell him so!"

"I wouldn't tell him anythin'. D'you mean to think he can come here and—"

"Oh, your damned stiff-necked pride, I suppose," said Mark with some heat. "I suppose you know that this silliness is apt to put us all in a very ticklish position?"

"You mean he can carry out his threats?"

Mark considered; he seemed to be trying to give a fair answer. "I don't know," he decided.

"Well, it's up to you to see that he doesn't," said Huston testily. "Finance is your end; steamboatin' is mine."

"That's all very well—if you'd stick to steamboating. But if you go pulling three or four banks down on our heads you're liable to find yourself without any steamboat. And putting the responsibility off on me isn't going to get her back, either."

"Well, what the devil do you think I can do about it?"

"If worst comes to worst you'll have to eat crow, that's what you'll have to do, my friend. You may have to apologize to him and ask him to call off his dogs."

"Can you imagine my doin' that, Mark?"

"I can imagine your breaking yourself and me, too, if you get one of your damned bull-headed streaks!"

"It isn't as if," said Huston soberly, "it would do any good if I did. You have no idea of the bitterness of that man."

"Oh, rubbish! A quarrel over a girl—"

"That has almost nothin' to do with it. My father and my uncle were bitter enemies before I was born. They—"

"Oh, another pack of rubbish!"

"Not altogether. The quarrel had its beginnin' in the existence of Will Huston himself."

"What has—"

"Will Huston thinks he's my cousin. He's not."

"He's not what?"

"He's not my cousin. We're closer than that, it happens. He's my half-brother."

"What?"

"Will's mother died at his birth. My uncle accepted Will as his son, knowing that he was no such thing."

"How do you know?"

"I have my father's word for it."

"But—"

"No one knows it but myself, now that my father and Dennison Huston are dead. I'm tellin' you now because you were gettin' ready to try to force a situation you knew nothin' about. Now, if you have the intelligence I credit you with, maybe you can imagine my uncle's bitterness toward my father and myself. Maybe you can appreciate their family religion—that

Anastasius Huston's breed is to be squelched at all costs."

They sat looking at each other. "Now," said Arnold, "what do you think of that?"

"I think," said Mark Wallace drily, "that I've bet into a stacked deck."

"You'll have to make the most of it!"

CHAPTER XVI

"YOU never come to see me any more," Jacqueline DuMoyne said.

Huston had visited her perhaps half a dozen times in the last two months. It seemed to him, however, as if he had haunted her beyond all reason. His days, and a good part of his nights, had been filled with the labor involved in the making ready of the *Frontier City*. He certainly had had enough to fill his mind and make dreamless his short hours of sleep. Yet each time he left her house he had immediately begun thinking about when he would see her again. He would put it off as long as he could, avoiding the issue from day to day, until he could deceive himself no more. His self-deception had been fairly successful, and the intervals between his visits correspondingly long. But she didn't know, of course, how many times, at late hours of the night, he had walked past that great arched door.

"I wonder that you let me come at all."

"I shouldn't, I know."

"Why?" he asked defiantly.

She ignored that. "Tell me about the boat."

"She'll launch Saturday."

"Captain! You sound as if you didn't care if she launched at all!"

"I'm tired, I guess. Getting old. I can't remember that I used to get tired at all."

"Old? At twenty-seven?" She always knew more about him than he had expected.

"I'm older than you are, anyway."

"Does that have to be so terribly old?"

He felt the blackness of a bitter mood closing on him as they sat down on the settee. It brought the bracketing lines to the corners of his mouth and made his eyes at once sultry and hard-edged. He sat rigidly, his knees crossed, staring out across the night-dimmed roofs to the river.

He was thinking of his father's words: "If you are going to hunt turmoil all the time, turmoil is going to begin hunting you. . . ."

This was the place where they always sat, where they could look out at the steamboats and the shipping. He thought it must be an interesting place to sit resting by daylight, when you could see the river traffic come and go; watching, perhaps, the deep-sea vessels starting for foreign ports and the busy steamboats beginning the daily race up-river. Probably you could see the sailors in the rigging, the pilots throwing their weight on the great wheels. But he had never been there except at night.

Often, on other nights, as he leaned on the rail of the *Frontier City* and drew deeply on a black cigar, he had thought of this settee and this window; but not in terms of the river. He had remembered rather the tones of Jacqueline DuMoyne's low voice, the darkness of her eyes, the sensitively changing expressions of her pale face, as delicately molded as a child's. These fancies had been pleasurable at first. When he tried to put them down they became a torment of his every idle moment.

He knew well enough what was the matter with him. Two months before it had been inconceivable to him that he should ever love anyone but Caroline Shepherd. He had loved her desperately enough for a while. Even after he had been wearied by her silly apprehensions for Will Huston's welfare and her blank-minded prejudice against the river, she still remained to him the embodiment of an ideal. He had judged all beauty as to what extent it was a modification of hers.

Jacqueline DuMoyne was in no sense a substitute for Caroline, but a personality entirely new to Huston's experience. Her attraction for him was a thing he had not sought nor desired. Rather some mysterious intoxicant that he felt in her presence had permeated him, making him see such depths of beauty in her as he knew it was impossible for a wholly sane man to perceive. It gave him a gnawing restlessness, so that when he was not grinding over paperwork at his desk he was never still for long.

One of his faculties had been an ability to rest completely when his work was done. That was gone now. Where once he had sat smoking and looking at the water, late at night before turning into his bunk, he now paced the guards, quarrelling with his own imaginings to all hours of the night. Some nights he gave up sleeping altogether, only flinging himself down, fully clothed, for an hour or two of restless dozing just before daylight. Sometimes he woke to find that he had rolled to his feet and gripped the mist-damp sill of his stateroom window in the moment of waking, as he had done the last night of the *Peter Swain*; but each time as he came to his senses it was to realize that it was not of fire that he had dreamed, nor of boats.

Reason told him that Jacqueline DuMoyne was not of his kind. She seemed subtly of a different race, an exotic thing that he could not hope fully to know or understand. She was almost as unreal to him as his ill-formed notions of the island from which she had come. Huston's background was of practical things. The people, the smells, the boats of the Mississippi were the normal, homely things of his life; familiarity had worn away the picturesqueness and romance that had lured him to the river as a child. His one creed was accomplishment, his one field of action the steamboat life of the river.

In this direct scheme of things Jacqueline DuMoyne had no previous counterpart. Only the sight of the Mississippi gave him any assurance of reality in this new phase of his experience. New Orleans was becoming a strange place to him. Its French-Spanish buildings took on a brooding and unfamiliar look, so that as he walked between them he felt a thousand miles away from the familiar plantations and the river towns of country-like homes or brawling dives.

It did not seem to him logical or reasonable that Jacqueline DuMoyne should ever become his wife. To imagine her settled in a Natchez home seemed preposterous. He certainly could not tolerate her merely as a friend. To think of her as more than a friend and less than a wife was incompatible with his view of her. However, he did not reason into that. He was sufficiently absorbed in his endeavor to suppress a passion which at its flood-tide would be too deep-flowing and strong of current for mastery. And he feared the growing hidden power of it as the steamboats themselves feared shoal water.

"What is to be the name of your new boat, Captain?"

"I wanted to ask you about that. I thought—I was thinkin' maybe you would give her a name."

"Oh, I'd have no right to do that."

"Right? Her name is what I choose. And if I want her to be what you call her—"

"No, no! I wouldn't feel I could. Don't you think Mark should be consulted? Perhaps he has something in mind."

The black mood was closing in. He felt a slow anger well up seething and fighting for expression. That single penetrating thing his father had said returned to him; and for an instant he sent a flash of dark hate after his father's ghost, almost believing that he had truly foreseen the torment in which his son sat tonight.

" 'If you are going to hunt turmoil all the time, turmoil is going to begin hunting you,' " Arnold muttered.

"What—why did you say that?" There was a breathless catch in her voice, so slight that he was not sure that he had detected it at all.

"I'm sorry; I reckon I didn't aim to speak aloud. What did you think I said?" He hardly ever spoke her name. He was too stiffly bound by convention to call her Jacqueline, and he would not say Madame DuMoyne.

"Why—nothing. I thought for a moment that you had said something that might have applied to me. It was nothing at all."

He wanted to probe that a little way, but the anger that had been aroused by the reference to his friend had left a lassitude upon him.

"You're paler than usual," he said when he turned to her again.

"I'm tired of this place." Her tone was not one of weariness. In it there was a hint of something, uneasiness perhaps, that made her words meaningless.

"What's worryin' you here?" he asked suddenly.

She gave him a startled flicker of a glance; but her eyes were immediately calm as she looked up at him again.

"What makes you ask that?"

He shrugged. He thought, "So something *is* worrying her." He was curiously indifferent, absorbed in his own mental disorders.

"Don't answer if you'd rather not." He had sense enough to add, "Whatever it is, I want you to know I'm sorry."

"There's nothing worrying me."

He looked at her searchingly, and found her eyes upon him with an odd quiet intensity. She looked sober, almost sorrowful. In her pale face her eyes were dark and deep, and he possessed no leadline for their fathoming. Some somber flame, he thought, was burning behind them. Its meaning he did not know, but he thought it was neither love nor hate; and it was too quiet for fear.

It seemed to him that he could not endure looking into her eyes, yet he could not look away. He freed himself with an almost physical wrench. The tumult of battle was in him, a battle over which hung the pall of coming defeat. He felt the desperate need of a drink; of a smoke.

"If you are going to hunt turmoil all the time—" The voice of his father, mouthing fatality.

No, he couldn't deceive himself. It was the woman he wanted. Her dark gown was close about her throat to-night; yet the white gleam of her shoulders tormented him, a memory clearer than vision. He wanted to press them with his lips.

He could turn and take her in his arms; but he intuitively believed that it would mean a defeat which he was by no means ready to bear. He suddenly got up.

She looked surprised. "You're going?"

"I've work to do. Got to get back to my boat."

"I never knew of a man working as you do."

"We're nearly done now."

Just as he left she said, "Please tell Mark I want to see him." Her voice was quiet; but there was in it, he thought, something as pleading as a cry. His imagination, perhaps, but it was enough to send him into another fit of jealous rage. What could Mark do for her that he could not?

He strode up and down for a long time on the levee, waiting for some boat to get ready to take him to the *Frontier City.* He smoked furiously, champing at the delay.

At last he flung down the cigar butt and tried to grind it out with his heel. It took refuge between the cobbles and lay staring up at him with its one foolish eye. Huston sat down on a stringpiece and rested his forehead on his hands.

"If you're going to hunt turmoil—"

CHAPTER XVII

It was about this time that Huston made his second visit to the swamp retreat of Walt Gunn. Certain supplies of molasses and cornmeal were three weeks late, and the riverman went to find out why.

As before, it was night when he landed from an up-river boat at the foot of that scratch of a road marking Gunn's landing. The night was cold and raw for that latitude, with a whisk of rain in the air. A perpetual wind fled through the cottonwoods with a faint whistling moan that always sounded far away, yet grew neither nearer nor farther as he walked inland. Miles overhead a mat of vast scudding clouds were perceivable, but so dimly that it seemed they were felt, rather than seen. On the earth lay an inky blackness, thickest near the ground, from which it seemed to rise like fur twenty feet deep.

The night birds were silent this time over the planted lands, and there was not even the voice of a frog in the swampy bottoms where the river once had run. But from a mile away he heard the voices of Gunn's dogs, a continual wailing and belling in twenty keys, so that a man less conversant with hound talk would have thought a big hunt was in progress. It made him uneasy.

The back-water was high in the old river bed that lay between the Mississippi and the cabins of Walt Gunn. Huston was in some doubt as to whether he would be able to reach the place at all. Certainly there was no hope of shouting across the half-mile of muck jungle for a boat. He found the water lapping over the edge of the road through the swamp; but it had been built high and well. If Walt Gunn had nothing else he at least had plenty of labor at his command. His road stood against the sluggish water.

At the lowest point the filled road was submerged. The blackness was so thick here that it seemed tangible, but Huston felt his way ahead. He waded through knee-deep water, knowing that at any minute the edge of the road might cave under him, sending him into soupy mud over his head. In the dark he splashed directly into the kingpost of the drowned bridge, damaging a knee. After that the road rose a little. Slogging in the mud, he reached the steep rise that had been the river's farther bank.

In the time that he had spent working his way over the last half-mile of swamp road the belling of the hounds had never ceased. It rose to a clamor as he climbed the rise, the poorer of the hounds breaking out of their long tonguing into frantic barkings and yelpings. He could hear a whole row of them on the crest of the rise ahead of him, and though he could not see them he knew they watched his approach. They gave back as he advanced.

The dark was impenetrable among Gunn's invisible cabins. Not a pin point of light, not a suggestion of the outline of a building was discernible.

"Hi!" he shouted. "Anyone home?"

No answer. He advanced slowly, feeling for the path, trying to remember exactly where Gunn's own cabin had been. The hounds retreated, maintaining a timorous distance, while their mad soprano bellowing killed even the sound of the wind. One deeper throat sounded over all the rest. Its interminable variations seemed never in need of breath, as if the dog were desperately pouring out some mournful explanation. "Howp, howoowhoop, yipooohoop, hooowowp, oooo—"

"Hullo! HEY! Walt Gunn!"

Still no response out of the inky black. He went forward shouting; and presently his groping hands found the lean-to's door. There he stood for a while, calling and kicking the boards. The splash through the swamp had been long and disagreeable; he was loath to turn back without result. He determined to enter the cabin, strike a light, and make himself at home, pending the return of someone who could at least give him information as to Gunn's whereabouts.

Nevertheless he did not step into the lean-to without some hesitation. The gun barrel that had jabbed into his middle the last time he had done so was clear in his memory. He half expected a recurrence of the incident, and his stomach muscles tightened as he crossed the threshold.

As he disappeared within the cabin the howling of the hounds diminished. On the outskirts of the cabin group they still gave tongue in long wails, as dogs howl at the moon; but they were quiet enough so that he could have heard even a small sound within.

The inner door was partly out of line with the door of the lean-to, and Huston crashed into the jamb. An oath escaped him before he could collect himself again.

"Walt Gunn!" he called. "It's Huston! Are you there?" Groping with one hand he started to step in.

Instantly a crashing explosion rocked him back upon his heels. Buckshot screamed past him, splintering the door jamb of the lean-to, rattling away into the foliage thirty yards beyond.

Huston's spring aside was purely instinctive. As he recovered from the daze of the shock he found himself flattened against the wall of the cabin, his pistol in his hand. Yet his reason had had no more part in putting him into that position than as if he had been lifted there by the heavy breath of the shotgun that had so nearly accounted for him.

His first emotion, when his hair had settled to his scalp again, was one of hot anger. He speculated for a moment or two as to what he should do, meantime listening for some stir of sound within the cabin that would tell him what his assailant meant to do next. Then he jammed his pistol back into the shoulder holster under his arm and stepped squarely into the opening of the door.

"Well, you damned fool," he said, his voice quivering with rage, "why don't you let go with the other barrel?"

No answer came out of the dark. The interior exhaled a faint breath of burnt gunpowder, mingling with a remembered smell of coffee grounds, old food, and sweat. But Huston could not hear so much as the stirring of a rat.

"I told you who I was," he went on loudly, "before I came to the door. You'll kill somebody with your damned foolishness, one of these days." No answer, no rustle of movement. "Well," he shouted, "are you going to answer me or not?"

The eery silence within remained unbroken. He produced a match; his fingers were trembling nervously as he ripped it along the wood. The match was wet, and its spongy head scraped off like damp bread, leaving a green streak of phosphorus glowing on the door jamb in the dark.

His impatience keyed to the breaking point as he failed with a second and a third. His bravado ebbed away, and he stiffly moved out of line with the door. As he stood with his back against the square-hewn logs of the wall he considered the advisability of carrying his investigation further. Reason counselled retreat.

Ahead of him was a pitch-black hole of a room from which he had already been fired upon without cause. It was not his cabin; conceivably he had no business in it without invitation. Walt Gunn, or whoever had fired upon him, was more than likely in a state of drunken insanity. Yet as he considered withdrawing he became aware that this in itself was a dangerous course. He decided he must finish what he had begun.

One by one he tested the matches. There were a half-dozen left. If they failed he would be faced by the task of walking into that black silent dark without a light. There were three left. There were two. The next to the last match flared, hissed, died; then sprang into flame again, and burned.

Instantly Huston stepped forward into the doorway. "Easy, now," he said, "easy!"

Immediately before him was the table; on it a dirty huddling shirt; a pile of clothes were mounded in one corner. But there was no one there.

That was all he saw before the match burned his fingers. He hastily lit the last match from the waning flame of the other, and held it high in cupped hands. On the rough plank that served as a mantelpiece stood a candle. Hurriedly, cuddling the feeble flame of the match stick in his hands, he stepped across the room and lit the wax.

By its light he perceived that there was a great ragged hole in the shirt upon the table; through it the muzzle of a shotgun glinted dully. He tossed the shirt aside. On the table lay that massive Bible that Gunn's hands had gripped and fondled the night of their conference. Across it the shotgun lay, braced by heavy nails and lashed down with leather cords. From the trigger ran a string, cunningly rigged and concealed, as if by a trapper's hands. His eye traced it to the doorway, where the end of it dangled broken.

Huston cursed in utter exasperation. There was a slab door in the back wall, with a hole in it that might have been intended for espionage. He supposed that he was being watched.

"Well, come on out!" he ordered. "D'you think I waded that damned swamp to stand here and be stared at?"

He persisted in regarding the gunplay as childish, unworthy of respectful treatment. He gave the rear door a terrific kick that would certainly have broken the nose of the watcher, had there been one. The door slatted open, revealing a back room that was smellier, if anything, than the one in which he stood. A cot, a stove, a broken chair, a cupboard, a litter of miscellaneous rubbish, were all it contained. Huston walked through it, and stood in the back door, swearing.

Outside the night seemed blacker than ever, after the temporary relief of the light. As his eyes became a little accustomed to the dark he could make out the ragged line of the tree-tops beyond, blacker than the pit-like sky. At the feet of the trees he thought he could detect a slight stirring of darkness in darkness where the hound pack shuffled itself, lurking on the extreme outskirts of his vision. Their weird yelling droned on without haste, without weariness; those dogs were professionals at that sort of work.

A shapeless form came writhing swiftly along the ground toward him, no more recognizable than some strange thing in a sack. Then the mystery came into the dim shaft of candle light from the door, and materialized into a great, floppy hound bitch. She wallowed slathering to his feet with whimpers that were suppressed howls. When he spoke kindly to her she moved close against his legs, never ceasing her deep-throated whines.

He turned back into the cabin in search of a lantern. The great floppy bitch crouched on the threshold trembling and belling hollowly in her throat. Huston found a certain comfort in her presence, useless as he knew she would be to him in any conceivable circumstance. She provided at least the companionship of a living and comprehensible thing. A certain sympathy for her was compelled by the fact that she had come seeking him as a friend.

"Come in here," he commanded.

The big loose-knit hound put one foot forward reluctantly; then drew back and turned away her face, low-headed with shame that she disobeyed him, but fearing some other thing more.

He found the lantern he sought, and with the stick of a burnt match transferred a flame to it from the candle's tip. Then he strode out the rear door toward the slave quarters. The dog slunk close to his legs, whimpering and nudging his knee repeatedly with her nose. So importunate was she that Huston thought the dog wished to take him to something; but when he stopped and asked her to lead the way she sat down, apparently desirous of nothing from him but the reassurance of his approval.

One advantage was brought to him by the hound bitch. Her dog-talk drew a great hulking mongrel from the ranks of the skulkers, a silent brute with a cold yellow eye and a perpetually bristling roach on his shoulders. This dog accompanied them at a little distance with suspicious snufflings. But at each of the cabins at which Huston paused the mongrel took the lead, walked through the black open doorways ahead of him, and for a few moments was lost to the lantern rays. He reappeared still bristling, still at a walk, but bearing the perfectly lucid information that the cabin was empty of life.

Huston made his way from one cabin to another, calling out, pounding on doors. His nose found the odor of unwashed negroes, molasses, old blankets, and dogs; but human beings there were none. Sometimes, not trusting the word of the mongrel who went ahead, he explored the interiors of the cabins on his own account. He found evidences that breakfast had been cooked that morning, but no meal since.

By some subtle chain of observations, perhaps influenced by the uncanny quality of the night, he gathered an impression of haste and disordered flight. In one negro cabin a rude chair lay overturned; in another, on a crumby table, lay a square of corn pone with one bite out of it, still showing the indentations of big teeth. Mice had been at it since. Across a threshold lay a pickaninny's doll, crudely made of a stick of wood, a strange little thing like an African idol; it lay dishevelled, abandoned, but grinning toothily yet.

At the farthest edge of the clearing Huston stood for a bit, staring moodily off into the night. Beyond him was a tangle of live oak and cottonwood undergrowth. The lantern light outlined a great down-sweeping live oak limb, twisting, aged, thick as a man's body. It drooped downward until it almost touched the ground, apparently overborne by its own weight; then curved upward high into the night like some monstrous seeking snake. The bearding moss trailed downward from its bark, gray, filmy, like the dust-dry residue of centuries of tears. It swung limply in the little wind that came under the trees, so that beyond, in the faint yellow light of the lantern, certain shadows swayed and shifted stealthily, the dimmest stirring of something half perceived.

The big-boned mongrel walked on, his shadow lengthening ahead of him, distorted on the bare sandy soil.

"Come back here!" Huston ordered. He had already decided to go no farther.

The yellow dog, choosing not to hear, went on with his stiff, unhurried strides. The whorls of hair on his haunches made them look ungainly, like a baboon's. He disappeared into the blackness, and did not return. There had been a certain detachment about that dog, even while he had been aiding Huston, as if he had slowly developing purposes of his own that were not to be suborned. The great hollow-throated bitch took a few steps after him, then sat down and howled once. She immediately returned to Huston, and resumed her inconvenient proximity to his legs.

Huston felt ironically disgusted with the whole situation. Even so, as he passed one after another of the silent shanties, he experienced a prickly sensation up and down his spine. He could not down the recurrent feeling that somewhere behind him a lurking enemy watched. Once he felt this so strongly that he turned and walked back to a cabin that he had passed, and entered its gaping door. A rat half the size of a cat leaped off a rickety table, plunked heavily on the slab floor, and scuttled away. He knew by its presence that nothing else had been there, and he went on, swearing at himself.

The candle light was still wavering in the cabin of Walt Gunn. When Huston had slammed the lantern onto the table with a jolt that nearly put it out, he lit a lean cigar and sat down beside the table with crossed knees. The big bitch once more remained moaning at the rear door with wide-braced forelegs, ears nearly touching the ground. This time he put her from his mind, along with the incessant eery clamor of the hounds.

He sat for a long time with his hands thrust deep into his pockets, scowling out into the dark. It did not occur to him that the trap in which he had almost lost his life was not as good a place in which to sit and think as any other. He champed his lean cigar, rolled it from one corner of his mouth to the other with his tongue.

He was lost in thought when something stirred behind him in the corner of the cabin. It seemed a stealthy movement over the floor, warningly subtle, yet so magnified by the silence that had prevailed in the room that Huston thought of no other possibility than that a man had moved there. He was instantly on his feet, pistol in hand, facing the corner from which the sound had come.

Behind him the cabin was as empty as ever. In the corner that great lumpy mound of dirty clothing lay as before. It was something of a shock to him to find that no one faced him there. The disquieting idea came to him that someone was concealed under that disproportionately large pile of clothes. He took a quick step toward it, but instantly checked with a feeling of revulsion as he saw disappearing under the clothing the scaly limp tail of a rat.

He blew a puff of breath at the guttering candle, and when it persisted to burn he swore and smashed it into a puddle of wax with the palm of his hand. Taking the lantern with him he strode out toward the river road.

CHAPTER XVIII

HUSTON caught a down-river boat a little before one o'clock.

The chill of the night had increased with the lateness of the hour. He got a blanket from his stateroom and flung it about his shoulders as he began his now almost habitual pacing of the guards. Aft to the hot oily breath of the engine-room ladder, forward to the bow rail; astern again. . . .

The Mississippi spread black under a starless sky.

The inky line of the shores, a mile apart, could hardly be seen by the casual eye. But there was no fog, and no precautions had been taken to dim the boat's lights nor the gleam from the fire alley that reddened the ripples of the black water.

Here and there in the main hall of the cabin a turned-down lamp glowed yellowly; below on the main deck the coals of a few pineknot braziers smouldered, waiting to be fanned into flame for the next landing, still glowing from the last. These gave the boat a dimly lighted existence in the blackness of the river, of a quality mournful beyond words.

There were few landings, and for hours the quiet of the boat was unbroken. The close-lipped poker players in the bar could not be heard. Not even the labor of the engines was audible up here on the boiler deck, except by the faint rattle of some loose bit of wood, a whisper that told off every fourth beat of the stroke.

Here in the silence of the lightless Mississippi Arnold Huston spent a long night. He dropped into a chair by the forward rail, after a while. He had more than enough to fill his thoughts.

Still river. . . .

He was soon to have his own boat. It had been a long time now since he had stood on the hurricane deck, hearing the harsh carrying drawl of his own commands: "Histe up. . . . Let 'er go! . . . Come on with your freight. . . ."

His debt to his dead father, if there had been one, was gone with the *Peter Swain.* Her engines rusted deep in the muck, her charred timbers had gone down with the river to the all-obliterating salt green of the sea. Her bones were scattered, denied the grave that took what was left of a man, purposelessly holding it in one place. Yet she had had as much of a personality as any man, one that he was not likely to forget.

If ever he had anything again, it would be by the labor of his own brain, results given for value received. Nothing yet. Debts. Seventy-five hundred in paper to Mark Wallace, in return for a means with which to pay it back. That was the kind of a load he could shoulder, though. At heart he had always felt a little defiant, the need of being a little harder, because he had got his start in steamboating partly from an inheritance. Presumably a dead man has no preferences. But Anastasius Huston had despised the river while he lived.

Still river, sweeping down the weary miles to the sea. . . .

Uprooted trees clutched for the mucky bottom with their limbs, became sawyer snags that fought the current, sometimes for years; then defeated, whirling on down to the sea with the rest in the end.

Meantime his quarrel with the other branch of the family went on. Will Huston, fruitlessly suing for the hand of Caroline Shepherd, conceived in his bafflement that it was Arnold who stood in his way. There was a smile in that, but with it there was a threat. Mark Wallace was none too happy in the shadow of Will's financial enmity.

Will's immediate quarrel was based on a misconception, of course. It was doubtful if his purpose would have changed had the occasion been removed. The enmity was too deep in the blood, always a brooding spark like a covered brazier, waiting for a breath to bring it into flame.

Now another mysterious threat rose, a threat no more clearly defined than the emptiness of the shadows about Walt Gunn's cabins. What situation lurked there no one could know—for a while. It would come out soon, a scandal of some sort that could not be hid. Perhaps his very presence there on this night would involve him inextricably. Meantime, what should he tell Mark? Nothing. That Gunn had not been home.

Still river, perpetual, unhurried, taking its broad bends with a strong swing and pull. . . .

Jacqueline DuMoyne. . . . The thought of her was a besieging thing, forever seeking the unguarded moments of his mind as the vast river, defeatable at any point yet indomitable at all, perpetually felt for the weaknesses in the levees, waiting its chances until no more than a crawfish hole let a little of the tawny water through; then surging through the widening crevasse, sweeping all before it, drowning, scouring, punishing, carrying off on its flood. And when it was diminished in strength by the very destruction it had wrought, permitting itself to be shut out again for a little while, leaving behind the receding hungry waters a blank mud plain of desolation and despair. . . .

It seemed to him that he would be satisfied never again to touch her hand, never to see her face, if only this bitter-hard work of his, this perpetual ebb and flow of battle for power on the river could be diverted to her use. If she could be made happy by his labors, it seemed to him that labor for her would be joy enough.

He was weary. A vast labor of preparation, of circumvention, of numberless motions in the putting down of obstacles, gained only a minute advantage at the end of it all: an inch, on a road that stretched ahead a thousand miles. Yet it was a labor of emptiness, having no more to do with her than the labors of a plow-horse in the Indiana fields.

She had made a shell out of him, a meaningless thing going through intricate motions to achieve futile ends. It was as if his whole spirit had gone out of him to her. The empty shell provided the *Frontier City* with what it needed, it satisfied the insatiable demands of MacMaugh. It was going to take to the river in a new boat.

Still river. . . .

A man can't stay awake forever.

When he roused himself there was a silver of frosty dew on the blanket over his shoulders. The twisting river was running northward now. On its right the sky was mauve, violet, and white gold. Nearer, on the left bank of the sweeping river, lay New Orleans. A west wind took the long dark pall of the steamboat smoke to the other shore, leaving the city minutely clear across the Mississippi reaches. The low-lying buildings were like flat cut-outs, looking bright and clean, pale violet against the dark western reflection of the dawn.

CHAPTER XIX

A LITTLE after dawn a drenching rain began to fall, in a heavy downpour at first, then slacking off into a steady pelt that promised to last a week. It was the middle of the morning when Huston, delayed by errands in the town, at last reached the *Frontier City* where she lay on the far side of the river, opposite New Orleans. She was in the water now, and her engines were in, great iron monsters twice the size of those she had had before. Two steam trials had been almost satisfactory, and MacMaugh and his mates were working on their last revisions.

Huston went directly to the boat's office in the forward part of the cabin.

To-day as he set his hand to the knob he was given pause by such a hideous muffled outcry from within as he would hardly have believed in a haunted house at night, let alone in gray daylight on his busy boat. In his astonishment he took an involuntary step backward; then, recovering himself, he thrust into the room.

In the middle of the carpeted floor lay the lank, high-hipped cat, stunned evidently, for the fluttering vibration of its ribs showed that it was not dead. Its head was such a mass of blood as to have been unrecognizable had it been seen alone.

In the best chair sat Mark Wallace, lounging with that habitual grace of his that made it seem impossible for him to take an awkward position. He was smoking with slow relish, and contemplating the ungainly lean body of the bloody cat. He glanced up as Huston came in, but did not appear disturbed. His sensitive face was quiet, composed. In his beautiful dark eyes some strange satisfaction glowed mistily, a keen hidden pleasure too fine-drawn to be called sensual, too languidly smouldering to be described in another way.

It was the expression Huston had seen fleetingly at the close of that fiasco of a duel, in the moment after Will Huston had fallen. It brought back the scene to him sharply, so that he could almost see the awkwardly sprawling figure, face down in the dirt under those brooding trees.

"What the devil have you been doin' to that cat?"

Wallace's answer, indifferently tossed off: "Amusing myself. Kick the thing out into the hall."

Huston opened his mouth to speak, but found that he had nothing to say. He took the animal up by the skin of its back, and handed it to a mulatto cabin boy in the hall.

"Wash that thing's head!" he ordered, thrusting the bleeding creature at the man so savagely that the negro started back.

"Sometimes," Huston said to Mark as he closed the door again, "I think I don't know you any better than I know the garfish under the boat."

"Cats are worthless," said Wallace indifferently. "I have no liking for cats."

"Is this the sort of thing you get out of your books?"

"I'm in no mood for accepting criticism of any kind whatsoever from you." His voice was so incongruously mild that Huston glanced at him sharply. The delicate incomprehensible pleasure had disappeared from Wallace's face, leaving his eyes more coldly bleak than Huston had ever seen them. A hint of some sort of danger came into the cold drenched air of the cabin.

"I'm here to tell you," Wallace went on, "that you sail to-morrow, not Saturday as you had supposed."

"Impossible," said Huston flatly.

"To-morrow's Friday. That shorts you only twenty-four hours. You'll have to arrange it."

"I told you it was impossible," Huston repeated.

"I'm not interested in impossibilities. I'm only telling you what has to be done. If you don't know how to get things accomplished that is no fault of mine."

"You haven't any notion of what you're talkin' about!"

"I respond to that," said Wallace, his voice softening almost to a purr, "by pointing out that you are rapidly proving yourself an ignorant fool."

Huston was not angry yet; only puzzled, and somewhat condescending to his friend's petulant whim. "Just where is the necessity for all this, Mark?"

"Quite of your own making. Since you found it desirable to brawl with your cousin over a towheaded girl in Mandeville, you thereby put us in a damned precarious position. I—"

"What the devil—"

"I mean to say I've spent a very pretty two or three days preventing about ten thousand dollars' worth of our notes being called."

"But if you prevented it—"

"Momentarily," Wallace qualified, biting his moustache. "I've saved our hides for the present by nothing in the world but face. If we get the boat into the river, and earning something, we may still be able to pull through."

"Still be able to pull through? It's as bad as that, is it?"

"Exactly."

A wave of anger swept Huston. "Then you're a damned sight weaker manager than you give yourself credit for," he growled. "The first breath of opposition finds you shakin' in your shoes. If that dough-faced cousin of mine really comes out with somethin' I suppose you'll curl up and quit like a cold-blood."

"I think not," said Mark incisively. "I'm holding up my end against a network of factors that you haven't the background to understand, even if I were interested in explaining it to you. Satisfy yourself that you pulled it down around our heads, that's all."

"Rubbish," Huston retorted. "D'you want me to come up and run your end of it, too?"

"I think you'd better learn your own end first. It seems to me, my friend, that I've supplied nothing less than everything this enterprise has had put into it so far. The first call on you for anything but the most mediocre effort has come now. Twenty-four hours' time looks a good deal like the line between success or failure. You sit there mouthing 'Impossible'!"

Huston was furious; but he held himself in check.

"Now you just make up your mind to pull yourself together," he told Mark harshly. "I'm not interested in your yellow streaks. The installation plans are not goin' to be changed; they couldn't be even if your silly notions were correct. Meantime, I have work to do. The boat leaves for Vicksburg Saturday."

"Whether she leaves before then or not, she certainly is not going to move Saturday."

"What do you mean?"

"There's a bankruptcy petition in the offing, my friend."

"We're no more bankrupt than—"

"Certainly not," Wallace interrupted bitingly. "That has nothing to do with the situation. It is a mere excuse upon which to base an injunction which will prevent the *Frontier City* from leaving her slip."

"If the petition is baseless, you'd better concern yourself in whipping it, and not—"

"You can't very well down the thing before it comes up. If I hadn't had underground wires out, I wouldn't know about it at all. Their play is to delay, and delay, whittling us down until they're ready; then they'll break us like squeezing an egg."

"Who the hell is 'they'?"

"Will Huston's crowd. Their injunction will be timed to the hour; there's such a thing as owning judges, you know, as well as boats. At best it would take perhaps a week to lift; at worst it'll drag on and on until they get something else to hold us with. They know to the rivet how far you've got with the remodelling of the *Frontier City*. Evidently they know you, too. They rest in confidence," he closed with cold sarcasm, "that nothing is likely to induce you to make a quick move."

Huston's lean cheek bones were scarlet. "Why didn't you say so in the first place?" he exploded. "You're goin' to go too far with me, Mark!"

There was a silence in which they sat looking at each other. Outside, the silver-gray rain pattered ceaselessly on the deck. It fell upon the river in a steep unvarying slant, with a steady wet whispering that lay as an impalpable background for all other sounds. Mark relaxed into a smile. His smile always had a suggestion of the beautiful in it, the subtly sensitive muscles of his face seeming capable of no other kind, regardless of the meaning behind.

"There's no need for us to quarrel," he said gently enough. "If we are going to fail, we're going to fail, and we may as well take it smiling."

"We're not goin' to fail," said Huston. But there was such an absence of conviction in his voice that Wallace glanced at him sharply.

The gray weariness had returned to Huston's face with the passing of his anger. His eyes were heavy and cold.

"Our success or failure," Mark Wallace said, "will depend on your activity. Or, rather, upon us both equally."

"That's a new idea to you, I take it," Huston commented drily. "A minute ago you said—"

"I spoke in haste," Mark conceded. "I've been under a very considerable strain, Arnold. It's up to me to accomplish certain difficult things; and it's up to you to get our boat into the water. We've got to pull together, Arn, and pull damned hard."

Huston saw no need for an answer to this. He sat relaxed, staring glumly out into the gray rain.

"You haven't told me," Mark suggested, "when the boat will move."

"Friday," said Arnold dully. The shadow of a smile widened his mouth. "Every nigger on the boat will jump over the side."

"Oh, I don't think so."

"The extra work will cost more, you know."

"I see that we can't avoid that."

They seemed to be on their old footing again. Arnold, harsh-tongued himself, was not inclined to remember the bitterness that had risen between them a few minutes before.

"Arn," said Wallace, "it'll be a relief to us both, and to you especially, I know, when this boat leaves the levee. The worst of this will soon be over, old man—far as you're concerned. I know you've worked yourself plumb to hell and back again, but—"

"I'm not tired."

"Yes, you are. You're as near under as I ever saw you, except that time after the burning of the *Peter Swain*. It shows in every muscle you've got. I know you've worried a good deal about the steamboat, but—"

"Hell, Mark, do you think I'm so poor at my job that a few details in gettin' a boat ready can put me under?"

Wallace said directly, "What's worrying you, Arn?"

Huston decided not to answer that. He stared off into the slanting shimmer of the rain, and half-smiled as he saw through Mark Wallace's questionings. His friend seemed to him singularly shallow, that his apparent concern should be so transparent. He saw that Mark regarded him merely as a factor in certain plans of his own. If some hidden thing was worrying Huston, it was to Wallace's interest to find it out, or at least to ascertain its nature. Huston wondered what underground machination Mark suspected him of. It was stupid of Wallace, he thought, to try to draw confidences on the heels of their quarrel.

His face sobered. He sat contemplating his own desolate plight as distantly as if Mark Wallace had been ten miles away. And thus, while it was still in his mind that Wallace was a stupid questioner, Mark trapped him.

"I saw Jacqueline DuMoyne to-day," Mark said.

"I wish to Christ," Huston burst out, "that you'd never taken me there!"

A swift chuckle, light and amused, brought Huston to earth.

"So that's all it is!"

"What d'you mean?"

"I thought maybe you had got yourself twisted into some underground rannykazoo. With Walt Gunn, for instance." Wallace was watching Huston's face.

"Yes?" Arnold's tone was cold and level.

"It's really a relief to me," Mark went on lightly, "to know that this spectacle is only the result of your falling in love."

Huston passed over "this spectacle" as he had passed over the reference to Walt Gunn. "You don't seem surprised," he said evenly.

"She told me," Mark said, "that she thought you were falling in love with her." Huston stirred. Wallace was going on: "She wanted to know what to do. I told her to let you—it would do you good."

"In what way?" Huston asked in a muffled voice.

"I told her I thought it would take some of the damned stiffness out of your neck to come a good sound cropper."

"I thought,—" Huston began. In the room before his eyes there was a shimmer like that of the outer rain, but he steadied himself and let his lids droop. "I thought—I had the idea that you had some interest in that quarter yourself."

"In your affairs? An entertained spectator, my child."

"In hers," Huston corrected him.

"Indeed?"

"I mean I thought you had plans of your own." With a flash of diplomacy he added, "Since you have not, of course that frees my hands."

"It happens that I do have plans of my own."

"Yet you suggested to her that she lead me on?"

"Say rather I advised her that it was hardly worth while to discourage you in the early stages."

"You give me carte blanche then, as far as you're concerned?" Huston believed that his anger was now so under control that he could meet Wallace's eyes without revealing it. Something akin to a cold shudder ran over him as he did do: he saw the same quiet face, the same sultry smoulder of amusement in the dark eyes with which Mark had gazed at that ghastly cat.

"I don't see that it is my place to give or withhold carte blanche on anything," Mark said.

"I think," Huston told him, "that your detachment is the best compliment you could pay me." He was feeling a keen revulsion for this odd man with the fine eyes and the beautiful smile.

"Don't deceive yourself," said Mark. "You'll never go further with this than I think useful to my interests."

"If you're speaking of your priority rights," said Huston, angrily in spite of himself, "I say there's no consideration comin' to you."

"I think you'll not find me asking for anything."

"You think it's impossible," said Huston, his voice quivering with his suppressed fury, "that you should lose out?"

"Not at all."

"Then you mean—"

"I mean that if ever I find you in my way I'll break you with no more compunction than I would anyone else."

"You think you could, do you!"

"Recall, my friend, that you were a pauper when I picked you up. You'll be a pauper again when I say the word. Everything that you have is by my sufferance. I had purposes in view when I gave you your chance. The fact that I was a fool to pick you, with your silly row on with your bastard brother, is beside the point. You're part owner of a steamboat—if you don't lose the steamboat—as long as I say you are. When I choose otherwise you'll be seventy-five hundred in my debt by your note of hand, and owner of nothing."

"The contract prevents that, I think!"

"Read it again." Mark Wallace rose, and began the graceful drawing on of his gloves. "You'd better be getting at your work."

That beautiful smile of his lightened his face; then it froze there, and changed to something else. His slight color went paler, and his hands checked in the drawing on of his gloves.

Into Huston had welled such a blind tumult of fury that he scarcely knew what he did or said. He felt himself slowly rise from his chair, his muscles taut springs. His lips drew away from his teeth in a mad grin. As he stepped toward Mark Wallace, his thigh struck the corner of the heavy table, and it tumbled aside like a straw thing, in a mess of papers and spilled ink.

Mark took a step backward, but the wall was there. Then the fingers of Huston's left hand twisted themselves into the pleated throat of his shirt, and he was jammed against the bulkhead. Wallace's face went white. There was the tinge of terror in the shock of his fury as he found his voice.

"This is preposterous! What is the meaning of this?"

Still the mad gleaming smile on Huston's face, the slow twist of his fingers in the neckband of the shirt. Wallace's face began to darken with the tightening check of the blood. He dizzied and a wild panic crept into him.

He screamed, "Let go, you fool!" His knuckles flailed in a sudden desperate struggle, but Huston's hand was like steel. Even as his eyes darkened and the terror of futility crushed him his mind was at work. He stopped struggling, and though he sagged as if he would fall he looked directly into Huston's mad eyes.

Wallace heard him say, "You poor cowardly fool, you'll never be master of any situation that I happen to be in."

Then he saw the madness in Huston's eyes give way to a gleam of triumph and a certain ironic amusement. The fingers slackened at his throat, so that he could get his breath again.

"You'll fight me for this!"

Huston laughed in his face. "No, I'm tired of fightin' cowards."

That irresistible hand flung Wallace staggering toward the door.

"Get out! Stay out! I've work to do."

WHEN Mark Wallace was gone Huston reached out the door and seized the arm of the mulatto cabin boy so suddenly that the negro almost sat down in his tracks.

"Tell every officer on the boat I want 'em here. Tell 'em to drop everythin' and come. Run!"

CHAPTER XX

At eight o'clock in the black rain Huston robbed his boat of two hours of his time to go to Jacqueline DuMoyne.

Every man in the boat's personnel had responded mightily to Huston's appeal for speed. An hour after Mark Wallace had left the boat Huston had been in overalls in the engine room. Both his mates were by that time out on errands; the second engineer had gone to word-lash a wood-barge from across the river, and to round up the last necessities. A Cajun boy who was an engine-room striker was bossing a gang of negroes with scrub brushes. To his surprise the spurred efforts of them all were outdone by the silent efficiency of that dour man of the engines, MacMaugh; after all, it was upon MacMaugh that all their chances turned.

Until noon Huston and MacMaugh labored alone. They were working on the "doctor," the fiddling pump that kept the water level in the boilers the same. MacMaugh had accepted Huston's services dubiously at first. He had heretofore been given no reason to think that his captain knew a boiler from a turbine. At the end of an hour he had no more doubt.

"If I'd had two men like you, we'd been up-river last week."

"Pass the graphite," said Huston.

Reinforcements came at noon, a first engineer borrowed from a friendly boat, and two others picked up in the town. They were an assorted-looking crew. One was a fat man with a walloping big moustache through which he shot tobacco juice with a whistling noise at intervals of one minute. Huston found himself timing his accomplishments by that whistling squirt of juice. Another was a little wisp of a man with glasses and a peaked face; his big bony hands were loosely affixed to his spindling forearms. The third was a thick-wristed Norwegian, whose methodical competence contrasted with the apparent blankness of his huge face.

These men started work slowly at first, with a detached interest. Then presently the close-lipped intensity of Huston and MacMaugh took them, and things began to get done. By the middle of the afternoon the five of them were working in a silent furor of speed emphasized by the clank of their tools and the short directions of MacMaugh. At six o'clock the Norwegian put down his tools and picked up his coat. No one followed his example. The fat engineer shot him a contemptuous glance, and whistled tobacco through his teeth. The Norwegian put down his coat, and did not again relinquish his wrenches that night.

They ate dinner standing, cramming their mouths with greasy hands, and in five minutes were back at their work.

During this time Arnold found himself.

There was something familiar and reassuring in the very hazard of the situation that had enveloped him. He was in a good position to lose everything that he cared about, with Will Huston bearing down hard with an unexpected financial strength, and his own partner so inconceivably changed that Arnold was at a loss to understand what had happened. Yet he found a new exhilaration in the extremity of his predicament. He was like a man who, about to succumb to the attack of a single adversary, fights with a surpassing fury upon finding himself beset by six.

How he was to master Mark Wallace and defeat Will Huston he had no idea. Nor did he have any illusions as to what chance he would have with Jacqueline DuMoyne if these things were done. The first thing was to get the steamboat up-river, so that her immediate usefulness would not be lost to both Mark and himself.

The steamboat men that he had gathered about him found him transfigured. There was no more humor in his face now than before, but there was a glint in his eye that goes with the love of battle in all men, let the devil-luck run as it may.

At eight o'clock he suddenly laid down his tools and kicked his overalls off onto the floor.

"I'll be gone for two hours," he said, "and be back for all night."

MacMaugh grunted; the others scarcely looked up. They didn't have time, knowing what was ahead of them in that night of rain. Huston raced upstairs to his stateroom, begrudging every moment that he lost. He had shaved that morning, and did not repeat the operation now. He scoured the grease from his face; it would not come off entirely from his hands. A black slicker was over his shoulders, but he was still tying his tie when a few minutes later he stepped into a skiff by the *Frontier City*'s side. A powerful negro was waiting at the oars.

"Now you move!" snapped Huston, pushing off with a shove that sent them three fathoms on their way; and the slave made the water foam from the bow.

In the streets of New Orleans the rain seemed thinner, yet possessed of dark misty depths. Here and there it glinted silver where shone a light. But the lights themselves glowed magically orange, each one doubled by a reflection of itself, below in the wet. On the Rue Chartres he was admitted to the small door in the timbered portal.

"WHAT was it," asked Jacqueline DuMoyne with a little smile, "that her name turned out to be?"

"Whose name?"

"Why, the name of your steamboat!"

Arnold smiled. "I don't know."

"But—Mark said she was to take to the river in the morning."

So he had been there, then! "Yes; I ought to be with her now. I'm goin' back in a minute."

"But it has to have a name!"

"Yes," he admitted. "I suppose so."

"You're not going to leave it *Frontier City*?"

"No; that's painted over. Anyway it wouldn't be good business, and the crew wouldn't like it. She has to have another. The carpenter was askin' just before I left. He's boss painter, too. He couldn't paint in the rain, but he'd made a pair of light signs, tall as a man, to be nailed to the paddleboxes, after bein' painted inside. And he wanted to know what her name was. I couldn't tell him. I told him to go ask the engineer, and put on whatever he said."

"I know what I would have named her."

"Why didn't you then?"

"I thought Mark—"

"I don't think Mark ever gave it a thought. Anyway, I forgot to ask him."

"I think," she said, "it should be called the *Arnold Huston.*"

He laughed softly, but so harshly that she looked at him in surprise.

"When you get back you'll probably find your engineer has named it just what I said," she told him.

"He'll more likely name her *'86-98 Stroke'*," Huston thought.

"Will the boat pass," she asked him, "out there where I can see it?"

"At about five o'clock in the mornin', I think."

"I'm going to watch it go by."

"She won't be much to look at, I'm afraid."

"But it's—" He had a fleeting impression that she had started to say "ours," but the sentence remained incomplete.

She suddenly extended her arm, and her soft fingers lifted his own. "Your hand is hurt!"

He wanted to grip her fingers, but he recognized her detached intention and withheld. His long corded hand lay relaxed, grimed with black engine grease. Its look of being worn and bent with toil was purely an illusion of its weariness; but of course she couldn't know that. A trace of blood had reappeared where the slip of a wrench had sent his fist crashing against a bolt head.

"Oh—I always hurt my hands."

Her fingers withdrew as gently as they had come.

"Mark told me," she said, "that—that you and he had quarrelled."

He drawled, "What else did he tell you?"

"That was all." She was timorous, hesitant; yet he felt that she was being drawn to him by an overwhelming pity.

He turned his face toward her with the slow shadow of a smile, warm, assured, faintly amused. For a brief interval they sat in silence.

He looked out toward the Mississippi. He could feel the river, invisible beyond the cloaking mists of dark rain. The strong swing and pull of the current surged in his blood.

"How many things happen," he said softly, "that a man knows nothin' of. Perhaps my fortunes have been discussed in this very room."

"Yes," she said.

"I think," he said levelly, his face still turned to the river rain, "I've been blindfolded, in some ways."

"Oh, poor Arnold," she burst out, "like a picador's horse!"

It was the first time she had used his name. An old fire that had long sulked blazed up, so that as he slowly turned his eyes to her they were full of flame.

He was in that mood of recklessness in which men of all times have walked into enemy gunfire. He felt a lift of proud power, edged by an utter indifference to catastrophe or loss. He would have walked directly into his death with that same glow in his eye, that same smile.

Because Mark Wallace had felt his strength, Jacqueline knew more than Huston suspected, more than Huston himself. Yet—

She could not look into his face and believe this man defeated. She thought, "He has something, knows something, that makes him master of them all." What it might be she could not imagine. But it was impossible to believe that this was not the man with the whip.

He said, "Perhaps the blindfold is off."

With a queer sense of distance he heard her say, "You can't let them down you—now."

They held each other's eyes until hers dropped. "One thing," he said, "is clear to us both."

A certain new quality in his voice carried to her such an inescapable significance that one hand fluttered to her throat, and she rose. Her eyes wavered on his. "What—"

He stood before her; his corded hands cupped her shoulders. Afterward she found that the hurt hand had left a touch of blood there.

"That I love you."

The hands from which Mark Wallace had been unable to free himself drew her against him. She was motionless as he kissed her mouth.

He let her drift from him a moment after that. But she swayed so that had he wished to release her shoulders he would not have dared, lest she fall. Her eyes brimmed, but there were no tears; and though her shoulders shook as with sobs, her lips were quiet and no sound came. Her head was a little to one side, and she was looking at him through eyes strangely narrowed, oblique dark slits in a face gone deathly white. They might have expressed terror—appeal—hate—some hard twisting emotion that he could not read. . . .

He never could remember just what she had said. The harsh, case-hardened shell of his own mood made him impervious to external things, even to his own effect upon her. He set her down among the cushions of the settee. She told him in a choked voice something to the effect that she wanted him to go away, to leave her to herself.

"You belong to me," he told her. "I'm not to be denied."

As he went out she called after him, in a small voice, "I'm going to watch for your boat."

She worried afterward as to what he might build out of that, but she could have spared herself the trouble. Huston was in no mood for the taking of soundings, and after a brief bitter smile let it drop from his mind. The one thing that he did not forget was the warmth of her lips under his.

CHAPTER XXI

FOR an hour the rain had been decreasing, first to a drizzle, then to a descending mist. As the gray dawn swelled rapidly into a universal bluish light it stopped altogether. The mild dark wood smoke from the stacks had been drifting down to touch the surface of the water, muffling close about the steamboat in the rain. Now it rose and drifted away, leaving the cool morning air lucid.

The carpenter's crew of blacks was struggling with the signboards that were for the present to bear the boat's name. Now that they had to be suspended and nailed to the paddleboxes the light signs seemed acres in extent. The negroes shuffled themselves, heaved, and cursed. There was a great stamping of bare feet, rattling of tackle, and whooping shouts.

MacMaugh came, and stood at Huston's elbow where he leaned on the rail. The engineer seemed unwearied by the night's exertions. He used no tobacco, and this, among men who were always smoking or chewing, gave him the appearance of never being thoroughly at leisure. His movements were economical of effort, and he knew how to rest as well as the next; yet he forever seemed to be doing something, about to do something, or planning to do something. When none of these attitudes were possible, it appeared that MacMaugh was waiting. Never under any circumstances did he seem to be merely taking his ease, as Huston looked when he leaned on the rail in the company of his cigar.

"How do you like it?" the engineer asked.

"Looks good; looks great. I'll have to see her lay against the current before I say for sure."

"I meant the boat's name," said MacMaugh.

"Oh—her name!" Huston chuckled drily in mockery of himself that he had forgotten to ask what it was. He experienced a moment of ironic panic, for fear that these steamboat men of his, in absence of any instruction from him, had given his boat some foolish label.

"Did you name her?" he asked.

"I understood that it had been left to me," said MacMaugh.

"It was."

"I see you don't think well of her name," said MacMaugh oddly. "Well, I named the name. I did not do so without consulting the other officers, these men of your own choosing. And if—"

"I don't even know what her name is," Huston put in.

"You had best be looking to see, then," MacMaugh advised.

Huston leaned far out over the rail, peering through the gray light of the dawn. At first he could not see the face of the huge wooden plate. Then it swung about on its spider webs of tackle, and he made out in letters black and red:

ARNOLD HUSTON

NEW ORLEANS

His emotion was one of embarrassment. He did not know what to say to MacMaugh, and remained for some moments staring blankly at the sign, as if it were almost beyond his capabilities to read two words.

"I don't think," he said at last, "it was hardly right to name her that."

He had been trying to decide whether or not he should allow the name to be put up, and was still uncertain. It was too late to paint another name now, and they could hardly take the rebuilt boat on her maiden trip with no name at all. It could have been worse; other men had given their own names to their boats before.

"I would not have thought you the man," MacMaugh was saying, "to begrudge his name to his boat."

"It isn't that," said Huston uncertainly.

"The *Huston* is a good boat," MacMaugh went on, using the new name already. "I am proud of her myself, what little part I have had to do with her in her powering. I don't know what she can do, no more than you; but this I can tell you, though she may be small, she is no boat that a man would be ashamed of. There are big names on the river, carried by boats that will not carry them as fast nor as neatly as she."

"I'm as strong for her as you are," Huston insisted, "but—"

"I thought you would be glad to honor the boat with your name," MacMaugh continued. The man seemed vaguely hurt, not at the questioning of his judgment, but as if some sort of offense had been offered the boat to which he had given his labor.

"The boat is worth any man's name," said Huston. "Only it doesn't look like I have the honor due me, hardly."

"Honor due?" It was apparent that MacMaugh had no conception of what Huston was talking about.

"That's it."

"It's the boat honored," said MacMaugh. "A man can honor a thing with his name. How can a thing honor a man? A thing is what men make it. Except the engines, which I sometimes think the devil made, or else got inside them afterward. If you don't like the name it is because you are dissatisfied with the work that has gone to make her. After all, let me ask you, whose name else did you have a right to give her?"

"Nobody's," Huston admitted. "I thought prob'ly the name of a place—"

"Argh," said MacMaugh, and went below.

They breakfasted immediately after that, grimed, tired men. Yet, in accordance with the etiquette of all good packets, the officers of the boat all wore their coats. Only Captain Pumpernickel came slopping to the breakfast table in a dirty undershirt and unlaced boots.

In fulfillment of his contract with the old man, Huston had assigned Pumpernickel an unimportant but comfortable stateroom, where he received the adequate service always accorded first-class passengers. He no longer ate breakfasts that had been cooked the night before, and his room was neatly kept. With the cares of life lifted from his shoulders, Pumpernickel applied himself to the task of keeping comfortably drunk at all hours, and staring at the people working on the boat. The old man had been de-flead along with the rest of the boat and her equipment including the cat. With this accomplished he was no longer an active menace. It appeared, however, that he might be a source of embarrassment in other ways.

"Huh-uh," said Huston, waving him away from the table.

"Lot o' noise last night," said Pumpernickel, his dry voice testy. "Man couldn't get any sleep. Like to know the sense—" He was about to sit down.

"Captain Pumpernickel!" said Huston. "You can't come to my table in that condition!"

"How?"

"You go get a collar and coat on!" Huston had a hard, resonant, slightly nasal voice when he gave commands. It cut through Pumpernickel's deafness.

"Who!" Pumpernickel exploded. His piercing glass-marble eyes popped at Huston.

"You know who I'm talkin' to!"

"Ye mean to say I can't come to my own table—"

"It ain't your table," Huston corrected him.

For a moment the small puckered mouth in Pumpernickel's loosely folded face expressed a frozen astonishment. Then with no other word he stumped off to his stateroom and his door slammed with a frightful bang behind him. He was not seen again until the rest had gone, when he slunk forth to eat with the second engineer.

There was little conversation at breakfast. They were a group of men various in degree of polish, age, character, and interest in the boat. Each was intrusted with some necessary function of the boat's existence as a working thing, although, since there were no uniforms among steamboat crews in those days, appearance did not distinguish one from another.

Huston sat at the head of the table. At his right hand, as befitting his acknowledged position, sat the "longest" of the two pilots, Harry Masters. He was a great thick mountain of a man, weighing only slightly under two hundred fifty pounds, with a good-humored blank face mounted between side whiskers. His eyes were prominent, at once bulging and heavy-lidded. Here was a man Huston was fortunate to get. In spite of his unwieldy mass he had a delicately skillful hand at the wheel, a fine instinct for a shifted channel, and an almost perfect sensitivity to the response of his boat.

Opposite him sat Nate Lacrosse, his mate, whose head was a close-cropped bullet with eyes so squinted and so deeply screwed into it that the man seemed to be in pain. A glimpse of them told better than words how the sunglare on the river could punish sensitive eyes. In contrast to the immaculate Harry Masters, Lacrosse wore his clothes in a way that enabled him always to look collarless, no matter what he might have on. This man was not quite so good by reputation as Harry Masters; but he knew his river, and his mishaps had been few. Considering the comparatively small size of the *Arnold Huston*, they were lucky to get him, too.

MacMaugh ranked next, of course, tall and dour, with a great disordered shock of hair above a rubbly face on which the bristle was seldom allowed to show. His eyes were like raw steel.

One other man was there at that breakfast table who later was able to influence Arnold Huston as much as any man ever could. He was the youth that Huston had chosen for mate. A good deal of a boy, some of the others thought him; but Arnold had been a mate himself at eighteen, and believed that he had discharged the duties thereof as well as most, and a good deal better than some.

The mate's name was Tommy Craig. He was of about Huston's size, and five years younger; but Huston looked by twenty years the more experienced man. Craig's hair was the color of dull brass, his eyes blue in a face whose complete homeliness was qualified only by the laughter that seemed never more than temporarily suppressed. The older men, with the exception of Huston, supposed him to be incompetent naturally: he did not have their experience on the river. But Craig nevertheless could fling a gang of negroes against a task with a speed which would have meant sulks and disorder under many an older man. The hookworm had passed him by, and a continual fear of missing something had slipped in instead. Consequently no emergency, in his watch or in anyone's else, was likely to find him in his bunk. And he did not seem to know the difference between a disagreeable task and one replete with interest.

There were a dozen others there, of varying importance to the boat: a knotty second mate; first, second, and third clerks; two watchmen who were hardly more than boys, in accordance with Huston's belief that greenness was preferable to defeated antiquity; a carpenter who was only a temporary fixture; a grizzled bartender who was in his own way the greatest individualist of them all, and one or two more.

They finished breakfast at last. It had been a dull necessity to some of them at least, though it had taken little time and less speech.

Huston said, "All right, boys."

They separated, going to their various posts. Those who were off duty drifted to the boiler deck. MacMaugh went down to his engines, the pilot aloft to his wheel, Tommy Craig to the forecastle, to direct the casting off. Huston himself went up on the hurricane roof, which was in reality the third deck above the water. As he stood at the forward rail the Texas house was behind him, abaft the two towering black stacks that rose abreast, one on each side of the boat. On top of the Texas towered the slender, well-glassed structure of the pilot house, highest of all.

Below, from the forward rail of the hurricane roof, Huston commanded a bird's view of the open forward section of the main deck, the clearing spot from which all cargo would be discharged or carried back into the depths of the deckroom or hold. Not all captains assumed this post when making or leaving a landing. Some preferred the closer surveillance possible from the boiler deck or even the main deck itself, from which latter point a whip could be applied to sluggish blacks upon occasion. To Huston the hurricane was a place from which he could send his voice battering down with heavy effect, yet without ever seeming to raise it above the tone, damaging enough, that the distance itself suggested.

Huston yanked a cord that was attached to the rail,

ready to his hand. At his feet the mellow dangling voice of his bell answered.

"Cast off!"

Running negroes cast loose the shore ends of the lines, others on the main deck coiled the ropes in.

"Take in your plank!"

"Bong!" said the bell, the signal to the pilot. The negroes who had cast off ran with that appearance of unperturbed leisure that is possible to no other race in the world, to leap the widening gap of brown water to the steamboat's guards. Tommy Craig was singing out in a hard drawling voice in imitation of Huston's own, getting the unwieldy stage plank aboard and into its place. A bell jangled in the engine room, and another. Down by the surface of the water, where the big engines lay, the voice of the steam began to speak in steady "whoofs" as she backed out: "Up—river; up—river; up—river!"

The bell in the engine room spoke again; the great paddle wheels idled and stopped. Still another bell—

What happened then was an impalpable thing, a transpiration of something more significant than the mere fact that the engines answered, that the steamboat surged easily against the current and began to walk upstream, gliding smoothly over the surface of the river. They all did that. It was the feel of her, the pulse of life and capability, that meant something to these men who had studied her and labored over her to make an old boat with a bad name into something new and good. It was the first expression of a newly powered steamboat, a boat whose engines had never before taken her into trade.

No one would have been surprised if, after progressing four miles upstream, MacMaugh had signalled to turn back. There are overhaulings, readjustments, and replacements in the building of a boat, as well as a first assembling of her component parts. Yet, in that initial movement of hers, when she first breasted the current and set her unfamiliar engines to kicking it away behind, it seemed to Huston that she gave him a lifting promise of unsuspected things.

The captain had no function on the hurricane roof after she had taken the stream. She was the boat of the pilot and engineer then, and until the next landing Huston would be needed no more. But for a long time he stood there, forgetful of the soot that sprinkled the shoulders of his coat and the carelessly slanted brim of his Panama. They were making their way up-river slowly, in deference to the newly installed engines, and he could tell nothing about her yet. But he was sensing the effortless drive of her engines, the faint smooth tremor of the superstructure to the pulse of the stream, the feel of her hull resistance to the churring paddles. Here, away from the rest, he was alone with his boat.

If ever a man loved a boat, Huston loved his namesake then: not with the slow habitual affection that long association brings, but with the thrill a man feels when new vistas open, promising the fulfillment of hopes only half existent because only half understood.

They made Baton Rouge with scarcely a pause, and there MacMaugh worked a day and a night. She went on effortlessly against the current to Natchez, to Vicksburg, to Greenville; and at last to Memphis, where she lay five days, and was completely overhauled.

There they turned back, and went booming downstream well-laden, with MacMaugh throwing her into long bursts of speed that surprised them all. They were nearly back to New Orleans before Huston drew from the dour engineer a definite prediction.

"MacMaugh," said the riverman, "can she beat the *Tennessee Governor*?"

"Handily," said MacMaugh, for the first time dropping evasion.

"The *Mount Haskett*?"

"She'll make a race out of it!"

Even Huston's optimism was skeptical in the face of the monotoned expectations of the engineer. Yet he placed this man's judgment above his own. He suddenly brought forth the name of the boat that had been in his mind from the beginning—that of Will Huston's fastest packet.

"Can she take the *Elizabeth Grey*?"

"The *'Galloping Betsy'*?" said MacMaugh. He did not answer at once. He seemed to be going into one of his spells of listening to the engines, his eyes hazy, his ears intent upon some hidden note in the voice of the oiled steel. "Mmmmm. . . ." he said at last. "No."

Huston turned away. Then MacMaugh suddenly burst out with a wholly unexpected contradiction:

"Yes, by God! I think she can!"

CHAPTER XXII

JACQUELINE, serenely graceful, came forward to receive him as he was let into that high room on the Rue Chartres; but in spite of the swift intoxication of her renewed nearness Huston was instantly aware of the presence of Mark Wallace, a shadowy form seated on the far side of the room. The man dominated the room like a statue of raw iron seen through gauze, as dark and hard and downbearing of mood as Jacqueline was light and lovely.

Wallace sat with his chin on his chest. His fine dark eyes, bleakly hard, indifferently forbidding, still retained that patrician keenness of perception which never entirely left them: yet they had the cold impersonality of the eyes of a cuttle fish. It was perhaps only a quarter of a minute in which he met Huston's gaze before he rose; but in that interval in which he remained a motionless figure of ebony and chalk, it seemed as though he were never going to move at all.

The gay cultured irony that had made Wallace's face charming was gone. In its absence an unsuspected appearance of strength was revealed in his features, as if the muscles over his cheekbones had become more noticeable, and his relaxed mouth ascetic and enduring. It was his face with the life gone out of it, leaving lineaments of strength that had been unperceived before.

Huston had time to note these things. The days in which they had been understanding friends seemed struck from the record, as if they had never been lived.

"Just in?" Wallace asked, rising at last. They shook hands with a specious sort of dry-palmed grasp.

"Not an hour."

"How is the *Arnold Huston*?" There was no emphasis in Mark's voice as he pronounced the name; he said it as he would have said *"Frontier City,"* or any other.

"Fast; faster than any of us believed."

"How was the trip?"

"We made expenses."

"Was that all?"

"Good God, man!" Arnold burst out uncontrollably, "we're lucky to avoid three months of trials and tinkerings!"

"Oh, of course," Wallace conceded lackadaisically.

"I was able," said Huston more equably, "to make arrangements that will make our next trip more profitable."

"That's good."

There had been an attempt at agreeableness in Wallace's voice every time he spoke, a concession that the presence of Jacqueline could not entirely account for. It was the sort of effort that Mark might have made in weariness to entertain a stranger. Huston felt more menace in this odd mannerliness of Mark's than there could have been in overt threats; it was as if the man felt it necessary to conceal behind this flimsy screen something too elemental in its potentialities to stand the light.

"I'm anxious to hear more of the trip," said Wallace

naturally, "as you can imagine. I hope you'll excuse me now. I'll appreciate it, Captain, if you'll call at my rooms as soon as you are at leisure."

"To-night?" With the news of New Orleans developments still unknown to him, Huston was nevertheless ready to match indifference with indifference.

Wallace shot him a curious glance. "Most assuredly, to-night."

"Very well."

"May I have a word with you, Madame?" said Mark distinctly.

That was really a statement to Huston, of course, that he had intruded before a conversation was complete. He took himself to the far corner of the room, where he stood looking out at the Mississippi shipping half seen in the light of the low-rising moon. He could hear the two of them whispering by the door, and he scorned himself that he should have to correct an instinctive attempt to hear what they said.

He did not turn as Mark left the room, but remained staring moodily out the window as Jacqueline came slowly across toward him. When he finally glanced at her he was shocked to see that her face was white with terror which she was evidently struggling to conceal. In his astonishment he stood gaping, without words at his command.

She paused uncertainly; but she was first to speak. "Oh, Arnold, I'm at my wits' end!"

Two strides brought him close to her. "Jacqueline, what is it?"

For all the peculiarity of the situation, he knew that

he would never again forget the sound of her voice as she spoke his name. There were tenderness and richness in the timbre of it, low in her throat, and the subtle suggestion of an accent not his own. For him there was in it an exquisite pain, at once the gift of a beauty beyond understanding and the suggestion of a beauty denied.

Slowly he ran his fingers through his hair. As his hand fell away he repeated: "Tell me what it is."

It seemed to him that he had croaked the words when he should have been pressing her gently in his arms, whispering tendernesses as his lips touched her hair. But his arms dangled woodenly at his sides, under his control only as far as the paddlewheels are in the control of the pilot, indirectly through cords and distant bells.

"Tell me what's the matter," he said again.

The sorrow that was in her eyes, as she turned them slowly to his, cut through him like the stroke of a blacksnake whip.

It is possible that in their brief silence she could see him understandingly, in lights which he never suspected: his rumpled unruly hair, his high-keyed countenance that the river had carved to suit its needs, his steel-gray eyes, his lean strong hands. Behind these things perhaps she felt the man's vital stubborn strength, the strength not of weight and mass but of pliant steel; and the deep welter of another emotion than that of pity, a thing possessed of a power that could turn all that gray steel in the man to molten flame, and stir a deep quiver of response within herself. . . .

These were things that Huston could not know. He saw himself only as an inarticulate yokel, hopelessly inadequate in the face of a situation the keys of which had been denied him. He groped uncertainly.

"If Mark has—" he began hesitantly, and stopped. But she had caught his meaning.

"No, no; Mark is doing the best he can."

There was despair in her voice; and his jealous resentment of Mark's greater privilege died away in such a surge of blindly understanding pity that he forgot the mystery from which he was debarred, forgot his own awkwardness, forgot everything except the unhappiness in the delicately contoured face and the depths of the dark eyes. Gently he took her slender hands in one of his own, and with an arm about her shoulders led her toward the settee, the river-window settee from which they had so often watched the boats.

He had meant to place her among the cushions there, to talk to her gently, soothingly, blindly comforting her hurt, trying to bring the color to her cheeks again, the smile back to the mouth he had kissed in a time that seemed ages ago. She had seemed apart from him to-night in spite of her lonely need, as if she had never been held in his arms. He had believed for a moment that all that was past; that he could comfort her as a brother might comfort a little girl. It was an illusion that crumpled, like tissue paper in flame, at the soft rondure of her shoulders within his arm, the slender softness of her fingers in his own.

He bit his lips, but even as he sought to steady himself she must have felt the quiver of his arm about her shoulders, and sensed the new racing of his pulse. Somehow he led her to the settee, though a heady dizziness swirled up out of the struggling emotion within so that his steps faltered. They were before the window where he had meant to put her down, to comfort her with words.

For an instant he wavered, and she looked up at him. In her face were wonderment, and acceptance, and a sadness tinged with fear. But in the depths of her wide eyes there was a new dark flame. For an instant the dark flame met and merged with the steel-gray glow.

Between them a barrier broke under the force of a flood released. He drew her against him; then her arms tightened about him, and her warm lips quivered under his own. . . .

Her face was quiet with the promise of a new peace as she presently leaned against him, their arms about each other, her forehead against his cheek. Over Huston there was a great glow of happiness, a surging, welling, soaring happiness, as unbelievable to him as the bitter abysses of the hells he had known in his unrequited desire of her. For a long time they stood together, too closely bound by the partial satisfaction of their contact to speak or move.

It was Jacqueline who finally spoke, her voice softly low and vibrant. “Where is our river?” She reached out slender uncertain fingers, and made a handbreadth opening in the mulberry curtains that until now had made the window opaque.

Suddenly he felt her body go rigid in his arms, and

her hand drew back as if it had been burnt. She drew a great shuddering breath, and gave him one upward glance so full of horror that his own body stiffened with shock; then she averted her face.

"Jacqueline! What is it?" There was no answer. "Darling, tell me!"

"Nothing, nothing—" She broke from him and dropped upon the settee, hiding her face in her arm.

Huston struck aside the curtains with a furious sweep of his arm. Beyond the roofs that shone vaguely in the light of the moon the ancient Mississippi lay silent under the still boats. Closer, below in the narrow canyon of the street, he could see the opposite banquette, where a single overcoated figure slowly walked, dim against the dark shadow of a great arch. Then there was the balcony immediately beyond the glass; only a segment of it could be seen.

He heard Jacqueline say, "No, no!" as he clapped his hand to the latch of the French window; but he wrenched it open and stepped out. The balcony was less extensive than he had supposed, shallow, and extending but a pace beyond the window itself on either side. It was empty. He whirled, and with his back against the curly wrought-iron of the rail he studied the bleak dormered eaves a long cat's leap above, under the formless impression that some unknown horror had been on the balcony and escaped that way. Then he turned back, leaned down, and searched the street below, empty as far as he could see save for that one inconspicuous figure across there, slowly making its way off.

He went back to her, softly latching the window behind him.

"It was nothing, my dearest," he said gently.

She was sitting up now, her face composed though very pale. It seemed to him the life had gone from it, even from the wonderful dark eyes. He would have sat beside her, but she slowly rose; and as he moved to take her in his arms she put her hands before her. He took them between his palms.

"Jacqueline!"

"Arnold"—there was a breathless catch in her voice— "You must go away—"

Suddenly the tears streamed down her face from the dark eyes, melting now, that had seemed brushed on delicate paper with dark ink.

"You're mine," he told her passionately, "you've got to be mine!"

"Sometime, perhaps, if God is good. But, my dearest, it can't be now. Please, please go!"

"But when am I to see you again?"

"Not—until I send."

He suddenly crushed her in his arms. She clung to him with upturned face as he kissed her eyes, her tear-wet cheeks.

CHAPTER XXIII

As the little door in the massive gate closed behind him, Huston felt an exulting sense of power which threatening difficulties, known and unknown, served only to whet. A joyous belligerency was in his blood, a need of battle; he felt that he could kill with his hands a man who so much as blundered into his path.

In this mood, his eye fell upon an overcoated figure standing hunched, cramped, in the corner of the gateway's thick arch. It was the man, Huston thought, that he had seen walking the other side of the street a little while before; though, since this seemed of no significance to him, his mind immediately dropped the fact. In his rashly war-like mood it was the attitude of the shadowed figure, at once appearing permanent and as if waiting, that irritated Huston.

The man was probably a beggar, he thought; but his mere presence under this particular arch, among all those that the city afforded, was sufficient excuse for Huston to pause a moment, staring angrily.

The high-flaring coat collar of the day was about the man's face, but over it a pair of bead-like pupils stared back at Huston from sagging whites. The riverman's resentment was increased by his inability to cut down those malignant eyes, as steady and unblinking as his own.

"What are you doin' here?" he growled.

There was a pause, so long that Huston was about to press his demand when the other suddenly spoke.

"I have as much right here," said the unknown, "as you have, and maybe more."

No breath of conciliation was in that cold voice, only a taunting insolence and a contradicting authority. Huston burst into fury.

"What do you mean, sir!" he snarled. With a quick

step and the reach of a lean arm he seized the other man by the front of his coat near the throat, jerking him roughly into a position in which he could see the face. To his suddenly increased anger, the twisting away of the coat lapels failed to reveal the features of the stranger. The moonlight into which he had stepped showed full insolent lips and those floating black pupils of eyes in dirty whites which the sagging lids exposed; but between mouth and eyes the face was concealed by a broad black band of cloth.

"Masked!" Huston burst out. "Masked, huh?" His fury at the presence of this lurker at Jacqueline's very doorstep now broke its last restraint. With an inarticulate oath he suddenly ripped the mask from the stranger's face. Soft black silk came away in his fingers.

Huston's grip relaxed, and he started back. Close before his own there was revealed a face so hideous in its mutilation, so utterly inhuman as to convey a ghastly shock. The nose, save for a bit of the bridge, was gone, revealing an unseen cavity, black in the uncertain light. Above, those haggard eyes, with the great sprawling whites undercircled in black; on either side, cadaverous cheeks, hollow and wasted in contrast to the loose full lips.

The lips now drew back from strong teeth in a leer so savage that Huston expected instant attack—until he realized that the man was laughing at him. While he still hesitated, revolted and uncertain, the death's head suddenly turned away, and the man walked rapidly toward the corner. Huston looked after him as a man hypnotized. Not until the apparition turned the corner and disappeared did Huston realize that if he had had reason for warning the man away before, it was doubled and tripled now.

He hastened after, only to find when he, too, had turned the corner that the fugitive had disappeared. Slowly he walked along the banquette, guessing as best he might into which of the doors the man had gone, more uncertain with every stride. For another twenty minutes he patroled that street, waiting for the man to reappear; in the end he had to concede that the trail was lost.

After he had given up and turned his steps toward Mark Wallace's rooms in the Rue Royale he turned back twice; once to patrol the side street again, to assure himself that the hideous stranger had not come out. And once on an impulse to see if Jacqueline was really safe—an intention that dissolved into a long gazing at her windows, and nothing more.

He put the inhuman face from his mind, and sought out Mark Wallace. Yet all that night he was haunted intermittently by visions of that isle of houses rising sheer above its stagnant gutters, its balconies overhanging the street; a great massive block of dwellings set wall to wall, roof to roof, court to court. What tortuous passages led from one to another, so that one who had access to one might, knowing his way, have access to nearly all? Somewhere in those contiguous rabbit-warrens was the most precious thing in life, the beloved one who to him was the heart of all beauty, the meaning of all things. And prowling some hidden passageway—how near?—an evil figure with a noseless death's-head face. . . .

CHAPTER XXIV

DUST, dust, dust over everything in the narrow room of Mark Wallace, an impalpable fragile film of it over the walls of books, over the bronze bust on the chimney shelf, over the transparent shade of the lamp. In the midst of these gray-filmed things, Mark Wallace's face, conspicuous by its nonrelation to the dust, like translucent porcelain, delicately tinted by the firelight.

Huston let himself in without summons; then for a few minutes stood leaning with his back against the closed door, looking at his friend—if the man could still be so described. Wallace looked up when he first came, and for a moment or two met Huston's eyes in a gaze without obvious meaning; then returned to looking at the red breathing coals.

It was hard for Huston to comprehend, as he gazed across at Mark's half-averted face, that they had quarrelled bitterly, that they were no longer the same intimate friends. Mark's face was quiet under the rumpled drape of his seal-brown hair: a sensitively beautiful face, for a man, with fine steady dark eyes. He looked as he had always looked, in the years in which they had been the closest of friends. A little finer drawn, perhaps, with a deeper shadow under the perceiving dark eyes.

"If ever you stand in my way—" It was almost

impossible to remember the insolence of Mark's voice, with a tinge of mockery in it, that day in the cabin with the rain outside. "If ever you stand in my way, I'll break you with no more compunction—" Hard to believe that Mark had said that. Yet Huston was almost in a mood to understand that, now. Within the hour Huston himself had felt the surge of battle, the eagerness for something in his way that he could break.

He tired of the silence at last. Coming forward, he dropped wearily into a chair and bit off the end of one of his lean cigars.

"Mark," he said with a touch of the vigor that every thought of MacMaugh's engines brought back to him, "we've got a fast boat there. She'll outdo 90 per cent. of the shipping on the river, I honestly believe."

Wallace did not answer at once. When he did speak his voice was dull. "I'm sorry to hear it," he stated.

"What!"

"I said I'm sorry to hear it," Mark repeated, pressing out his voice a little more strongly.

"What the devil's the matter with you?" Huston demanded.

"I'm not interested," said Mark, still dully, "in what sort of performance the boat will turn in for the benefit of your bastard brother."

The beginning of a flush tinted Arnold's cheekbones. "Whipped, are you?"

Wallace glanced at the riverman, and stirred. "There's a point," he answered, with such a flat defeated somberness that Huston cooled, "there's a point beyond which I cannot offset the difficulties which you bring onto us."

"What's happened while I was gone? Are your notes called?"

The faintest sort of bitter smile altered the modelling of Mark's face.

"Look here!" said Huston. "If your financing has been so damned weak that it's collapsed and undermined all the work we've been to, you'd better come out with it!"

"The notes are not called," said Mark distinctly. "I don't know why they're not, or why we're not bankrupt to-day, as the result of your entanglement with Will Huston. Suffice it that I was temporarily able to controvert that. God alone knows how."

Huston opened his mouth to speak, but there were no words there. Mark's face was quiet, his voice was his own; yet there came from him such a conviction of unavoidable defeat, defeat beyond hope, defeat beyond recrimination, that Huston was checked. He was thinking of those steady pulsing engines of the *Arnold Huston*, of her full-powered answer to the pilot's bell, and the ease with which she kicked the river miles away behind her. But beyond that he was thinking of the financial salvation her labors would mean in a time comparatively short, if she were only given that time; and of the river victory whose beginning she was to be.

He told himself that they couldn't get her from him now. She was more than a steamboat, she was a golden stroke of fortune, a victory in herself and a mother of victories. With the *Arnold Huston* under steam, no power that Will could bring to bear could cancel away the income nor the prestige of their fast packet. Yet—there was that finality of defeat in Mark Wallace's figure, in his relaxed hands, in the room itself with its gray shrouding dust.

The possibility occurred to him that Mark was lying down, quitting, as a result of sheer exhaustion. Yet Mark, even more than he, was staking everything on the success of this enterprise. If they lost, Huston would be penniless, with a heavy debt; but he had had little enough to lose. Mark, too, would be penniless, with the makings of a fortune lost, and greater debts than his own.

"Can you raise any money?" Wallace murmured.

"Not a picayune, and you know it, and you've known it from the start!"

The other did not demur. Silence returned to the room, the soft silence of the dust. Huston was gathering himself for a verbal attack, phrasing in his mind what he should say to this man to bring him out of his accursed lethargy. If the situation was as bad as Mark's attitude implied, they needed to thrash it out, set new forces moving, retrench at once for a new and more bitter fight. But before he was ready, Mark spoke a single sentence in such an unexpectedly strong voice that Huston was startled.

"Walt Gunn is dead."

"What?"

Wallace did not repeat.

Huston's momentary surprise did not long engage

his attention. He was thinking not of Walt Gunn's mishaps, but of the future of the *Arnold Huston*. "What has that to do with us?" he asked impatiently.

"Do you mean to say that you don't know?"

"Our contract holds good with his estate, I presume, if you're worryin' about that passel of niggers."

"You mean to say you didn't know that every one of those blacks you've got there is stolen property?"

"Stolen? Those niggers?"

"That's what I said."

"I? Knew it?"

"You understood me."

Huston blazed. "Of course I mean to say that I didn't know it! What sort of fool do you take me for?" A swift suspicion burst upon him. "Wallace, if you sent me there to fetch stolen slaves I'll—"

"You fool, d'you think I'm as short-sighted as that?"

"Well, what's the answer?"

"Gunn's death gave away his game. It means that we haven't a deckhand, a fireman, a cook, or a steward, is all. No, it isn't all. It means that you are implicated for receiving stolen property; and consequently that I am implicated, with the *Arnold Huston* back of us for forfeit."

Huston sat silent for a moment, glaring. Then: "We'll fight, of course. By the time it's been through every court in the land we'll damn well see—"

"Fight with what? Oh, we'll clear our name. A blank reputation is good for something, thank God. Unfortunately, your next slip will find us with no reputation at all. However, I hardly think there will be a next time, in the case of the *Arnold Huston.*"

"Well, if we don't fight, just what the hell are we goin' to do for hands?"

"What are we going to do anyway? You realize, of course, that the law, with a little prompting from the Will Huston interests, will tie the slaves up anyway. Don't deceive yourself that we would have the use of them while the court action dragged through!"

"But—"

"I have no intention of arguing with you. By accepting the situation and handing over the blacks we clear our skirts. Which is exactly what I have guaranteed to do."

"You've guaranteed—" Huston stammered with anger—"you've— D'you think you can give away— Damn you, if you've double-crossed—"

"Now you look here," said Wallace with cold bitterness. "There's a thing or two in this that will stand explaining from your angle. Just exactly what did you find when you last visited Walt Gunn's?"

Mark's narrowed eyes lay against Huston's like razor blades, and Arnold was checked. He considered whether it were worth while to answer this question completely; then contemptuously put aside subterfuge.

"I found desertion," he said.

"What else?" Wallace pressed him.

"What the devil do you expect I found?"

"I think," said Wallace, "that I know you well enough to forecast your actions." Suddenly he whipped out, "You went into Gunn's cabin, did you not?"

"Certainly I did."
"And found there?"
"Nothin'! What'd you think?"
"I thought perhaps," said Mark coolly, "that you might have noticed the corpse of Walt Gunn."
Huston hesitated. "It wasn't in his bed," he stated.
"Gunn, of course, was not murdered in his bed."
"Murdered?"
"Certainly!"
"You said nothin' about murder!"
"You did not perceive," said Mark, "by the appearance of the corpse, that the man had been murdered?"
"I tell you," said Huston, between anger and puzzlement, "I saw no corpse!"
"You were in the cabin?"
"I prob'ly sat there for over an hour."
"In the front room?"
"Certainly."
"Then the remains of Gunn were in the room with you at the time."
"That's—" Huston started to say. There suddenly came back to him with a chilling vividness the cabin in the deserted clearing, the wavering light of the candle, the heavy creaking chair—and, with a gruesome shock, that great shapeless mound of dirty clothes in the corner, hiding the work of a stirring rat—
"Good God!" Huston ejaculated. A shudder passed over him. He almost jumped to his feet, but settled back.
"Hm," said Wallace. "I see you didn't realize what

you were in the presence of. You haven't lied to me as much as I supposed."

Huston let that pass. They sat in silence for a time, while Mark gazed into the faint ebb and swell of the fire's glow.

"Well," said Huston at last. "We'll have to scramble for some more niggers, I suppose."

"We haven't heard the last of it, you know."

"What do you mean?"

"If any one wants to press the case against us, I fancy a very pretty case can be made to show that we have been accessories to nigger stealing. Will Huston will see that it is pressed, trust it."

"But our contract with Gunn—"

"You have it in writing? I thought that in dealing with Gunn—"

"No," Huston conceded, "it isn't in writin'. But surely—"

"Oh, I didn't say the case would hold. Only sap time and money, and increase the instability of our position. It'll just throw the balance, that's all. Our hands are in the trap, my friend."

"I'm damned if they are!"

"Yes?"

"I'll round up another batch of niggers—"

"Can you?"

"By God, I've *got* to!"

Wallace smiled.

"You h'ist up on your end, Mark. Play the game out, man! And if I get the niggers, and you hold out for two months more, the *Arnold Huston* will have earned enough to—"

"If, if!"

"We're not whipped yet!"

Wallace did not answer. Huston waited for further remark until he was tired of it. Sarcastically he said at last, "Is that all?"

"No," said Wallace.

"Well—let's have it." Huston's voice was becoming increasingly ugly.

"Will Huston has purchased our notes."

"You fool," Huston shouted, "why didn't you say so!"

Wallace shrugged contemptuously.

"When?" Arnold demanded.

"To-day."

"What amount?"

"Nearly ten thousand."

They eyed each other blackly until Huston's glare bludgeoned down Wallace's eyes. There was a long silence.

"A wonderful botch you've made of your end of this," Huston said at last. "How much grace can you force out of him?"

"None."

"None? Any court in—"

"If we do get grace he'll tie up the boat with court actions—"

"They'll have to catch her first! We can take to the upper river, or the Ohio. Thirty days' trade would give us—"

"Catch her?" sneered Mark. "You don't know what

you're talking about."

Huston gnawed his lips, and fell silent.

"There is just one chance in the world—no, two chances—of saving ourselves from ruin," Wallace said slowly and intensely. "The first is that you go to Will Huston, conciliate him, concede him whatever it is he wants, apologize to him, and induce him to call off his damned dogs. Reveal your relationship, perhaps—but that's up to you. With that done, our financial situation is clear and the Walt Gunn episode becomes trivial.

"It's the force behind these things, supplied by Will Huston's money and political pressure, that makes them dangerous." Wallace suddenly burst out vehemently, all his slow poise forgotten. "For God's sake, Arn, have you no sense at all? Haven't you any obligation to me? We've got the start of a fortune in that boat—are you going to lose it for both of us in a silly quarrel that doesn't amount to two pins outside of your infernal pride—" Mark's face was white, his eyes glittering.

"You're talkin' rubbish," said Huston.

"You mean that with everything in the balance you wouldn't—"

"No," said Huston.

"To save my fortune and yours, to pave the way for God knows what success—"

"No," said Huston again.

Mark Wallace's tortured eyes blazed at Huston helplessly.

"Your fortune—"

"Nothing of mine will ever be built on the gift of Will Huston," said Arnold.

"Mine, then—"

"Let me tell you somethin' I got from you. 'If ever you stand in my way, I'll break you without—' "

"You're determined to hold to your suicidal—"

"Yes."

"Then," said Mark, suddenly quiet, but whiter still, "there is one other way out."

"That's—?"

"To sell your note to Will Huston."

There was a long silence. When Mark Wallace had looked into Huston's steady steel eyes as long as he could bear, he settled back and lit a cigar with shaking hands.

Then Huston smiled, and a new gleam came into his eyes. "Yeah," he said, "I thought you'd come out with that."

The smile baffled Wallace. "Perhaps," he said ironically, "you failed to grasp the trend of what I was just saying."

"No; you were threatenin' to sell me out to Will Huston. I understood you well enough."

"You thought I was joking, perhaps?"

"No, you were in deadly earnest."

"If you think you have grounds to fight—"

"None at all."

He drew a folded paper from his pocket, and handed it to Mark. "I want you to sign that."

"What is it?"

"That's a ninety-day option on your interest in the

Arnold Huston, at a price of ten thousand dollars."

"It's not the slightest use to you."

"Sign it." Huston rose.

"What the devil do you think you can do with—"

"I've given you your chance," said Arnold, "and I'm sick of you. Now you can take your little fiddlin' profit and get out."

"What makes you think I'll—"

"Because you're yellow to the core, and glad to get out of this with your skin. And because I'm not goin' to pull the chestnuts out of the fire until you do!"

"There's nothing you can do, anyway!"

"No?" Huston's smile was bitter as gall. "I advise you to sign."

"You are a fool," said Mark contemptuously. But he obeyed.

CHAPTER XXV

THOUGH it was after two o'clock when Huston left Mark Wallace's room, he was up at seven, slowly bathing in cold water. He shaved with the utmost care, chose the best shirt that he owned. His eyes were calm, his hands steady and slow. At eight he downed a breakfast consisting of more Creole coffee than food; and at nine thirty, fresh-skinned and assured, he strolled into the office of Will Huston.

Arnold thrust directly into the inner office where, in accordance with the regular habits that were at once his hobby and his leading asset, Will Huston sat reading his mail. He did not look up as Arnold came in.

It was a plainer office than Huston had expected to find. There were no rugs on the floor, no vast open spaces, no row of clerks. The small room was made stuffy by the heavy black walnut cabinets and desk filigreed with pinnacle upon pinnacle of turned and jigsawed wood.

Will sat at a plain table, his papers littered in front of him. His head was bowed, and though he faced the door he appeared not to hear the sound of the latch, for he did not look up. It was such an office, and such an attitude, Arnold thought, as old Dennison Huston would have liked. In exteriors, at least, Dennison had done his work well in the moulding of this son of his that in reality had never been his son.

"Well, you ass?"

At Huston's voice Will looked up suddenly, startled. But the expression that immediately replaced that of surprise was noncommittal except for a certain eye-gleam that bespoke a malicious pleasure.

"To what am I indebted," he began with a beautifully simulated politeness that Huston was forced to admire.

"Why, thank you, I will," Arnold smiled, seating himself. He drew out and lit a cigar like a railroad spike.

"What can I do for you?"

"As we were sayin'," Huston began. "Come to think of it, what were we sayin' the other day on the boat, when you had to rush off? Somethin' about your breakin' me, wasn't it?"

"I've quite forgotten," said Will without expression.

His pale rounded face was politely indifferent. There was a steadiness of eye, Arnold thought, that he had not noted before. Business seemed to be agreeing with Will, now that he had some authority of his own. Agreeing a little too well, perhaps, to judge by the increasing puffiness under Will's chin.

"Seems like to me," said Arnold, "that when you make threats you ought to jot 'em down. Can't carry 'em out if you can't remember 'em."

Will Huston's long full lips formed a smile so like that of their father that a queer sensation ran through Arnold, almost as if his father's ghost had appeared between them.

"I had a burst of temper, perhaps," Will said. "I don't recall what I may have said. Nothing offensive, I hope. If so I will withdraw it, if you like."

The cool hypocrisy of the man surprised Arnold, almost delighted him. He felt a momentary curiosity to see what strain the attitude could bear.

"You guess Caroline Shepherd is safe, then, for the time bein'?"

A swift shadow passed over Will's countenance, as if for an instant Arnold could see into hidden depths of anger, despair, and hate. He was instantly assured that whatever front Will wished to place before himself, the elemental factors beneath remained unchanged.

The shadow passed, leaving Will's face as politely expressionless as before. There was only a shade of stiffness in his voice as he answered, "I'd rather not discuss that."

"I see where you've laid down a trap or two for my

boat," said Arnold.

Will did not conceal that he was slightly annoyed. This was not the way business matters were approached. Arnold knew that as well as Will. Yet it was impossible for him to take a different attitude toward his half-brother after their years of submerged war. It was only open to him to go on, playing this new game in their old way, Will evasively treacherous, Arnold striking directly at the point with a swaggering contempt for the other's reactions.

Will Huston's eyebrows raised in question.

"You know what I'm talkin' about," Arnold grinned.

"I haven't the faintest idea," Will answered.

"But I'm ready to tell you," Arnold went on, "that the fish has slipped through the net. You'll have to come again, old man!"

Will smiled. Knowing the workings of the man's mind, Arnold knew that Will was contemptuous of what appeared to be his shallow bluff. Arnold grinned. "I happen to know that you hold quite a lot of our notes."

"Oh, that," said Will, stirring perfunctorily. "An agent of mine was instructed to acquire a small amount of commercial paper, for investment purposes. Imagine my irritation to find that he had bought some of yours! Ridiculous. A dead loss, I haven't the least doubt."

"You're callin' the notes, of course."

"There is hardly anything else to do. We must take a certain loss—but cover what we can before it is too late," said Will, judicially detached.

"Then why do you say that you didn't try to catch my boat—hadn't any idea of what I was referrin' to?"

"You don't mean," said Will, affecting surprise, "that you have to liquidate the boat in order to cover?"

"You know damned well we can't cover any other way, my little man."

"Really," said Will, smiling. "Now that's too bad!"

"It is, in a way," said Arnold. "She isn't an easy boat to replace. Still, it clears the financial situation."

"Yes?"

"We're lucky," Arnold went on, "to be sellin' the boat high where we bought her low. Even with the notes covered, we'll be able to equip another, of a sort, on a much firmer basis. But—"

"You have a purchaser?"

"Why certainly."

There was a stilted silence. Will's eyes were steady on Huston's face, and by the very texture of the quiet Arnold knew that headway had been gained.

"Your maneuver did one thing for me," he said. "It scared Mark Wallace out. I have his quit claim on payment of what he put into it. Damned glad he was to get out, too. So that the profit necessarily falls to me, in return for my acceptance of the risk."

"Oh, nonsense," said Will, laughing outright. "How could you 'accept a risk'? You couldn't accept a risk to cover the shoes you stand in."

"Would you like to see Wallace's signed agreement?"

"Certainly not. I'm not interested in your antics from any standpoint whatsoever."

"You'll just have to make a guess," said Arnold, "as to whether I'm lyin' or not. If I was you, I would assume that I am."

"I do."

The momentary uncertainty to which Will had been compelled had now dissolved. Inwardly Arnold faltered; yet his grin was no less malicious than the half-smile with which it was returned.

"And now," said Will, "the proposition?" There was in Will's eyes the sensuous keenness with which a cat plays with a mouse.

"Oh," said Arnold, "you knew I had a proposition?"

"Of course," said Will with a contemptuous chuckle. "Otherwise why would you be here?"

"How smart you are," said Arnold, careful that his sarcasm should be devoid of any trace of bitterness. "I do have a proposition."

"I'm waiting to reject it."

"You're a fool," answered Arnold brazenly, "if you don't."

"Then why do you offer it?"

"Because that's exactly what I take you for."

Will flipped the pencil in irritation. "Come, come, you're wasting my time," he complained. "Why are you here?"

"I'm a pig," said Huston gratuitously.

"I realized that."

Arnold grinned, and put the grin away, its service done. But for a few moments he retained a slight smile, as the gray steel of his eyes became shrewd, boring into Will Huston's.

"I'm not satisfied with my profit, so long as there is a chance for more. It happens that I know you almost as well as you think you know me. You possess one good trait that I know of, which your best efforts have failed to suppress." He paused.

"And that is?" Will's lurking smile of anticipation returned.

"Not generosity to the fallen," said Arnold, "like you thought I was goin' to say. There aren't any fallen. But you're a gambler. A trait that gets you into trouble and therefore compels my admiration."

"Yes?"

"You have one fairly fast boat," said Huston. "That's the *Elizabeth Grey.* My own boat—"

"*Your* own boat?"

"I'm speakin' for Mark Wallace as well as myself. He's goin' out of steamboatin'."

"Well?"

"I thought you might like to own a faster boat than the *Elizabeth Grey.*"

"Faster than the *Galloping Betsy*? Your old tub, I suppose? This is rich!" Will laughed insolently, but with a genuine enjoyment. "Go on, say it! For a slight advance over and above your notes, you'll sell me the *Arnold Huston*, letting down the other buyer, won't you? Yes, like hell!"

"Like hell is right," said Arnold.

"Well, I won't buy—"

"You haven't the chance."

"Good! Hahahaha—" Will's enjoyment of what he conceived was Arnold's last play exceeded all bounds.

"I started to say," Arnold went on, "that the *Huston* can beat the *Grey* to Memphis with a five-hour handicap. And we'll bet our boat against the *Grey*—"

"You'll what!" Will Huston was brought to consideration at last.

"We'll give you a match race, winner to take both boats!"

"You're crazy!"

A certain confusion in Will's eyes told Arnold that the man was hastily trying to compute what this new possibility might mean to himself. The game was in the balance. As Will Huston decided, so the cards would fall.

As a silence came between them, Arnold felt suddenly that his plan, which had seemed so brilliantly daring to him upon its conception, was only a pitiful subterfuge, hopeless, an obvious last resort. Will Huston already had them in his pocket; why should he risk their escape now?

Then, with swift acceleration of the pulse, he saw that his half-brother had taken the other line. Watching him keenly, understanding the man to the core, he could almost check off Will's ideas one by one as they went through the other's head. If the notes he held put Wallace and Arnold Huston under, how much worse would they be broken if the value of their boat were also subtracted? If indeed they had obtained a buyer who would pay an exorbitant price—by no means impossible—it meant that they might slip through his fingers altogether. The doubt that Huston's poker face had instilled was, after all, getting in its work.

Arnold's heart suddenly gave a great bound. Into Will's face was coming a new smile, the smile of a man who has had his enemy delivered into his hands with a completeness beyond all expectation or reason. Even before Will spoke, Arnold knew that he had learned the time of the *Arnold Huston* in her up-river stages, that no doubt for an instant entered Will's head that his *Galloping Betsy* could swim circles around Huston's aged boat, let the mishaps fall as they might!

"We'll just put that in writing," said Will, drawing paper toward him.

On the spur of the moment Arnold daringly pushed his success.

"I'll want odds, of course," he said reservedly.

"Odds?"

"You'll have ten thousand additional upon the *Grey*."

"In addition to the boat herself? Ridiculous." Will flung down the pen he had caught up.

Arnold rose. "Oh, well—no bet, if you don't want it."

Will reluctantly picked up the pen again. After all, it was not as if he had believed there were a possibility for him to lose. "Have it your own way!"

CHAPTER XXVI

THE Mississippi swept around its bends with a strong swing and pull, the river under the boats and the river in Huston's blood. He strode down the dark Rue Chartres lightly, with only the slightest hint in his long-legged walk of the swagger that is never quite separable from Irish blood. He was fresh from a full twelve-hour sleep, though he had been dog-tired before that. They had made another trip to Memphis since Arnold had caught Will Huston in the wager that was to be the salvation of their boat. He had insisted on the prerogative of that last trip before the race, and Will, eager in his belief that his relative was under the heel at last, had been forced to concede.

Huston and Arthur MacMaugh had made a long trip of it, laying up twice for engine work. At Baton Rouge, on the downstream run, they had lain over for days, and had had the engines down until hardly a bolt and nut had remained together. Then, with the complete assurance that she was right, they had slowly drifted her down to New Orleans, refusing passengers, hardly more than dipping her paddle buckets in the current. More than three thousand miles of travel since the engine installation had taken the stiffness out of her. The iron monsters in the engine room were working effortlessly; even MacMaugh's rockbound face showed a glow of anticipatory pride.

Above all, they had assured themselves of the *Arnold Huston*'s upstream speed. MacMaugh's final verdict was in, more assuring to Arnold than his own: "She'll never fail us; she'll do it, man! . . . If God wills. . . ."

He had been unable to see Jacqueline again before the hasty departure on that upstream trip, though he had three times gone to knock at that great arched gate in the Rue Chartres. The black wizened face at the wicket had turned him away each time. He had been forced to content himself by sending her no less than four laboriously composed notes within twenty-four hours. It might have worried him that he received no reply; but he had other things to worry about then.

They had labored longer than they had expected at Baton Rouge, with the result that as they at last made the levee before the New Orleans Place d'Armes it was dusk on the eve of the race. Huston, wakened from daylight sleep by the ringing of the final bells, ate dinner alone, while MacMaugh returned to his engines and his grease. The engineer contemplated taking down that water-feeding "doctor" again, to scrape and tinker at some minor bearing that another man would have been glad to let alone.

The stars were out as Huston went ashore, turning his steps directly to Jacqueline's home. In the morning the boat of his name was to begin her great effort, the long grind that was to establish them once and for all, and so clear the path to greater things.

He left behind him a steady seethe of labor on the *Arnold Huston.* The slaves that he had obtained from Walt Gunn were gone, held in idleness, most of them, while litigation sought to assort them among owners who had not seen the play of their muscles in many a long day. In their places labored a new picked crew, "free men of color," most of them borrowed from the captains or owners of other steamboats. Huston still had friends on the river, men who would put themselves out of their way to help him in a pinch.

The new borrowed gangs were working in long files,

unloading the cargo of slow freight that the *Huston* had brought down from Baton Rouge. They trotted, bent under their burdens, in long lurching strides timed to the jouncing spring of the stage plank, big hands flopping, heels flung out on every step. The negroes whose job it was to lift the heavy burdens to the shoulders of the others sang at their work. Long after Huston had left the boat he could hear one great baritone voice that must have rung far up and down the river: "Come a long way! . . . Come a long way!" A rhythmic cry, timing the heave of the load, falling into that steadier rhythm of the broad bare feet on the plank. . . .

It followed after him, that careless negro voice, melodious and strong, expressive of brute strength, and the joy in strength. Somehow like the voice of the Mississippi, like the voice of his steamboat, now gathering herself to churn the heart out of her in his behalf. After he could hear the singing rhythmic voice no more he found there was going through his brain a song the roustabouts had sung in the loading at Baton Rouge, an improvised song, without rhyme or fixed text, full of repetitions and a jogging, jouncing refrain, timed to the lilt of the stage plank and the black bare feet:

"Steamboat *Arn Huston*,
She haht made out ob arn,
Big ol' arn gizzard,
Big ol' arn lights,
Gwine a-whoopin' up de ribba
Fo' to beat de hot-foot *Betsy*,
Come along you niggas to de promis' lan'!

"Steamboat *Arn Huston*,
She haht all gol' an' arn,
Golden arn gizzard,
Golden arn lights.
See dem whoopin' niggas
On de Hot-uh Foot-uh *Betsy*!
Ain't a gwine a git dah,
'Cause she ain't got time!"

In his stride there was the resilient swing of the youth that was still his. Never in his life had Huston been happier than he was to-night in the opposed lights of love and coming battle, with his future wavering in the balance and his fortune more than ever an uncertain thing.

He knocked lightly at the great gate of the house in which Jacqueline lived, and almost instantly the little iron door behind the grilled wicket flicked back, revealing the wizened face, dim beneath the glint of the bald black head.

"Huston," he said.

There was that momentary rattle of bars behind the small door in the great one, and he was let in. As he stepped over the foot-high threshold of that tiny door a pulse of emotion undermined the rigid mood of war in which his absent interval had been lived. On the up-river trip Jacqueline had been to him a constant warmth within, a beacon light of promised things; yet she had seemed distant, somehow, her voice half lost to him in the constant driving demands of his toils. The turmoil that his father had predicted for him had increased about him, partly drowning out the overtones of his beloved dream. But as he stepped into the great flagged hallway he felt suddenly the nearness of her again; and he was near to being overcome by the realization that she was here, and he was to see her again, and hear her voice.

The door above was held open for him by the slave; and as he entered he hardly dared lift his eyes lest they find Jacqueline not there, and the room as empty and meaningless as all places without her had come to be. Then he saw her standing near the middle of the room, leaning on the table of the lamp, and his heart leaped—and fell.

She seemed infinitely tired as she stood there, her figure drooped and somehow worn. There were dark smudges under the faintly slanted eyes in a face always pale, but paler now than he had ever seen it before. She was more than ever like a drawing in delicate pencil, with the eyes brushed in with black ink. And in her dark eyes he read such an inexpressible despair that for an instant the life went out of him, as if steam that moved him upcurrent had suddenly died away. He recovered himself immediately.

"Jacqueline!" he cried out. "What is it?"

She yielded to him as he swept her into his arms. Once more, as when they had last parted, he kissed her eyes, her cheeks, her hair. She leaned nervelessly against him, supported by his arms.

"In God's name, Jacqueline, tell me what's happened!"

It was moments before she answered him; and

when she spoke she only said: "I knew you would be here soon. I saw the *Huston* go down-river to her landing, and I listened to her whistle. I could hear her bells tinkle; it almost seemed to me I could hear your voice. . . ."

He remained silent, holding her close, clumsily comforting her with his hands. When at last he drew his breath to question her again she startled him by suddenly crying out: "I can't tell you!"

"But—"

"I can't, I can't!"

"If you'll only tell me what it is, I'll—"

"There's nothing on the living earth that you or anyone can do."

He tried to answer her and found himself wordless, checked by the finality of her tone. Looking suddenly up into his face she saw, unbelievably, the most incongruous thing she had ever known; the gray eyes filled with tears. The answering tears welled into her own. Trembling, she hid her face against his coat.

"Oh my dearest," she cried, suddenly clinging to him, "you must love me so!"

"This will work out," said Arnold. "When we've whipped Will Huston's *Gallopin' Betsy*, nothin' will be able to stop us, nothin' on the river or any place else. If you can't tell me what's hurt you, that's all right. But we'll beat this thing—"

She slowly shook her head. "I can't see you any more. You must never come here again."

"Jacqueline!"

"It's true. You—"

"I'll accept no such circumstance," he told her calmly. "I'm not to be turned aside."

They were silent. Her voice presently came to him small and muffled.

"There is one thing you can do that I will bless you for."

"Name it."

"We have only a little while left to us; perhaps a quarter of an hour more. Be kind to me, tell me that you love me. For just this little while let's forget everything, and pretend that it's to be forever."

He wanted to tell her that it was to be forever, but he felt that he must humor her until she should be less weary and distraught. He bowed his head.

Below and beyond the river window where they sat spread the quilted pattern of the roofs, their slopes and counter slopes reflecting with varying radiance the little light of the sickle moon. Beyond that, the pale pilot houses of the levee-nosing steamboats rose like watch towers before the red and green riding lights of half-seen ships. Under the still-riding ships Huston could sense the invisible Mississippi's turgid current, wheeling the broad flood around the bends with a strong swing and pull. A grave sadness was upon them; yet they were happy for a little while. . . .

Jacqueline suddenly sprang to her feet, wrenching herself from his arms.

In the next few moments no reasonable thought found time to trace its way through Huston's mind. For an instant he stood beside her, his arms pressed against his sides, seeking to snatch some explanation of her movement from her face. His eyes jerked away to follow her terror-stricken gaze and saw only the gray masking curtain of the farther door from which she had always appeared. As he looked, the gray folds moved ever so slightly, no more than as if they had been touched by a faint breath; and then hung still.

Huston's thin lips drew back from his teeth. It was pure instinct that made him vault the settee, charge across the room, and dash the curtain aside.

The elbow of an unlit passageway opened before him, empty, black. Its emptiness mocked him as for an instant he stood and listened. From the throat of the passage, like the touch of a whisper, came the faint sound of a retreating step.

Jacqueline's cry rang in his ears as his sudden burst of fury carried him into the narrow-walled dark. He ran cat-footed, on the balls of his feet, his hands in front of him to find the turn of the wall. One of his hands made a motion toward the shoulder holster, but checked as he remembered, even in his madness, that it was not there.

The passageway angled twice, and let him into a high hallway, dimly lit. On either side were evenly spaced white doors, silent and fixed, as if they had never been opened since time began. From the far end of the hall a narrow curved stairway led up into impenetrable dark. He was forced to pause, listening for a sound that might indicate which way he must go.

From the stairway came the sound of climbing feet, regular, plodding, without haste or stealth. In the baffling dimness at the upper bend of the stair his searching eyes imagined a slowly moving shadow, seen momentarily before it merged itself with the blackness above. Not running now, but with long quick strides, Huston gained the stairs and went up them three at a time. Under an unseen door in the musty blackness of the upper hall there showed a dim crack of light.

His shoulder crashed against the panels as his hand found and twisted the knob. The unlocked door shuddered as it swung wide. Huston stopped, breathless, and stood swaying on widespread legs; and a terrible cold chill went over him at what he saw.

Behind a heavy oaken table a figure sat with casually crossed legs. Across the middle of the face, flat where the nose should have been, lay a black silk bandage such as had come away in Huston's fingers once before. The fish-cold eyes pressed unfaltering and expressionless against his, and the full lips below the mask stirred in an odd smile.

Huston sickened under the disgust and horror of his discovery. The heat of his fury died in the chill, but beneath his revulsion he was as hard as if he had been a tool in the hands of powers outside of himself. His baffled mind conceived but one idea clearly: that this mysterious, unbelievable menace with the death's-head face must be destroyed, done away with forever.

The fighting part of him was trying to decide swiftly what his move should be. The position of the man's arms suggested that there might be a pistol in the hands hidden by the table's edge, but he was undeterred by that. He took a slow step forward, a creature of instinct without plan, moved only by the feeling that it was necessary to get closer before he should strike. The death's head spoke, its voice formless and blurred.

"Well, Captain Huston?"

"I think," Huston heard his own ironic voice say, "you have the advantage of me."

As Huston advanced another slow stride the muffled, noseless voice answered, "Your conclusion is correct."

There was a step at the door, and the rustle of full-billowing skirts. He knew that Jacqueline was at his shoulder.

"Want to explain yourself?" Huston said steadily, moving closer again as he spoke. Two paces more—

The death's head laughed, a laugh as blurred and noseless as its voice. Huston advanced a step.

He felt Jacqueline's fingers on his arm; then suddenly she was between them, her back to the table, her eyes dark slanting slits in her white face.

"What are you doing?" she demanded in a voice so cold and low that he could not believe that it was hers.

"What—" he gasped. He stood staring at her, utterly dazed. He collected himself with a supreme effort to say, "Who is this man?"

"He is my husband—DuMoyne."

In the silence that followed all the reality of his surroundings dropped away from him, as if he had come to the climax of an impossibly evil dream. He swirled, lost in bottomless space, out of touch with all reasonable things. He struggled to recover himself, groping for understanding. His eyes searched her face and found nothing there that was akin to what had gone before.

"You mean—"

"I mean that you are the intruder here."

The moment of silence was ended by that hideously soft, muffled laugh. "I've had enough of you," DuMoyne said. "Now get out!"

The red despairing wrath surged up into Huston again, and he raised his hand to thrust Jacqueline aside, to fling himself upon the monster beyond. But his hand fell away again, and he stood bewildered.

"Madame DuMoyne and I understand each other," said the noseless voice. "You are quite superfluous here."

"Do you expect me to—" Huston began.

Jacqueline answered: "I expect you to do exactly as he said: get out!"

"How can I leave you with this—"

"Get out!"

He desperately searched her face for a contradiction of her words, then turned and sought the darkness of the hall. Somehow he found the dim well of the stair.

CHAPTER XXVII

THE wizened guardian of the lower gate peered at him curiously as he swung open the small door for Huston to pass out, but the riverman did not see. He stepped slowly over the high-timbered threshold of the door in the gate, his muscles moving as if against their will. He wanted to rush out, to go plunging away, escaping the horror of the house that no longer held anything for him except disaster; but he was unable to stir his limbs to haste.

His heel caught on the high threshold, so that he stumbled. Then he leaned in the corner of the gate, in the very shadows where he had first seen the grotesque figure of DuMoyne—and laughed. The bitter laughter welled out of him peal upon peal through the throat that had laughed so easily all his life, until he could only gasp and suck in deep breaths of the misty river air to satisfy the exhausted shudder in his chest. And with that done he strode off hatless up Chartres, his gait loose-muscled and swaggery, without a thought for where he went.

There must have been a glint of that crazy laughter in his eyes when he rolled at random into some water-front saloon, for at the sight of him a group of rivermen, nondescript officers of nondescript boats, burst into a genial cheer.

"Cap'n Huston of the *Huston*, by God!" roared a liquory voice.

"Toughest damned skipper of the fastest damned boat that ever—"

"Up with the *Huston*! To hell with the *Betsy Grey*!"

The race between the *Arnold Huston* and the *Elizabeth Grey* for both boats or nothing had been the leading fuel for argument all night. Half a dozen of his acquaintances and friends, all looking alike to him to-night, rushed to drag him forward with rough, friendly hands. They were half-seas over already, most of them; the whiteness about Arnold's mouth assured them that he was the same. He let them haul him up to the bar, grinning back at them with a show of teeth that passed for good-humor. He cared nothing for what he did or how he might appear.

"Hooray fer Huston of the *Huston*!" There were answering bawls.

Some drunkard of other alliances recklessly raised his voice in behalf of the captain of the *Grey*.

"Hooray fer Sawkes of the *Betsy*!"

"And a rope to hang him!" shouted another.

"Who said that?"

"Me!" three voices instantly answered. A thundering brawl began in the middle of the floor, went muddling and thumping toward the door, and swiftly ended with the ejection of the staggering miscreant. A maudlin figure or two rolled in the sawdust, fumbled up, and reeled back to the support of the bar.

A tall tumbler of whisky was poured for him, and he gulped it down. It was not the last. As the vertiginous warmth of the liquor rose to his brain he laughed with the others, joked uproariously, slapped backs, sang. Then in a brief silence in which they paused to raise glasses to their lips, the death's-head face swam before his eyes again, crossed by a black silk bandage where the nose should have been. It leered at him over the tiny pool of his whisky glass, freezing the unnatural laughter on his lips.

He disentangled himself from the drunken rivermen presently, under circumstances which he never remembered. Indeed, there was little in the next few hours that he could ever again recall.

He remembered afterward that a thick figure of a man with a blurred face and sharp glittering eyes had stepped near him in some other saloon, somewhere along the levee front. He could see the big red mouth, blaring words.

"A-hey, Huston! Pretty sick, ay? Wish the *Betsy* was safe on a mud-bar, ay? Ha, ha, ha, ha—"

He stood staring at the man, with what sort of an expression he never knew. He was trying to make out the man's features, the truth of the matter was. He didn't know why he was presently moving toward the thick figure, nor what his intentions were. But the man spoke hasty apologies, and, glancing back warily over his shoulder, lost himself in the crowd.

Again, in some half-deserted bar, he remembered that the bartender had dared pour his second drink for him after Huston had slopped the counter pretty thoroughly in pouring his first. He dashed the whisky glass into the bartender's face, wrenched the bottle from a fat hand, and went lurching out. Someone opposed him at the door, mouthing something about the color of his money. Huston swung the bottle at the man's head, smashing it against the jamb of the door. Then he walked out into the night, unchallenged.

Sometimes he was aware that a group in some hazy bar was looking at him curiously. Sometimes a man followed him with his eyes, and muttered to a neighbor behind his hand. Fixed lights swirled and moiled before his eyes. Within, the black desolation lay undiminished—grew, if that were possible—and the horror of it remained undulled.

Burning sickish liquor, hopeless emptiness of crowded places, reeling lights, blurred vacant faces, lurching steps, meaningless moving forms. Jacqueline . . . where have you gone? . . . Cold desolate madness, a leering death's-head face. . . .

It was beyond midnight. Where his insensate feet had guided him he had not cared. If he had consciously sought any certain place, it is doubtful if they would have carried him there. He didn't recall going down the slant of the cobbled levee, nor lurching across the stage plank of his boat, with those borrowed niggers shuffling out of his way. He was there, though, in his stateroom on the *Arnold Huston*, the boat of his name.

There were faces about him in the light of his lamp. Tommy Craig was there, and the three clerks, the open-mouthed steward, both watchmen, and a smudged engine striker from below. Well-known faces, all of them, yet strangely unfamiliar, too. He sat sprawled with dangling arms, staring at them senselessly from under his brows.

"Jee-*eez*us!" said a voice. "What a bun *he's* got on!"

"Tighter'n a drum."

"Paralyzed."

"Peetrified!"

"Shut up!" snapped Tommy Craig. "Captain Huston!" he called, tentatively, as a man calls into the dark. There was no answer. Craig with blasting oaths herded out the crowd that had bulged in the door to stare, and slammed the door. "Hey, you! Come to life, will you, Huston!"

He shook Arnold roughly by the shoulders without eliciting reply.

"Fer God's sake what's the matter with you? Is the bet off?"

Craig shook him again, this time with all his strength.

"Off what?" said Huston thickly.

Tommy Craig stepped back in despair. He flung open the door, and the steward, who had leaned his ear too heavily against it, tumbled in. Craig brought him upright by the collar.

"Here, you! Gimmy gallon o' black coffee. Dick! Dip up a bucket o' water! Two-three buckets!"

" 'Tain't no use. He's peetrified. You'll never bring *him* to!"

"It's a God damned lie! I've got to."

They loitered. "You'll never—"

Tommy Craig leaped at them, sending the nearest of them reeling with his fist. He turned furiously upon the others, but they were on their way. Savage with a night's overwork and worry, Craig returned to Huston. "Now, you cheap rumhound!"

With two or three wrenches that spared no buttons Craig stripped Huston to the waist. He got one of Huston's arms over his shoulder, and half led, half carried his captain to the deck. The buckets he had called for were ready now. He lifted one of them as if it had been a cup, and forced Huston to drink until he choked. Then he flung Huston on his stomach over the rail of the guards, and with one hand forced into his throat emptied him as if he had been an old sack.

Pulling him inboard again he jammed the captain's back against the rail, held him by the belt, and three times smashed him across the face with his open hand. Huston's head went up, and the first light of fire came into his eye.

"Now," Craig commanded, "let fly with them buckets."

They "let fly" gladly enough, putting the zest into it that underlings always feel in any temporary humiliation of one superior to them in command. Four buckets of cold water poured over Huston's head and naked torso, silvery cascades of liquid ice. Huston gasped, spluttered, shook his head, and flung Craig back; but he let the mate lead him back to his stateroom.

"That coffee ready?"

Coffee was always ready, a great hot boiler of it on the galley stove in which the fires never entirely died. Craig, having slammed the door again in the faces of the crew, scrubbed his captain with a rough towel. When he had got half a quart of coffee into him, bitter black, Huston shook his head, and grinned like a man coming out of sleep.

"Well, are you there?" demanded Craig at last.

"Seem to be."

"Then for God's sake," burst out the youngster, "tell me over again how you want this thing ballasted!"

Huston smiled. Craig's terrific earnestness made him repentant and ashamed.

"I guess I misunderstood you," Craig rushed on. "When I come to load her like you said, it seemed like all the strain come in one place and her nose rode as high as ever."

Huston got paper and pencil, and with shaking hands drew diagrams. His brain was far from clear, and he was shivering under the damp towel with which his shoulders were draped; but the explanations that the mate wanted came steadily enough. The points in question were fixed things in his mind, deeply staked there by the long study he had given them. They discussed the ballasting until Craig understood. It took about fifteen minutes for that.

"Why didn't you ask MacMaugh?" said Huston when it was done. "He knows that stuff better than I do."

"MacMaugh has the whole guts of her apart," Craig told him. "He told me to see you, he didn't have time." The young man added, "If I was you I'd go check up on that old boy—if you're able. Don't look to me like he's goin' to have her ready to go."

Huston smiled again, sardonically. He could picture himself checking up on MacMaugh. "Well, is that all?"

"Well—here's a letter for you." He produced it as an afterthought, and handed it to the captain. It was addressed in Mark's hand.

"Wait a minute," said Huston.

He ripped the envelope, rubbed his eyes with his fingers, leaned close to the light, and read:

WELL ARN, OLD MAN:

Jacqueline tells me that you know about DuMoyne now. I have known of his return for weeks, though he did not actually intrude himself until to-day. I gather that she treated you rather brutally. She wants you to know that she was sorry to do that, but you were on the point of making a corpse of yourself, or words to that effect, for DuMoyne was armed.

This thing has been a good deal of a nightmare to me, as you can very well imagine. It excuses, I think, my rather uncertain mood lately and my apparent loss of interest in the boat.

I am fighting DuMoyne to-night, and will appreciate your attendance as my second, inasmuch as the arrangements, while a little out of the ordinary, are of a conclusive nature. The messenger who brings this will bring you to where I am.

I realize that you have had something of a shock, and I beg of you that you try to pull yourself together enough to win this race with the *Galloping Betsy.* Now that the uncertainty of the thing is over, you should be able to see that there is nothing so frightfully extraordinary about a man's getting hit in the nose with a knife.

Ever your obedient servant,

W.

Huston raised his eyes to Tommy Craig. "Where's the man that brought this?"

"It wasn't a man, it was a nigger. He—"

"Where is he?"

"I'm tellin' you, damn it!" The old hero-worshipping Craig was gone, leaving only a habit of obedience and an impatience to get at his job. "He left."

"What!"

"He left, I said!"

"What do you mean, sir!" The thickness went out of Huston's tongue, and a familiar fire kindled in his eyes. "What business had you, sir, dismissin' my niggers?"

"He wasn't—" began Craig sullenly.

"You stand up to me, sir?" Huston blazed. The youngster's tune changed.

"I didn't know you wanted him," he said.

"How long ago did he leave?"

"Nearly an hour, sir."

"You don't know where he went, I suppose?"

"I ain't any idea, sir."

"What the devil did he look like? Had you ever seen him before?"

"No, sir. He was dressed somethin' like a house nigger, and he had a broad nose, and thick lips—"

"Bah! Get out of the way!"

Craig jumped to the door. "Is that all you want of—"

"Go on to your work!"

Huston followed him out, putting on his shirt and coat as he went. Hatless and dishevelled, but with the color coming back to his cheekbones, he strode up into the town.

CHAPTER XXVIII

THE cool breath of the river was in the town, faintly rimy with the mist that rose almost nightly from the Mississippi. It cooled Huston's blood as he walked, so that his step quickened and his sluggish veins stirred to new life. The drunken moil of despair was past, behind him like a mucky river bar over which a boat has floundered into clear water again.

He was returning to himself, though the dark mood remained even when all heat had gone. He was cool and possessed, far less fatigued than he had thought. The greatest change that the night had brought him was that his mind was functioning shallowly, as if a blank wall stood where before he had perceived depths of mysterious beauty and hope.

He reached the house in the Rue Royale where Mark Wallace had his rooms, and obtained admittance at the lower gate. Rapidly he climbed the steep winding stair into the unlit blackness under the eaves. The door of Mark Wallace's study was locked, and there was no answer to his knock. Without hesitation he burst in the door with his shoulder and struck a light.

Dust, dust over everything in the narrow familiar room, over the walls of books, the bronze bust on the chimneypiece, the unlit shade of the lamp. Across the floor a water roach as big as a mouse fled silently, out of dust into dust beyond. On the tabouret a pipe spilled its ashes into the open pages of a book printed in some unfamiliar tongue. Huston struck a second match, searching for some message that might tell him where the owner had gone. There was nothing, though, to so much as indicate that Wallace had been in the room since Huston had last seen him there.

Huston swore, and returned to the street. Systematically, with a conscientious thoroughness rather than a hope of success, he set out to search for Mark Wallace. Since the negro messenger had returned without him, Wallace had probably procured a substitute second. He therefore first sought certain men whom he thought it likely that Mark would choose. A round dozen men were routed out of their beds that night to greet a tousle-headed figure, clothes rumpled and tie askew. They were unanimous in their ignorance of the whereabouts of Mark Wallace; unanimous, too, in the opinion as they went grumbling back to their beds that Captain Huston was maudlin drunk on the eve of the race that was to decide his fortune.

He made the rounds of the livery stables next. At the first he hired a saddle horse from a reluctant stable hand who, though suspicious of both Huston's identity and his mission, finally let him have a decrepit beast in exchange for cash in advance. In response to his questions, designed to find out whether Wallace and DuMoyne had left the city streets by road or water, he obtained stares of curiosity and avowals of ignorance wherever he went.

He decided that they had gone off by water, probably. It was hopeless, if that were the case. The all-night coming and going on the levee made all inquiry futile. Remembering the manner in which DuMoyne had fought before, in a deserted house somewhere on the bayous, he went with little hope to the lugger basin, and learned nothing from the watchmen there.

All this took time, and his soberness was an aging reality as his search neared what promised to be a futile end. Toward the last of it he had begun to feel, as the result of his very efforts, that he had desired intensely to be with Wallace, rendering him whatever aid he could. After all, in spite of their quarrels and the parting of the ways which they had reached and separately passed, Mark Wallace was at heart his friend, one of the oldest and most valued he had known. A great proportion of the affection Huston had once held for Wallace came furtively back now that Mark was in the presence of what might be his death.

A terrible sense of mystery and desolation increased about him as he galloped those empty narrow streets without result. It was as if the antagonists had disappeared utterly by some hidden means which he, perpetually doomed to be uninitiate, could not know.

It was curious, and yet typical of the new shallowness of his guiding mind, that while he sought with increasing desperation for some remote clue, the thought of going to the house of Jacqueline DuMoyne occurred to him last. He swore at his obtuseness when this most obvious of all expedients came to him. The night was old by then. Even as he flogged the listless mount to a renewed effort Huston felt that he was too late, that there was no longer any reason why he should go to the place that should have been first in his thoughts.

He hauled the aged animal to a sliding stop before the house in the Rue Chartres, and left it with the reins on its neck. Then he sprang across gutter and banquette to the arched gate. He struck the little door in the great gate heavily with his foot, to rouse the old man within; and under the impact of his boot the unbarred door swung wide.

He stepped unaccosted into the vaulted carriageway, where a smudgy lantern with an untrimmed wick still burned.

"Hallo!" he shouted. "Hi there!" and loudly shook the bar of the door.

His voice reverberated hollowly in the passage, in the courtyard beyond; but there was no answer, nor so much as the stir of an answering foot.

He strode forward over the flags, the ring of his heels echoing from the vaulted stone above. An ugly anger came into his movements, attesting to the waking of emotions that had three hours before seemed dead. As the black courtyard opened before him he stopped and raised his voice again. The feeble yellow rays of the smoky lantern were powerless to penetrate the dark, but the sky seemed less black than he had thought. By its faint light he could partly make out architectural forms, the black cave-mouthed arches where the stables were, and the galleries before the slave quarters. It was to these last that he angrily turned his voice.

"Well," he shouted, "are you going to let anybody come and go that wants to?"

Silence, complete, unwhispering. Not even the guilty creak of a negro's cot. Unreasoning, he strode across the courtyard and ran up the flimsy stairs to the pigeon-loft slave quarters above the stables. He kicked open the nearest door.

"Come out of it!" he snapped. "Move, now!"

No answer. He swung up the lantern and stepped in.

It was vacant of human life. He grunted and stepped on to the next.

The house of Jacqueline DuMoyne had once been a pretentious establishment, and the quarters for slaves were many. Two layers of small rooms, the second and third floors above the stables, ran around three sides of the courtyard's well, their walls joining to the house in front. He explored them rapidly, a glance sufficing for most. Many were storage rooms now, padlocked from without, and that saved time. A few held the stuffy warm odors of recent occupation; all were empty now.

Huston stood on the top gallery at last, and stared across the court at the fanlighted windows of the house, dark and still. A cold fear touched his face with damp hands. Where were the slaves? Certainly not in the silent brooding house. Some terror had come upon them, so sudden and so great that they had forgotten all consequences and loyalties, and fled. To that superstitious race a glimpse of the death's-head face would have been enough to accomplish that. Its effect had been to leave Jacqueline without so much as a black man's hand to be raised in her defense.

His anger rose, mingling with that increasing fear. The blank wall in his mind crumpled like a curtain dropped by a breaking string. A great rush of remorse overwhelmed him as he saw what he had done. DuMoyne was a maniac, for all he knew, warped in mind by his ghastly deformity. She had stepped out of Huston's arms, turned, and used a pathetic subterfuge to shield him from danger; he had left her with the knife-maimed man. Mark Wallace might have been dead these many hours if his written account of the situation meant anything. Where was DuMoyne, and where was she?

He rushed down the flimsy wooden stairs, across the courtyard to the house, and up to the second floor, calling her name. He strode madly through the echoing rooms, fearing unguessed horrors to be revealed behind every door. Leaving the second floor half-searched he took the curved dark stair leading to the top floor, and went driving into the room where DuMoyne and Jacqueline had last been seen.

Nothing there, no sign. He ransacked the entire top floor, finding only echoes and dust. If at any instant an insane figure with a noseless face had flung upon him out of the dark he would have been unsurprised, yet for himself he was devoid of fear. The terror that stiffened his throat was for Jacqueline alone, for his beautiful one that he had so lately held safe in his arms and now was lost to him in the ominous mystery of the silence and the dark.

He returned to the second floor, searching anew. Not a room, not a closet remained closed to him now. Their dark caverns made his voice sound hollow and terrible as he called her name. He came to a locked door, and using his shoulder as a ram, smashed it open, splintering the wood about the lock. For a moment he paused on the threshold, trying to steady the jerk of his ragged nerves.

The shadowy room he had opened exhaled a faint fragrance that instantly made his blood leap. He had not noticed that she had used a perfume, yet now that it came to his nostrils it made the memory of her poignantly vivid.

"Jacqueline!" he cried again; and raising the lantern high he pressed into the dark, dreading what he might find there.

It was her room. Her bed was there, untouched. His eyes ran hastily over the furniture, the rich and dainty things that had had the infinite privilege of living intimately with her. There was no closet, only a massive carved armoire. But forcing himself to leave no possibility unprobed, he opened that. Like everywhere else he had looked, it was devoid of any sign of evil, or of news.

A delicate silk garment brushed the back of his hand. He paused to touch it with his fingers, held by the feeling that it bore an intimate kinship because it had been close to her. He was thinking that this soft thing of silk had once rested within the curve of his arms, had been warm under his hand. Suddenly he gathered it between his palms and buried his face in its folds. . . .

CHAPTER XXIX

HE stepped out through the little door in the great gate at last, at once relieved and hopeless in the certainty that nothing further was to be learned within. The sky was graying with the approach of dawn. The faces of the buildings across the street, that had been only black hulks before, were beginning to show contour and detail, patterned in blocked tones of gray. He realized that it must be five o'clock. The horse he had ridden was gone.

He leaned once more in the corner of the gate. At six o'clock the *Arnold Huston* and the *Elizabeth Grey* were to start their long upstream grind that was to change the ownership of a steamboat and decide the fortunes of Huston and Wallace. He could not, he told himself, go with his steamboat now, leaving his search unfinished. Yet there was work to be done.

He walked to the moorage of the *Arnold Huston* and paused for a moment at the top of the levee. All up and down the river front figures moved in the bustle preparatory to the starting of boats. Before the *Arnold Huston* a small throng was gathering, drawn by news of the race.

She lay white in the gray of the dawn, his boat that he had worked for and loved. His eye ran over her clean strong lines, smooth, compact, balanced. The *Elizabeth Grey* had pulled in alongside in a berth readily conceded by a neighboring boat in honor of the race that was soon to commence. The rival boat was bigger than the *Huston*, with bluff square lines, tall and rugged. She towered over the lesser boat: bigger paddleboxes, wider guards, greater stacks, bigger everything. Her scrubbed paint was older and duller, so that she looked like a great veteran of a boat that was about to put a young upstart in its place.

A gaunt skeletonesque look about the *Grey* immediately caught Huston's eye. He suddenly raised an eyebrow as he saw that not a door nor a window on the

Elizabeth Grey contained a panel or a fragment of glass. She was stripped to her frame; the wind would blow through her woodwork as through a picket fence. He had looked for something of the sort, and was not disturbed.

He strode down the levee and joined Tommy Craig on the forward deck. The young mate was waiting for him in an angry mood. He was in shirt sleeves, as usual, his brown corded arms bare; his tangled hair was like dull ragged brass, and a trace of red touched the blue of his eyes.

"So you're here at last!" the youngster burst out. "Good God, man, it's damn near time!"

"Oh, I beg your pardon," said Huston with humorless sarcasm. He suddenly felt infinitely lonely. The realization swept him that these men who had given their best to the boat believed that he had lain down, failed to back them in their strenuous efforts to win for him. It was his name that would ring up and down the river if the *Huston* won, and his pocket that the advantage would go into. He could not blame them for their resentment that he alone, of them all, should have drunk and caroused the precious night away, putting himself out of condition for the emergencies that would fall to his decision, leaving them undirected in their labors for his boat. No word from him, no possible explanation could make them forgive him for what they thought he had done. It wouldn't be his name that they would vote to put on his boat if they had it to do over now.

"D'you see the *Grey*?" Craig went on. "Naked as a

lizard, not a door or a piece of glass in her! The wind'll go through her like a tin horn, while we go blowin' around like a paper sack! That's what they call racin' a 'regular run,' is it? Are we goin' to stand—"

"No," said Huston. "That's easily remedied."

"Shall I get axes and—"

"Not now."

"But—"

"Give 'em the satisfaction of imitatin' them in dock? We'll be a furlong ahead of 'em in half an hour; then out with everythin' that'll move. That's what'll drive 'em crazy, instead of givin' 'em a laugh."

"All right, that's only the beginnin'—d'you know how she's goin' to load wood? Our niggers got it from their niggers. What d'yuh think they've done?"

"What?"

"They've got barges waitin' at every wood yard they'll touch; they're goin' to lash the barges astern and toss on wood goin' full steam! While we—"

Huston smiled. "You must think I'm a fool. We've got as many pine knots as they have, an' oil to boot. I saw to that last trip."

"Why the devil can't you tell a man?"

"I didn't tell anybody I didn't have to; I kept my mouth shut in hopes that Sawkes might not think of it. Is that all the bad news?"

"No, by God. A nigger just come runnin' with word from Harry Masters."

"What!"

"He was throwed by his horse as he was ridin' in this mornin' from the plantation where he stayed overnight. Hit his head on a tree, and ain't conscious yet. They think he's got a stove skull. May pull through and may not. I—"

"When did that message come?"

"Fifteen minutes ago. He said—"

"Have you sent for another pilot?"

"No. Who the devil is there that can handle it? I thought—"

"You wasted fifteen minutes?" Huston bellowed. His mind was racing now. For one thing he could have killed Tommy Craig for blurting out that deathly story in front of the hands. Whites of eyes were showing in the black faces here and there. Every negro aboard would be certain in his conviction that the boat was voodooed. Huston's odd behavior had already prepared them for that. The starch would be out of them now; probably the whip would be singing before they were four miles up the river. This in place of the singing gang that had shouted *"Arn steamboat"* the night before!

All that was only in the tail of his mind. What he was trying to concentrate every mental effort on was the name of a pilot then in New Orleans, a long pilot of long pilots, a man who could instantly be found.

"Jean Brule!" he yelled suddenly; and his third clerk, a hatchet-faced Cajun boy whom he happened to know could run like a deer, leaped up almost at his elbow.

"Yessuh!"

"You know where Madame Fanchon's boarding house is, in Bourbon Street? Run like the devil was after you, get into the house if you have to smash the door, and jerk Cyrus Meller out of bed with your own hands. If he can get here in fifteen minutes his price is his own. Bring him just as he is—you know what's happened. He can put on my clothes when he gets here. Now, run! Petrie! Run to the Place d'Armes, get a coach, an' flog as hard as the horses can pelt after Jean, to bring Meller back. Move!"

They were on their way, Brule already out of sight over the levee. Craig exploded bitterly.

"Cy Meller couldn't get a rowboat over to Algiers!"

Huston couldn't bring himself to order the boy silent. "He's a good long pilot," he answered; "the best I know of in New Orleans to-day that isn't tied up with some boat. If we had two hours, I'd beg a pilot from some other boat here. We haven't time to even find out who come in durin' the night, let alone find him."

"You're a pilot yourself," Craig came out flatly, his reddened blue eyes burning with impotent fury. Older men would have stood back, but every known responsibility made itself felt on Tommy Craig's shoulders then. "I know what kind of a pilot you are, and you know. I don't care what you say."

Craig's voice was low, suppressed. The *Elizabeth Grey*'s guards almost touched those of the *Huston.* The crew of the *Grey* probably knew the predicament their rivals were in now, but Craig's instinct was to rob them of all the satisfaction that he could.

"Goin' up-river this last trip," Craig rushed on, "I saw you lay her square in her marks in the hardest crossin' this river's got. You got the feel of the boat, Cy Meller hasn't; he couldn't steer the race you can even if he was anywhere near the pilot, which he ain't!"

Huston's cheeks were sucked in between his teeth. What little color he had had when he came aboard had now slowly drained away, leaving his face gray. He shot his eyes to Craig's for a moment before he turned away, but the youngster read nothing there.

Not once since Huston had left the silent house on Chartres had he considered the possibility of his making the trip upstream. That his absence might lose them the race, their fortune, their boat, he had recognized as a foregone likelihood, yet one which he gave no weight. If he had known that Mark Wallace was with Jacqueline it would have been another thing. But no word from Wallace had come.

With Jacqueline's whereabouts a mystery and Mark Wallace's fate unknown, he felt he would have seen the river dry and all boats rotted before he would have abandoned his search.

The sun was rising now, through the wisping river mist. The clean bright rays scintillated over the wavelets where the wind played, and gleamed along the white paint of the boat. In the new sunlight he was almost able to persuade himself that his fears of the night had been futile things. Almost—not quite. If Will Huston insisted on forfeit—and Arnold thought he would—Huston would sacrifice the boat; but he could not go with her now.

He had the strength, though, to make light of their

hazards for a few moments yet. His smile was not far from convincing.

"You're powerful anxious to captain this boat, aren't you?" he said gently.

"Captain, it ain't that," Tommy began.

"Well," said Huston, "it may come to that, like as not."

He turned and climbed the stairway to the boiler deck. Across the rail, so little higher that they were almost on a level, lay the boiler deck of the *Elizabeth Grey.* Captain Sawkes was there, talking to Will Huston; they were smiling, conversing in low voices. As Sawkes saw the Captain of the *Huston* he instantly raised his hand and came forward smiling, but Will strolled away. The captains exchanged genial greetings.

"Your old tub is looking all-fired handy," said Sawkes pleasantly. "I was just saying to Mr. Huston, the *Betsy* has a race on her hands if ever she had one. I wouldn't give odds to any man, I'm telling you frankly." Sawkes had a full-blooded, vital face, gray hair, a merrily sharp brown eye. Huston thought him a good riverman.

"Well," said Huston agreeably, "we'll do our best to make it an interestin' trip for you, Captain; I *think* she'll hold together to Natchez, providin' we can find the way."

"We'll be glad to show you the way," Sawkes grinned, "no trouble at all!"

"How d'you want to make the start?" Huston asked.

"I'm upstream of you, so I'll back to the outside.

That gives you the slack water—what do you think of that? If the current starts carrying us downstream, I better drop in behind you, huh?"

"Fair enough."

They completed their last-minute arrangements. It was only a few minutes before the appointed time. Long since both steamboats had gathered their full poundages of steam. The heavy smoke rolled from their stacks; from below came the clump of passed wood, the voices of negroes, the clang of fire doors. In a few minutes, bells and whistles, unless—

Unless Cy Meller failed to come. If that happened, what explanations could he give, what arrangements could he attempt? Will Huston was there. He might or might not claim forfeit. Tommy Craig was at his elbow, but Huston did not feel he could face him. He turned sick at the thought of the man of the engines below. Everything was ready, now, with all that they had fought and labored for wavering on the scales. They would have to take their chance on Will's accepting a postponement, that was all.

Over the top of the levee, four hundred yards downstream, he suddenly caught sight of Jean Brule, running—alone. Sickness took away Huston's strength. He felt that he must at least for a moment be alone. Hurriedly he shook hands with Captain Sawkes, mumbled something, turned away. Unsteadily he walked to his stateroom. Only a moment to steady himself, alone. Nate Lacrosse was in the pilot house, MacMaugh below at his levers, Craig was running up the steps to the hurricane roof, assuming the only thing they all could assume, knowing that Huston was a licensed pilot: that he would take his trick at the wheel.

His head was down as he fumbled open his stateroom door. Then he froze motionless on the threshold as there came to his nostrils a faint perfume, a thin suggestion of a fragrance that he would never forget. He lifted blank eyes.

Jacqueline was there.

She said, "I'm ready to go where you go. I couldn't stand that empty house any more."

"Where's Mark?"

"I don't know."

CHAPTER XXX

TOMMY CRAIG stood on the rim of the boiler deck, leaning on the forward rail. In spite of his all-night labors he felt no weariness; only a deep disgust and a revolted dismay. Captain Huston should have been the backbone of his boat, the very heart of her effort; instead, he had won the contempt of them all. Yet the boat was the thing, the same boat that they had given their labors to, unchanged by the defection of her captain. Craig was loyal to her still, with the loyalty of the young.

Ashore the crowd had grown in the last few minutes, increasing with startling suddenness from the two score loafers that had been there since daylight to a mob of several hundreds. Groups were on the *Elizabeth Grey*, chatting excitedly with the officers. Groups on the *Arnold Huston*, friends of the crew. A hum of voices rose from the people on the boats and the crowd on the slope of the cobbled levee, a continual mutter laced with shouts of encouragement, disparagement, humorous advice.

Suddenly there was the rumble of a bass drum and a bursting blare of brass. A band that had straggled down the levee had formed in front of the *Elizabeth Grey* and now exploded into tumult. The swinging beat of an old marching song swayed the crowd ashore. On the *Elizabeth Grey* gay pennons blossomed. Long strings of them, red, blue, orange, purple, green, gold, ran up all over the boat, reeled into place by waiting hands. Will Huston was a showman! The crowd burst into cheers above the music as the stars and stripes ran up the *Grey*'s jackstaff.

Aboard the *Huston* there were no pennons, no band, only the flag that had fluttered from the jackstaff since dawn. Even that would have been forgotten, except that a watchman had thought of it.

For the spectacular success of the *Grey*'s display Tommy Craig felt a curling contempt. Even so, there was something daunting in the cheers of the crowd, the blare of the band, and the new gayety of the skeleton *Betsy*, as if she were decked with victory already. Something daunting, but lifting, too, a challenge to be answered by the *Huston*'s engines.

Craig's head was up, his lower lip thrust out; his reddened eyes smouldered and burned in his head, and from behind his face every trace of the ubiquitous laughter was gone. A spirit of supreme recklessness was upon him. He was acting captain now, more of a captain, he felt, than Huston would be again. The man whose name she carried had done what he could to take the living heart out of her, but it couldn't be done. They'd flog and batter her through to victory somehow. Braced with coffee and lashed with words Huston would have to be made to steer an even channel though he had failed them in every other thing.

Captain Sawkes came running up to his boiler deck, knowing, as every one on the river did, where Huston would be found when he was in command. "Where's your captain?" he called across, coming to the rail.

"He's pilotin': Harry Masters has smashed his head and is like to die. Huston has pilot's papers and I have captain's. You and me for it, Sawkes." He added, "Huston's takin' the second watch," in answer to Sawkes' glance to the pilot house where Nate Lacrosse stood.

"The devil," said Sawkes, sincerely sympathetic. "I'm sorry to hear that. How'd it happen?"

"Fell off his horse on the way here," Craig told him.

"Isn't that hell? Like to die, you say. Good man, Masters. Hope this doesn't put you boys out too much."

"We'll have to worry along," said Craig levelly. "Personally, I'd rather have Huston up than Masters, given the choice. Nice hand on the spokes."

"It's a damned shame, anyway. . . ." Sawkes' thick gold watch was in his hand. "Well, first boat to

Natchez, is that right?"

"That's my understandin'."

"I wish they'd made the race to Memphis, like they started to. Well, maybe Natchez will be far enough. Are we ready?"

Craig yelled up to Nate Lacrosse. "MacMaugh ready? Tell him 'Stand by!' "

"He's standin' by," Lacrosse called back.

Sawkes smiled, perhaps at Craig's nervousness, perhaps at the looseness of the *Huston*'s coördination. "Well, let's get going, then. Natchez it is! You're to back inshore, and I offshore, you know. You ring when you're clear, and I'll ring when I'm up; and the brawl is on. Right?"

"Right." Their voices were almost drowned in the blare of the band.

"Well, good luck—Captain!"

"Good luck to you." They leaned far out over the rails to clasp hands.

A moment later the captain's bell on the *Grey* rang heavily, paused, spoke three times more. Answering jingles through the pilot house to the engine room. Sawkes disappeared to the boiler deck, where he preferred to stand. There was a shouting of her mate, a stamping of bare feet, and slowly the *Betsy Grey* wangled herself free of the *Huston*, free of the levee, drawing herself with a surprising swift strength backward out into the stream.

Craig waited. Then the *Huston*'s bells went through their routine, Craig shouting from above. With smooth ease the *Huston* sent the levee drifting rapidly away from her. Craig thrilled to the whoofing snort of her steam: "Up—river! Up—river!" They were on their way. . . .

There was sunlight on the river as Huston appeared on deck again, shimmering sunlight all up and down the reaches of the Mississippi, making the memory of the night mist seem an impossible thing. The coffee-colored flood flowed smooth under the sun, rippled only enough by the larboard breeze to make it glint and spark in the morning light. The vast river swept past under them with a strong swing and pull, mud-colored, glimmering, silently parading its broad waters to the sea as it does to-day, as it had done for a thousand years.

How long Huston had been in his stateroom he did not know. Nor did the others on the boat, for their interest had now been engaged in a happening more dramatic than the vagaries of this man whom they no longer hoped to understand. That he had not been on deck at the start of the race was outrageous to them, incomprehensible. They did not hope to account for anything further he might do.

Yet there was not one of them who looked him in the face who could fail to perceive that—most incomprehensible circumstance of all—Huston came out of his room a changed man. "Drugs," whispered Jean Brule. "He's loaded to the guards with some kind o' drug!" And that was what they were forced to believe. In the hours that followed, when Huston had disproved that theory beyond all doubt, they gave up the understanding of him forever.

Tommy Craig, who met him on the boiler deck as he stepped from the cabin, instantly noticed the change. Huston was washed and combed, dressed now as a captain on a packet should have been on the great day of his boat. Craig, embittered almost past recall, sneered to himself: "When the boat is startin' out to run her heart out for him, and everybody else is standin' by with his guts in his teeth, this buzzard is changin' his collar!" But the collar was not all.

The heavy spider-webbed shadow that had lain on Huston's face was gone. In its place was a new quiet: the quiet of a fatality that was at once a forecast and a demand. It was as if there was now stone behind the face where there had been only river water before. A man hardly noticed that the whites were bloodshot in those steel eyes, so level, so quiet, so hard, that they gave the illusion of being clear.

Huston's eyes struck into Craig's face for a moment in an unreadable gaze. He could read the contempt, the puzzlement behind a certain desperation in the eyes of the mate; it gave him a sense of distance and detachment from the youngster he had known so well, whose character he had helped to make. He felt that he would never have Craig's confidence again. Yet there was no hope of explanation, nothing he could say. It was only left to hold his old air of command, colder and harder now, where grins and reckless swagger had served before.

All this passed through his mind in the instant it took the tail of his eye to catch the position of the *Betsy Grey.* There was no room there for personal things after that. By their place in the river he knew that they were less than an hour under way. Incredibly, that short interval had been enough to put Will Huston's boat in the lead.

The great square-standing bulk of the *Elizabeth Grey* lay close off their larboard bow, so near that the curved guards of her stern were hardly five fathoms away. She was holding as close inshore as she dared, but not quite able yet to swing across in front of them into the slightly slacker water in which the *Huston* ran. If she continued to gain as she must have in the hour past they would soon be trailing in her wake. Already the living hills of water that the *Grey*'s starboard paddles churned up were breaking against the *Huston*'s bow.

He stared for perhaps a full minute before he walked to the rail with fixed eyes, like a man asleep. The expression of his face did not change, except by that fixety itself; but long minutes more passed while he studied that gap of brown water between, trying to judge whether or not she still gained. His voice was quiet and level as he turned at last to Tommy Craig.

"How did this happen?"

"It ain't Nate Lacrosse's fault," Craig instantly defended. "That Bob Carey they got pilotin' the *Grey* is a fool for luck and a dog for guts, that's all. You know what he did? He turned straight for the middle o' that bluff reef off Saul's Point, where everybody hugs the shore. And got by, by God! That's how he gained the distance on us. Lacrosse took his own channel. He done right. Carey'll pile his boat up, if he plays the fool like that!"

There was a little too much gusto in Craig's defense, casting a suspicion on the sincerity he sought to feel. In his heart he must have blamed Lacrosse for this first edge the *Betsy* gained, but above all he was against the captain, the dominating man whom he could not understand.

"There couldn't 'a' been half a finger between her keel and the reef at this stage," Craig piled on. He swung to another tune. "This here breeze is heavin' us into the bank, we're blowin' crosswise like we had sails. How the hell can we make time with the engines fightin' the rudder every stroke?"

It was a gross exaggeration, but it had a grain of truth. Anyway, it seemed to serve.

"Get the axes," said Huston. "Smash out every window she's got, sash and all. The doors are all right hooked back as they are. Wait a minute! Leave the windows in my stateroom and in the one opposite, and see that those doors are closed. Everythin' else out, includin' pilot house and galley."

"Why d'you want to leave—" Craig began.

"Wind balances, like cargo," Huston suggested, "bow and stern. You've already forgotten what I told you about loadin' a steamboat."

"Crazy as a whirligig," Craig grumbled to himself as he turned away. But he did as he was told, and no more.

While the axes rang to the splintering of wood and the crashing of glass, Huston walked slowly over the boat. If there was a tenseness of nerves in his body it was shown in the stiffness of his walk, curiously like that of a strange dog who circles another. They had never seen his face harsher, more austere. The spark in the gray of his eye had a deeper, more smouldering source than the blaze of instant command. The fatality was strong in his face now. Even the negroes sensed it. It carried them along, held them to their work.

"Your fool in the pilot house knows nothing of his river," said MacMaugh. "You see what he's lost us already, man? If we lose in the end the fault will be his!"

Before Huston's eyes the irony in MacMaugh's gave way to an expression which he could not read. The truth was that it was merely of puzzlement, such as came into all who faced him now. They cursed and sneered at him behind his back; and to his face they were confused, seeking to cover the suspicion that they now held in common—all but MacMaugh, whose reasonings were more obscure.

"I'm takin' the wheel in a minute," said Huston. "It'll be a different story then."

"Well," said MacMaugh, "we'll see."

He approached the pilot house at last, while from below continued the complaint of shattered wood and the cracking ring of falling glass. He climbed slowly, still walking like an inspecting dog who keeps long lips over his teeth, yet seems so deadly close to baring his fangs in a belly-ripping snap that others near him walk carefully, watching what they do. He had often run up those stairs before. In spite of his controlled tensity he was trying to husband his strength, saving everything he had for the work ahead.

In the high-standing square cage, axes had already knocked out the sides of glass. The twelve-foot wheel stood from its slot in the floor like a rising moon, its lower half invisible below; at one side of it Nate Lacrosse stood uneasily. His close-cropped bullet head was bare, and the collar had been ripped from his sun-coarsened neck. He turned to Huston a muscly face in which the squinted eyes seemed sunk with a nail punch, and shook his head.

"She's pullin' out on us," he said.

"Why?" said Huston.

"God knows," said Lacrosse uncertainly; "mebbe we ain't got the guts under us." Huston said nothing to that. Lacrosse added, "Mebbe we'll cetch 'em in the night stretch. I dunno how Bob Carey's doin' some o' the things he's done, 'less it's by lookin' at the water an' guessin'. I say he's guessin' wrong; luck may break on him an' pile him up. Off Saul's Point—"

"I heard about that," said Huston.

"Well, we'll see what they got in the night run. Might outfox 'em, they're so damned smart."

Huston stood leaning against one of the high seats along the side of the house, his face quiet with that odd combination of grimness and peace. He studied the river. For a long time his eyes never left the surface of the glinting brown water.

Slowly, almost imperceptibly, yet definitely as the long miles passed, the *Elizabeth Grey* was pulling away. A foot gained; a yard; a fathom; a rod. She no longer lay to the larboard of the *Huston*, but dead ahead; a narrow crossing had accomplished that. For an hour he watched that widening gap, until he could endure it no more.

"Let me hold her a minute, Nate."

The man with the sun-tortured eyes relinquished the wheel and sat down. Lacrosse talked no more; out of sight behind Huston's back he was forgotten, no more in Huston's mind than as if he had been a plowman in a cotton field miles back from the river.

Craig, his work of demolition done, climbed to the pilot house and sat unheeded beside Lacrosse. Others came, clerks, watchmen, the engineer off duty. They stood behind Huston, watching the *Elizabeth Grey*, studying the water. Occasionally they talked in low mumbles. For Huston they might not have been there.

At the end of an hour Lacrosse said, "Want me—"

For an instant Huston's eyes returned to the man as if puzzled that he was still there. "I'll stand this watch, Nate. Get some rest."

It was a long time before anyone spoke to him again. It was the river, more even than the ascendant rival boat, that held their eyes. Under the mile-wide surface of the flood lay a single twisting channel, and one only; forking sometimes, but always with only one way that was best. It crossed invisible under the river, it traced close along thicket-dense shores where branches touched the stanchions over the guards, it wavered in midstream, or struck squarely, sometimes, to the river's opposite side.

Among the ten or eleven in the pilot house now perhaps one, besides Huston and Lacrosse, knew that hidden channel under the breadth of the river so that he could have followed it at night. Of the rest, nearly every one could tell its general curve by treacherous surface indications which only experienced rivermen could read. It was the battle of the opposed pilots that they were watching now. The great engines in both boats were already giving everything they had, laboring at a pace that they must hold for eighteen hours yet before the end would begin to be near.

From time to time they turned to hold for a moment each other's eyes, or to mutter behind their hands. Huston was out-piloting Bob Carey: not conspicuously—no man could have done that—but so definitely that it was apparent to them all. A few feet cut off here, a moment's hesitation saved there—he was saving his boat all a man could. The *Huston* lay true in her marks, her rudder idle during every moment it could be spared.

Yet—the *Elizabeth Grey* pulled away.

They knew what manner of night Huston had spent. They knew, or thought they did, what had been his best piloting before now. Once more he was surprising them, this time by piloting better than he himself knew that he could. He was giving the boat more than he knew he had, that over-the-head effort that a man sometimes achieves when all he has is called for and he finds that he can give more. Not an effort of brawn—Nate Lacrosse was there to help spin the stubborn wheel when she had to go hard over; only the hour-after-hour application of infinite judgment, delicately balanced skill, and the nervous tension that saps the brain and heart out of a man and leaves him an empty shell of muscle and bone.

"This is an iron man," said a whispering voice.

"Drugs—goin' to wear off," said Brule.

"He'll crack up pretty quick," Craig murmured. "It ain't in him to go like that long."

He didn't crack nor waver; the hour stretched to two, three, four; it was noon. The *Grey* had opened a considerable stretch of water by then. They saw figures on the *Elizabeth Grey*, where before they had seen faces and the color of eyes.

"Ain'tcha goin' to go eat?" asked Lacrosse.

"You eat," said Huston. Lacrosse went without demur. He was soon back.

"I'll take her now."

"Get some coffee up here," said Huston. "I'll finish a six-hour watch."

He could not bear to leave the wheel with the *Grey* pulling away. He drank his coffee slowly, in an easy stretch of water; but the sandwiches they brought him remained untouched.

Two hours more. A widened gap. If Huston's face had been grim before, it was now drawn and gripped as if under invisible harsh hands.

"Oh, Christ!" Craig suddenly burst out as they momentarily lost the *Grey* around a bend. "She's got us!"

"We've got a long run yet."

"We'll see come night," Lacrosse began again, and his voice mumbled and trailed off. He drew himself up from the bench as wearily as if it had been himself who had stood the six-hour watch. Indeed there had been no decision, no press of the wheel which he had not vicariously shared. "Your watch is up, Captain. I'll take her now."

"No," said Huston. "We'll be in the Sangamon reach pretty soon. I've got a trick I'll spring on him there. Your chance is coming, Nate. Get some rest."

Sangamon reach was an hour away. Glances shuttled back and forth, silently formed words. There was no argument, though. It had not been dope on which Huston had taken his brace; they could see that now. Dope would long ago have worn off, and the *Huston* was lying deadly true in her marks.

"Get out those axes, Tommy," said Huston unexpectedly. "Strip her clean as a hound's tooth."

"Strip—?"

"Get off that filigree stuff—rails—anything that will come clear that catches an inch of breeze."

For half an hour after that the axes rang again, smashing away an acre or so of gingerbread and jigsawed rail, all the white-painted lacy wood that was the pride, in those days, of the river boats. She was a sorry sight when the axes were done, looking naked and wrecked; but they imagined, at least, that the breeze troubled her less. And still the *Elizabeth Grey* pulled away. She gained a fifth of a mile.

Sangamon reach came and went. Nothing gained there. They knew that Mike O'Farrell had replaced Bob Carey at the *Grey*'s wheel by now, and he knew a trick or two as well. Nate fidgeted.

"There's the reach behind us," he said. "Yo're tard.

Lemme swing her some."

Huston said, "Not yet." They brought him coffee again. He remembered to drink it by the time it was almost cold.

Ten hours at the wheel, a hard stretch from the viewpoint of physical effort alone, in those days before automatic control, when a man turned a boat with his hands. He could not let her go, give her up to other hands while she was losing so, take away from her the supreme effort that he could trust only himself to give. Not yet. He did not reason that. He could not bear to turn from her, that was all.

"Captain, you better lemme—"

"I'll finish out this watch, Nate. Get some rest. Only a little while more."

"It's two hours more to the regular end of the watch, figgerin' two men's watches from where you started from, an' I—"

"I know."

Again those shuttling glances among the men that crowded the pilot house. They had eaten twice, and come and gone and returned again while he stood there at the great wheel with gray, bitter-carved face and undershadowed eyes. He steered her though, no man could deny him that. Huston whistled through the speaking tube to MacMaugh for the first time since he had taken the wheel.

They could hear the engineer's voice answer, unfamiliar as it came pinched through the tube. "Aye."

"Throw in your oil."

Thin through the tube: "Aye."

The watchers in the pilot house stirred. They had been waiting for that. A new suspense, a forlorn hope that now the tables would turn, came over them all.

The *Huston* did not respond at once. The new fuel meant greater heat, more steam, supposedly more speed. It took time for that, though. The sun was down, and the dusk thickening. Faint streamers of mist were rising from the river in long upward-swooping veils, to lose themselves like smoke in the dusk. Against the crimson afterglow the smoke of the *Elizabeth Grey* trailed fuzzily black, a long slow blur of darkness like the ghost of a mammoth rope. Through the glassless frame of the pilot house the light wind swept with a new damp chill.

Their eyes were on the mouths of the *Huston*'s stacks, where the heavy perpetual rolls of smoke poured from the coroneted tops of the black twin columns, five fathoms forward, to their right and left. Presently they saw it subtly change to greasier billows, heavier, thicker, more profuse. The oil was in. A rattling bit of wood fell silent, and another, of higher, thinner voice, took up the song. A new tremor came into the timbers of the *Huston.* The men who watched behind the wheel stirred, sat silent with strained eyes.

Twenty minutes without perceptible change. Then, as they steamed plowing around a bend, the *Grey* came into view again, closer, more distinct than before. Perceptibly the *Huston* had gained.

A half hour, forty minutes, while the humped, long-lived hills of water from the *Huston*'s paddles dropped away behind, and the ancient undying current slid silently under them with a strong swing and pull. A trace of foam, a thin line of turned-over water showed at the *Huston*'s bow beyond the guards. And she crept up, and crept up, and crept up, with a new power as if she were never again to be denied. In that hour a full fourth of her lost distance was regained.

Thickening dusk. Not so easy to read the surface of the water now. Nate Lacrosse rose, paced, sat down; it seemed to him that the iron man of a pilot was taking long chances now, was going to throw away his boat in the very hour that the song of victory was surging up from her engines and the love of won battle was breathing in the murmur of her steam. And still they gained, and gained, and gained. Incredibly a third of the hated gap was eaten by the furious iron monsters below.

In the dusk, as Huston turned his back to the wheel to sight astern, his eyes seemed set in black hollows in which they were visible only as half-hidden gleams. No sign of exultation there, while the rest were coming joyfully to their feet, gripping each other's arms, muttering oaths in sheer blessing of the living hope that had died to rise again. No sign in Huston's face, unless it was in the increased grip of that devouring strain of giving better than he owned. Eleven hours at the wheel now, twenty-seven on his feet, and: "God, man, how she lays in her marks!"

From below arose the chanting of negroes, now a single ringing tenor voice alone, now the swell of a roaring score, a great surge of sound twisted with weird primitive harmonies, powerful in a rhythm like a tomtom beat.

> "Ol' Arn steamboat,
> Golden Arn steamboat,
> *Come along, come along home!*
>
> "Whoopin' up de ribba,
> Push away dat ribba,
> *Come along, come along home!*"

Breathless voices, most of those in the chorus, breathless with long back-breaking toil, yet booming with the jungle lust of the chase, pouring something indescribable into the soul of the boat herself along with the wrung sweat from their bodies that went with the fuel into the inferno. They knew down there, they knew what their fresh work had done; and out of the sweat and the stench and the fire-glare heat of the boilers came that booming voice of the pack, lifting the spirit of the boat on its crest as the fires that they fed drove her engines on. . . .

In the thickening dark they could no longer see the smoke of the *Elizabeth Grey* when the other boat began to drench her fires in oil, yet they sensed that it was done. A silence fell in the pilot house again as they strained their eyes to verify, by the running lights of the *Grey*, what their riverman's sixth sense told them: that the *Huston* had ceased to gain.

The chant from below had fallen away, exhausted, by the time it was certain to them all that the *Grey* was once more pulling away.

There was one hour more, Huston's twelfth hour at the wheel in that insane watch, wherein he tried to bring his boat up by his own skill alone. Slowly, slowly the *Grey* pulled away, more slowly indeed than the *Huston* had come up; yet perceptibly, inexorably, while the *Huston* was giving all she had. The man at the wheel turned once to the tube, but turned away again without signalling below. Without turning for foolish verification to MacMaugh he knew definitely and finally that there was nothing more in the world that they could do except to go on, and go on, and go on, through the hours of the night, to the end already written by the fates.

Yet he played out that hour, in one final effort guiding his boat as she never was steered before, and not again, frozen to the wheel, unable to give up. Until at last, as they made the bend into a long reach in which they had been certain they would sight the *Galloping Betsy*, their searching eyes found only the lanterns of a raft, and a wallowing scow.

Silence, with underneath it the droning, murmuring song of the boat and the steam. Then: "Nate."

Huston's arms dropped as Lacrosse sprang to the wheel. He turned, and for a moment stood swaying on his legs, looking from one to the other, meeting their eyes. His face was terrible in its grayness, in its immeasurably advanced age; the gleams in the dark hollows of his eyes were surface lights now. He stood looking at them, and they thought he was going to speak, but he did not.

Unsteadily he found the door and went lurching and

stumbling down the steps, his hand gripping the rail.

Behind him in the pilot house silence, while none stirred except the bullet-headed man at the wheel who threw his weight on the spokes, wheeling her into yet another crossing that lengthened their way. Then suddenly Craig sprang up and raced down the steps after Huston.

He overtook him on the hurricane roof. His arm went about the captain's body. "It ain't your fault," he blurted out. "God knows no pilot ever stood a better watch than that there!"

"Almighty Christ," said Huston in a dead voice, "how that boat can run. . . ."

A vile reek of burnt oil, blurred lights of lanterns, a long black hulk of shore drifting downstream with the flood; beneath their feet the tremor of the boat that was giving the very soul of her without avail. . . .

CHAPTER XXXI

HE had forgotten Jacqueline until he entered his stateroom again, and found her there. It was typical of the man that his instant thought as his eyes found her again was of the pressure of the steam.

"Here," he said almost brusquely; "come with me."

He took her to the farthest stateroom at the rear of the boat, a narrow little cell above the transom of the hull.

"Why did you do that?"

"My stateroom is over the boilers," he told her. Then

with the fragment of a one-sided smile, "I think it should be cooler for you here."

He closed the door after them, and stood leaning with his back against it.

"Is—" she started to ask him about the boat, but the question died, for she could read the answer in his face. In her eyes there was infinite pity.

"I'm afraid," he said, "you haven't had anything to eat all day."

"I couldn't touch anything, dear."

For a moment, in his weariness, he took her at her word, though he said, "I'll get something in a minute."

She was standing before him relaxed, her veined slender hands quiet at her sides, her solemn eyes caressing his face. He was wondering at the beauty of her, the delicate sensitiveness of her pale face, the gentleness of her dark eyes. He was aware of other things: the rounded modelling of her shoulders, the dark softness of her hair, the tiny pulse that beat in the hollow of her throat like the heart of a bird.

He knew how he must appear as he stood before her now, sooted, dishevelled, unshaven, with hollow dull eyes. There was no question, either, that his defeat was shown in every line. There would have been no concealing that, even had he desired it in time.

He said, "I'd give my life to win for you to-night."

Her eyes melted, and she leaned toward him with such appeal that he caught her in his arms. He kissed her, but even as their lips met he was swayed by a weary dizziness, so that she had to steady him in her arms.

A powerful realization welled up into him that she loved him in spite of the dirt, and the ugly weariness, and the defeat; loved this empty worthless shell of a man, whipped and broken on the very flood of the river that he loved, the only field of action in which he could pretend to amount to a damn.

"Poor Arnold; you must lie down."

Absently he said, "I'll have another watch to stand."

"All the more reason."

"If I once give in and sleep—"

Her gentle soft hands covered his face. "Pretty soon we'll be in Natchez—" Natchez, Natchez, rang in his head: how he had longed to make fast time to Natchez!—"I'll see the house where you were born, and where you lived when you were a little boy; and all this struggle will be done with, and we'll start life over again, a new life, together. . . . Now, lie down. . . ."

Her voice was quieting him as it had so long ago when first he met her, at the end of those black sleepless hours following the loss of the *Swain.* Under the touch of her voice and hands the grip of the battle strain subtly loosened, like harsh biting chains that were falling away. Yet the habits of his mind were strong, and a moment later she knew that he was listening to the engines again. Slowly she felt him stiffen under her hands.

"Arnold! What is it?"

"Listen!"

She heard nothing but the perpetual churr of the water from the wheels, the vibrant moan of the striving boat. But to his ears had come a new note, a hidden grinding complaint scarcely audible under the muffling drone of sound, some warning voice that came to his ears alone.

"Something—something in the engines," he told her vaguely.

"You mustn't worry about that now. Your other watch—"

He gently freed himself of her arms. In his weariness the habit of his thought channelled irrevocably in old grooves. The race was lost; it did not matter what new thing was wrong, or where. Yet he answered the engines' call like a mechanical thing, a tired animal trained to old ways. . . .

Below, in the engine room, the tall gangling form of MacMaugh stood with arms loosely folded, slouched against a stanchion in the lantern light. The shag of his forelock was matted black with grease where his oily hands had run through it; it hung stringily before the steel eyes in the craggy face. One cheek was distended by a great chew of tobacco, the first Huston had ever seen him use. About him throbbed and groaned and pulsed a vortex of sound, the organ-thunder of the fighting engines.

There was more than weariness in the droop of MacMaugh's shoulders; the attitude of momentary waiting was gone from his bearing. Incongruously, in that labored room in the heart of the boat, MacMaugh seemed for once in his life at rest. It was a moment's illusion, soon gone. As Huston stepped into the thick oil-reeking heat MacMaugh lifted his eyes, hard and sharp through his forelock, eyes bleak and cold with the torment of an acceptance that could no longer be postponed.

The engineer's eyes dropped again, as if he had not recognized the captain's hag-ridden face. Huston's glance drifted over the moving shadows of the engine room, subconsciously noticing certain things: MacMaugh's hat hung over the face of the steam gauge, a heavy block of wood driven fast between the arm of the safety valve and the beam above. What hazardous pressure she was carrying no one knew nor cared; the block holding down the valve arm assured that no consideration of caution should let a pound of power escape.

Huston's ears were hearing only that new grinding sound that had come into the engine chorus.

"What is it?"

"Wrist pin in the starboard cylinder." Close-lipped words, low-mumbled, more read from the lips than heard.

"She sounds," said Huston, "as if she was carvin' out her guts."

MacMaugh slowly shook his head. "Ain't as bad as it sounds. She'll last the trip—in her way."

Huston did not make out what he said, but he did not ask to be told again. "Nothin' to do," he stated dully.

Again MacMaugh slowly shook his head.

The captain's voice came harsh and bitter through the smother of sound.

"You know what I say?" he grated with a sudden momentary flame of savagery. "I say she's a hog, a wallerin' hog!"

MacMaugh's eyes lifted, slow, hard, vacant through the greasy forelock shag, regarding Huston. "She's what we made."

"Then we made a damned wallerin' hog," Huston answered as he turned away.

A bottomless sense of helplessness undermined him, so that he did not care whether he moved or stayed; one place was like another now, so long as he need stand no more. There was a greasy chair against a stanchion, where the second engineer usually rested, and Huston dropped into that.

About him the wheeling thick rhythm of sound, the groan and chuck of moving parts, the formless full note of rushing imprisoned steam. A great whirling toil of giants, a vast soul-cracking labor without meaning, that must be carried through to the end. . . .

From up forward in the main-deck bow rose a great ringing shout, a second, and a third; then a sudden tumult, a surging roar of voices, the bellowing cries of the roustabouts on the forward deck. MacMaugh lifted his head, Huston stirred. A black figure came catapulting back along the guards, in its head a gleaming flash of teeth. It danced, gesticulated wildly, pointing up-river.

"D'*Betsy*, d'*Betsy*!" the negro shouted. "De gawallopin' *Betsy* 'e show!"

"What the devil are you talkin' about?" Huston demanded savagely. "What's broke loose up there?"

A tumble of unintelligible words came through the noise of the engines, and the figure was gone, racing forward again. The tube from the pilot house whistled shrilly. “Fool niggers see a steamboat,” MacMaugh tossed over his shoulder as he turned to the tube. “Think they see the *Betsy*, that’s all.” Then to the tube, “Aye?”

From the megaphone in which the pilot’s tube ended came the voice of Nate Lacrosse, contradicting MacMaugh. “The *Grey* is in sight at a quarter of a mile!”

The eyes of Huston and MacMaugh met and locked in a long gaze. Huston broke the silence at last. “She stuck herself on a bar some place,” he said. “Ask Nate if she’s clear.”

“Is she aground?” MacMaugh shouted through the tube.

“Not now she ain’t,” came the voice.

Once more they looked at each other; presently their eyes fell away. “If she’s clear we’ll lose her again,” said Huston; and the engineer nodded, and spat.

But from the forecastle the joyful yells of the roustabouts continued, overlapping, rising in brief choruses, never still. A stench of scorched oil drifted back to them, telling them that the striker had of his own initiative ordered in resin. Periodically came the gruffer chorusing yells of the firemen as they fed the flames, coughing shouts in rhythm as they frantically stoked, racing to get the doors shut again, conserving the precious draft.

The continual clamor forward stirred the captain and the engineer in spite of themselves, tormenting them with the nagging ghosts of hopes that were dead. They remained in their places, grim, inert under the pall of their defeat. Fifteen minutes passed, while the new heat of the resin told its story in the increased tempo of the rhythms and the heavier churr of her paddle-wheels.

"We'll make Natchez in twenty hours for the run," said MacMaugh at last. "A good, clean effort for any man's boat. It's a good steamboat we've lost, between us."

"Yes," said Huston listlessly out of his fatigue. The anger in which he had cursed her was gone. "She's a good boat."

Forward, continually, these lifting yells, now and then breaking into the syncopated beat of songs:

> "Beat, man, dat steamin' steamboat—
> *Cross-cross-cross oba Jordan ribba!*
> Beat her now or blow to Hallelujah—
> *One mo' ribba to cross!*"

Again the speaking tube whistle blew shrilly, cutting through the vortex of sound. "Aye?"

"We're pullin' up hand over hand!" said Nate's voice.

For a moment Huston sat dazed, uncomprehending. Then he leaped to his feet.

"WHAT?"

Lacrosse heard him above, through the tubes. "We're gainin' hand over fist," he yelled down. "We'll take her inside the hour!"

A moment's dazed unbelief. Huston licked dry lips, then: "Nate! It ain't her! How the hell can it be her!"

"It is her, I tell you!" came that distant voice through

me had shot out of the firedoor from a bursting sin lump, driving flaming bits like burning shot into e eyes and face and throat of the man before. The urt man reeled away from his furnace in an agony of ain and terror, caromed with driving skull from a tanchion, plunged toward the guards.

Craig was there already. He seized the big negro ıbout the waist, struggling to hold him as he drove across the guards. A backward swung fist like a maul caught the mate in the temple, dropping him in a dazed huddle. The rail crashed and shuddered as the stricken fireman struck it; then the man plunged over into the black water that swirled past under the chocks. For a moment they glimpsed a bobbing bullet head that seemed fleeing suddenly astern, like a passed snag; then the paddles of the thirty-foot wheel struck it out of sight forever into the thrashed water below. . . .

The engine striker's eyes were held only for a moment by the sudden touch of death; he whirled, thinking instantly and only of his fires, and those gaping unfed doors that let the cold air through, spoiling the underdraft that was the racing steamboat's breath of life. His furious yell rang through the silence hat overlaid the droning song of the boat.

"Fire your doors! Fire your doors! You—" His comnand exploded into a wild splatter of oaths.

The row of firemen hesitated, looming grotesquely, ack silhouettes bordered with wet flame. Two or ree stooped uncertainly to their work. The engine iker sprang at the nearest black, striking with a

the tube. "Don't I know her by now?"

"You *sure?*"

"Hellamighty! Look fer yerself!"

Huston sprang for the guards, followed by the dazed eyes of MacMaugh who dared not leave his controls. He raced forward, fatigue forgotten.

Up the black river, less than a quarter of a mile away, shone the lights of the *Betsy Grey*. By the spacing of those far pin-holes in the darkness, by the showers of sparks that perpetually erupted from her stacks, he knew that it was she. Her red larboard light, by some whim hung lower than the green light on her starboard stack, identified her past doubt.

Still dazed, he turned to the fireroom. Craig was there, grinning; it had been he who ordered in that oil. Craig and the engine striker who directed the firing were dancing grotesquely in each other's arms. The mate flung away from the striker to rush to Huston and exuberantly grip his hand.

"The *Grey* is feedin' resin!" Craig yelled. "Look at them sparks! It ain't doin' her no good! We can whip her hands down without resin or oil!"

"If she's layin' back—" Huston faltered.

"With *resin* on?" Craig shouted. "She can't *raise* no more steam than she's doin'! . . . Look at the heat we got! Them stacks is damn close to red!"

"Are they watchin'—"

"Niggers with water buckets is on both upper decks sousing the stacks when the color shows. Ain't nothin' will stop us now!"

An open barrel of whisky with a string of tin cups at

its side stood on the forecastle forward of the fire-room. Between their spasms of frantic firing the firemen drank there at will. They threw open the doors now, six white-blazing maws that exhaled such a withering blast of heat as to force the white men bodily back. In the sudden blaze of light the half-naked blacks worked frantically. They were picked men, great bullet-headed Congos with muscles like writhing snakes. The sweat poured over their faces, ran over the wet black skin of their torsos in rivulets that glinted in the blazelight, molten silver and gold. A few moments of mad motion, like men fighting for their lives, while the ready-piled allotment of oil-soaked knots flung hissing into the inferno; then the clang of the iron doors, and an end to the eye-stinging glare.

The firemen turned stoop-shouldered away, shaking the sweat from their eyes, wide mouths gulping cooler air. Black faces, bleared with weariness, some of them, with rolling eyes; two or three lurched to the whisky barrel. Then the straining eyes of all of them peered forward through the rows of stanchions to the far lights of the *Grey.* No need of the whip here! They gave the best they had, now.

"Is this the best watch?" Huston asked, his eyes ablaze.

"The best o' both," said Craig. "Some come on ten hours ago. Lord, can't change now! Ain't a man in the line can be replaced with another as good. The whisky's holdin' 'em up; but they was ready for the whip when we raised the *Betsy*'s lights!"

Huston paced to the bow, his eyes on the
Grey. A sudden complete silence had falle
gang of roustabouts gathered ahead. Then a sw
lant negro voice:

"Ah kin heah it, heah plain! She's throwed a
bucket, mebbe two!"

"G'long, nigga, no man can't heah thataway!'

"Ah cain so! Dat *Betsy* chewin' herse'f up ev'y
She done fo' now!"

Again the freed rabble of jubilant voices, bul
through with high, mellow whoops of negro laugh

"Beat, man, dat steamin' steamboat—
Cross-cross-cross oba Jordan ribba!
Beat her now or blow to hallelujah—
ONE mo' ribba to cross!"

"Look," yelled Craig at his elbow. "Look! She
closer! See how we've come up, just since you be
here! God, Nate's steerin' a great race! She's do
We've got her! We've got her sure!"

Dancing, whooping, singing, heel-thump
negroes; jubilation, glory, victory come out of
grave! Flash came the blaze of the opening inf
doors—

A mad scream from the frantically working r
firemen before the furnace mouths, a scream of
pain that clapped silence of ice over the s
negroes. It lifted the heads of the firemen fro
work, made them falter and raise, and turned
to the big black on number six. A reaching

pistol whose muzzle opened the side of the negro's face. "Fire your doors!"—a savage snarl. The fireman staggered, shielded his head with his arms; then, panic-stricken, caught between gun butt and furnace, the black swung gorilla-like with an arm like a great club, smashing the white man to the deck.

Craig was down, and the striker; the firemen drew together, their work forgotten. Half mad with whisky, with fatigue and heat, terrified by the flash of death that had cut away number six as with the stroke of a knife, dazed by the collapse of the white men that had gone down by their hands, they huddled together in the scorch of the white light, uncertain. In another moment they would have bolted, killing anything that stood in the way, leaping over the side—anything to be out of the crush of mad fear that had come upon them like the pressure of a mammoth down-cupped hand.

Then Huston was in front of them, coming up with measured stiff steps like a great ready dog, his teeth gleaming bare, his face and voice terrible. Yet his voice was somehow the same as when it had come lashing down from the hurricane, driving them hard in the routine of ordinary trips; harsher and colder and heavier than ever before, yet still drawling, measured, contemptuous: "Fire your doors!"

His shirt front was ripped open, where he had torn his pistol out. The white rolling eyes caught the gleam of it at his side. They moved to the doors, frantically stoked. Number one made a break for the guards; the flame of Huston's pistol stabbed, and number one flailed down, sliding in a heap over the boards.

"You, Martin! Fred! Take one and six!"

A moment of silence without movement among the negroes that stared from the bow; but he knew that they had heard, and disdained to turn. Then the two he had called took their places, and worked with the rest.

Raggedly the doors closed at last, badly stoked. They needed more fuel than they had, yet he must leave a moment for the draft to take hold. "Stand to your doors! Now stay there!" Still the hard drawl in the harsh, coldly savage voice. "I'll kill the black bastard that moves from his door!"

He turned his back on them, knowing he was master, knowing that they knew. He walked forward into the curve of the bow. The striker moaned, huddled where he had fallen. At the rail of the guards Tommy Craig, white-faced, was dragging himself doggedly to his feet. Huston had no eyes for them; he was seeking the lights of the *Betsy Grey.* At first his eyes found only the empty black of the river ahead. Then the laboring *Arnold Huston* cleared a wooded island, and the lights of the *Grey* rose up, near, near, nearer than he had dared to hope. Good God, how she had gained! Hand over hand, up, and up, and up—it seemed that he could see the *Huston* gain in the moments that he watched. The battle song of his fighting engines surged up through his body in a great tide.

Like a man possessed he whirled and shouted from where he stood. The hard voice rang over the surface of the river, through the stripped aisles of his boat. They said afterward that they heard him aboard the faltering *Betsy Grey.*

"Fire your doors! Now, stoke, you black sons of bitches, stoke!"

Six furnace mouths blazed open as one; for an instant the frantic silhouettes flickered before the ports of white light. Then—

The boilers let go with a blast like the splitting apart of a world, leaving a great sky-gaping pit open to heaven where the forward cabin had been, a pit from which rolled a vast unfolding cloud of steam. Over the empty steam the pilot house tottered hesitating, a weakened tower. Before the furnaces shone a great moiling bed of scattered coals, where the firemen had stood. A shuddering scream ended in a deep-chested sob and choked. Then silence, deep, solid, unbroken by the thrum of engines, purl of water, or murmur of the boat. In the deathly stillness the steam rolled over the surface of the river in vast billowing forms. Somewhere underneath the mask of the steam the wreckage of the *Arnold Huston* began to turn slowly to soft sheathing flame.

For a moment after the explosion Huston stood, stunned with shock, but upright still. Then—"Jacqueline!" the name rushed through his mind, burst from his lips. The peeling steam folded over him, and he strangled. He took two blind strides directly into the heart of the steam toward the place where the stair had been; then crashed forward onto his face.

CHAPTER XXXII

THE mile-wide coffee-colored flood of the Mississippi, mighty in its high-water stages, rushed perpetually toward the sea, taking its broad bends with a strong swing and pull. The turgid current gnawed and fretted, its eddying mass of water powerful enough to pull under a horse or a man, or swing a great steamboat smashing against the bank. Spring was coming into the ancient river to make it young again, as it does every year, as it had done for ten thousand years before the steamboats came.

Under ninety feet of moving water, sinking deep into the muck of the bottom, lay the engines that had been the pride and the labor of MacMaugh. They were not alone; for twelve hundred miles the rushing tawny waters hid the iron hearts of other ships, rusting in the graveyard of the muck. The charred broken timbers of steamboats went down with the river to the final oblivion of the sea, among them the bits of wood that had carried Huston's name.

Arnold Huston was conscious of none of that, nor of where he was, or who. Over him rolled vast illusory masses of steam, blinding him, strangling his tortured lungs. Through the steam he struggled endlessly, calling Jacqueline's name. . . . Sometimes phantom shapes moved grotesquely about him in the fog of steam, among them one with a death's-head face.

Sometimes it was day, sometimes it was night; he could recognize that, though the steam was always there, its endless masses rolling over him like clouds of living pain. They had bound him down, but he fought the bonds, shouting deliriously, cursing the phantom shapes. When he lapsed into unconsciousness, borne down by pain, it was only to wake fighting, struggling against his bonds and the formless steam.

It could not last forever; a man must either live or die.

THE room in which Jacqueline received Mark Wallace was large, high-ceilinged, but poorly and skimpily furnished. It was the house of a man whose ambitions had struck high but whose fortunes had fallen short of them; so that he had been forced to retreat from plans begun, leaving unfinished works to decay in order that others might be saved. Horsehair furniture ranged scatteringly along the walls, maintaining a meagre austerity; the worn hooked rugs on the floor were too small for their work, the salvage of a smaller house.

Beyond the windows the plantation lay, wooded here and there with cottonwoods half grown. A score of figures moved erratically on the distant levee, here and there among them a team of mules. The people of the plantation were making their semi-annual fight against the voracious river.

And above, in a four-poster bed with a frayed white counterpane, Huston lay asleep, exhausted by his delirium and his brief wretched struggles against his bonds.

The pallor of Jacqueline DuMoyne's thin face had increased almost to translucency; violet smudges underlaid her eyes, softening their dark contrast. But she was steady and calm, her hands quiet at her sides. It was characteristic of her that she, almost alone among the women of her day and class, could stand with quiet hands, fidgeting with nothing. She appeared to Wallace more delicate, more fragile than before, and hence more precious, more difficult to lose. It was an ominous humiliation to him that he should find her here, yet he was glad to find her at all.

As for Mark Wallace, he was haggard; though this was partly concealed by his perfect grooming. There was, too, an unnatural brightness in his eyes, and his cheeks showed spots of color—perhaps from his ride. As Jacqueline appeared he snapped his quirt once against his boots, then flung it to the floor. He strode straight across to her, his hands extended to take hers. She permitted this, while remaining relaxed, apathetic, almost. He thought that her breathing quickened a trifle; but he could be sure only that veils seemed to draw behind her eyes, so that he could read nothing.

"Jacqueline, Jacqueline, in God's name, where have you been?"

Her eyes for an instant shifted from his, and her lips moved as if to form an evasion. Then she looked at him again, and gave him a deeper answer than he had asked.

"Where I always intend to be, Mark."

He brushed past that without probing. "How's Huston?"

"He has a chance."

"Then he'll live. The man is half alligator. You couldn't kill him with a—"

She cut through his nervously racing words. "Where is—" She hesitated.

"DuMoyne? Dead."

There was a pause, in which she drew away her hands. Then Jacqueline said in a flat voice: "God rest his soul."

"I doubt it."

She shot him a look darkly unreadable. Her eyes appeared to blur as if she were about to weep; but they were clear again the next moment. Then: "Does anyone know?"

"Everybody knows. But it is thought that he was killed in a quarrel with his confederates."

"Confederates?"

"The facts are out, now," Wallace explained with a disinterested impatience. "He's been engaged in smuggling, as I suspected in the beginning."

"In the beginning? In the beginning, and always, until a little while ago, you said that you believed him killed in that first duel."

He jerked his fingers in an impatient gesture. "We have other things to think of now."

"Of course."

"You must get your things together." He spoke gently, as if he were carefully threading his way; yet with the perfect assurance of a man who bases his plans on firm-grounded assumptions.

"What do you mean?"

"I'll find a carriage. We've got to get out of this."

She drew away. "I'm not leaving, Mark."

Mark Wallace started to speak, checked, then said evenly: "This has gone far enough, Jacqueline."

"I'll be the judge of that."

He scanned her face but found there no wavering hint of flexibility. That his case was all but hopeless he must have known before he came there, for he was a thinking man. Even so, as he now found himself balked, resourceless, the dark blood flowed up into his face, and he was forced to turn away to compose himself. He stood with his face averted from her, looking out through the window across the fields, across the black broken muck to those scattered hurrying groups that fought the river. There was a steamboat there now that brought sacks, and sand on a barge; its superstructure thrust up oddly above the levee, its hull many feet above the levee-guarded cotton land below.

When he turned to her again the dark flush was gone. Much of the haggardness seemed to have disappeared also, and the harsh lines of weariness were blurred out by a returning light within. His face was beautiful again, as she had seen it when she had first known him: delicately strong, sensitive, so quickly perceptive of beauty that it seemed itself to reflect the beauty that he saw.

"You are tired," he said softly. "Sit here."

She remained standing. "I must go back to Arnold in a minute."

He hesitated a little longer, his eyes unseeing upon the quirt he had flung down. He seemed to be carefully gathering himself, choosing his words. He smiled a little as he looked up, and his words came gently, slowly, the picked words of a thinker, an actor, a lover of beauty, a man who was putting everything he had into a supreme effort. In his own way Mark Wallace was making a game final struggle for victory against odds that had turned overwhelmingly against him.

"Look at those gray clouds out there," he said, "full of rain, always more rain. The river's up, up higher than it's been for years. A dozen towns are under water; all up and down the river they're fighting for their homes, just as they are out there. And still it rains. One vast swamp, that's what this country is, built on wet reeking muck. The black damp creeps up the walls in New Orleans, into the houses, into the people themselves. It's all one bog, a nightmare of a country."

He paused a moment, changed pace, and went on. "It isn't all like this; there are other countries where it's beautiful, and the air is clean. Sunshine, sand beaches, wind from the mountain tops. Hills that rise from the sea. Towns that build up and up those hills, full of a kind of life that these fever-struck bogs can't ever know. I've had enough of this country. Haven't you?"

He stopped, and for a few moments looked out the window again. As she was about to speak he turned suddenly and came directly to her.

"Dear heart, come with me! Let's leave this damned swamp country, go together to some far-away place where we can find the beauty of life again—Paris, Florence, Madrid—some place where life is, where we can put all this behind us forever! We can be married to-day, and take ship to-morrow. We can—"

He was pleading with her now, gesturing with tense, outstretched hands. He had tried to take her in his arms, but she had drawn back, so that he stood still now, approaching her no more. His words rushed out, tumbling over each other. "There's no tie in the world to keep us here any longer. I've loved you as no man has ever loved a woman. Four years of my life have been yours. Guardian of your interests—"

"Self-appointed." Her voice cut in, low, but very clear. He was checked for an instant, and she struck in. "Why did you deceive me about my husband? Why did you lie to me, telling me he was dead when you knew he was alive?"

"Lie? Why, Jacqueline—"

"You said only a moment ago—"

"What does it matter, now that he's dead?"

"It was you," she said, "that arranged his death, and accomplished it."

"You know as well as I," he reminded her, amazed at her illogic, "that in this last duel I only removed a menace to you."

"This last duel?" she asked suddenly. "What—"

He interrupted her. "Have you forgotten the fear, the horror, with which you confronted him, with his ghastly destroyed face—"

The tears had suddenly appeared in her eyes, and her hands twisted themselves together. She murmured, "I can't forget—can't ever forget—that once he was beautiful, and strong. That terrible disfiguring duel—before that—" Her voice trailed off.

A sort of velvety hardness came into Wallace's eyes, making him look unfamiliar. "I think your memory fails you. As I recall, before that first duel he had already become distinctly intolerable."

She blazed at him. "Who is to be the judge of that? . . . There are things one is willing to forget."

"So I perceive."

A silence fell between them, which Mark Wallace presently broke.

"Jacqueline, what is it that's standing between us? Can it be that—"

"More than you would believe," she answered. "Things that can never be crossed over."

"Do you mean that you can't—"

"It's impossible, what you propose," she told him. "Impossible!"

Such a black fury welled up into Mark Wallace's face as she would not have believed possible there. His skin purpled, and the veins swelled in his forehead until they caught the angled light in shadowed sculpture. Her eyes widened, and she started back, shocked by the contorting savagery of his passion. She half expected his hands to rush at her throat. But when his anger found expression it was in words again, lashing words that sought to cut and hurt.

"You empty wench, you flitter-brained ungrateful fool! You as good as set me on your worthless scum of a husband in the first place, it was you that turned Arn

Huston on me, you came to me to defend you from your precious DuMoyne when he came back with his face off, and now you stand there snivelling over him because I've finished the work I began for you! You—"

She cried out: "Finished the work you began—"

"I fought him with knives in a dark room, way back in the beginning. I sunk my blade in the bones of him. Liked the effect, didn't you? And now that I've killed him with pistols at five paces, you pretend you suspected nothing of the first duel. Who did you think was this Fouchet that no one ever heard of? Who were the authorities with whom he left word of what he had done? Why should I have been the only one who knew everything about it to the last detail? Twice I've risked my life for you under circumstances few men could face. And now you, like any shameless quadroon, slink off on a steamboat with my closest enemy; and when I've forgiven that—"

The fury ebbed out of him, leaving him white and quivering, without strength. He turned away, sickened by his own emotion. In the silence that followed he could barely hear her voice, low and full of horror, saying over and over: "Beast—beast—beast—"

It could not last forever; a man must either live or die.

At the end of untold ages, the steam rifted, thinned, and was finally gone. The phantom shapes dimmed, and Huston no longer saw the death's-head face. He ceased to struggle. It seemed the river was under him again, its current majestic, perpetual, unhurried, taking